the
marriage
pass

BRIANA COLE

www.kensingtonbooks.com

DAFINA BOOKS are published by

Kensington Publishing Corp.
119 West 40th Street
New York, NY 10018

All Kensington titles, imprints, and distributed lines are available at special quantity discounts for bulk purchases for sales promotion, premiums, fundraising, and educational or institutional use.

Special book excerpts or customized printings can also be created to fit specific needs. For details, write or phone the office of the Kensington Sales Manager: Kensington Publishing Corp., 119 West 40th Street, New York, NY 10018. Attn. Sales Department. Phone: 1-800-221-2647.

The Dafina logo is a trademark of Kensington Publishing Corp.

ISBN-13: 978-1-4967-2955-2
ISBN-10: 1-4967-2955-2
First Kensington Trade Paperback Printing: March 2021

ISBN-13: 978-1-4967-2956-9 (ebook)
ISBN-10: 1-4967-2956-0 (ebook)
First Kensington Electronic Edition: March 2021

10 9 8 7 6 5 4 3 2 1

Printed in the United States of America

the marriage pass

Also by Briana Cole:

The Wives We Play

The Vows We Break

The Hearts We Burn

Chapter One

Today seemed like the perfect day to go to jail.

It was cold, too damn cold for an April morning in Atlanta. The low temperature, combined with the rain pelting the Jeep Cherokee in sheets so thick it was nearly blinding, seemed to heighten Shantae's anxiety, and thus her urgency to get to the Southside Women's Correctional Facility. If the weather had been anything other than uncooperative, she would have reneged on her promise altogether. The last thing she wanted to do was spend her Saturday going through the routine security checks and sitting in that musty visiting room while the guards showed entirely too much interest in her modest attire. So honestly, the terrible weather had forced her to make the trip, because like her mother had reminded her only a few hours prior, what else did she have planned? Besides, she needed to get a few things off her chest.

Shantae steered her car up the slick roadway, flashing her ID briefly at the entrance before letting the guard direct her to the visitors' parking lot.

By the time she had fumbled with her umbrella and made a

mad dash for the front door, Shantae's sweat suit was completely soaked through and hung on her petite frame. Though she couldn't see herself, she knew she probably looked a mess between her paled mahogany complexion and sloppy ponytail. But that was honestly the least of her concerns. And apparently from the appreciative stare of the guard at the first checkpoint, her hasty appearance didn't even matter.

"How you doing?" The guard's snaggletooth winked at Shantae as he smiled in her direction. She tried not to be disgusted.

"Fine," she murmured, obediently setting her purse on the conveyer belt.

"What's your name?" he pressed.

"Shaunie." It was a nickname she hated, one she never would have answered to, but it was better than divulging her real name to yuck mouth.

"You too pretty to be frowning up like that."

It took everything in her not to roll her eyes. Shantae spared the guard an absent glance, long enough to catch his name and badge number just in case he didn't stay in his place. She almost laughed out loud. *No, his name is not Denzel. His mama must have a sense of humor.*

"You must got a man or something," Denzel went on.

"I do." Shantae stepped through the metal detector and lifted her purse from the bucket.

"The nigga probably in jail, huh? You seem like you used to this."

Shantae didn't bother responding as she headed down the familiar corridor. The idiot had one thing right. She was used to this.

Shantae followed a small group of people into a visiting room with tables, chairs, and cement floors. The air felt like it was on full blast, which chilled her damp clothes and was enough to sting her skin. She had a seat on one of the benches and waited. Pretty soon, the idle chatter ceased, the door swung open, and a line of female inmates in orange jumpsuits with handcuffs binding their wrists trudged into the room. Shantae's eyes swept over the faces before she settled on one in particular.

Not even incarceration could mask the woman's sex appeal. She was short, like Shantae, with the same rich mahogany complexion and slanted eyes. She had put her braids up in a messy bun, and though her jumper was a few sizes too big, her curves were still just as prominent. Plus, Shantae knew her sister because despite the circumstances, only Reagan had a sway like she was strutting on a catwalk, and a slight smirk that was so subtle, Shantae only knew it was there from the little sexy dimple winking at her cheek.

Shantae could only shake her head as Reagan headed toward her. It was clear she wasn't taking this latest arrest any more seriously than the first six. The girl was young, reckless, and in more ways than their five-year age difference could justify.

"I didn't know you were coming," Reagan said, sliding in the chair across the table.

"Of course you did. I told you I would."

Reagan shrugged absently, as if those words meant nothing. "Still," she said. "Figured you would change your mind."

"Well, do you want me to leave?"

Another shrug, this time accompanied with a slight eye roll. Funny how she was the one that got herself in the situation, and yet she had the nerve to be frustrated.

"I don't know why you got an attitude with me," Shantae said, nodding toward the handcuffs binding her sister's wrists. "This is nobody's fault but your own."

"Oh, so now you're trying to lecture somebody? I thought you had my back?"

"I'm here, ain't I?"

Reagan pursed her lips, unable to argue with that comment. She sighed and lowered her eyes. "Yeah," she murmured.

Brief silence stretched between them, and for a moment, all

that could be heard were the hushed voices of surrounding inmates and their visitors. Another chill had Shantae shivering in her damp attire.

"So what happened this time?" Shantae asked when her sister made no move to speak.

"Just'. . . stupid shit."

Shantae could only stare in disbelief. She wondered if it was "stupid shit" when Reagan had written all those bad checks before, or "stupid shit" when she'd been booked on credit card fraud after opening up a ton of them in their mama's name. Or maybe she considered the time she forged their dad's signature to refinance the house "stupid shit." It was all minor to her, and her spending a few weeks or a few months in jail was only a temporary inconvenience.

"So what you been up to, sis?" Reagan's lips lifted into a mischievous smirk.

"Nothing. Just work."

"Oh yeah? What do you do now?"

Shantae lifted a brow, partially because she knew Reagan was really trying to get an idea of how much money she was making. Baby sis couldn't care less if she was selling drugs, hair, or life insurance. As long as the funds were flowing.

"Banking," she answered.

"Ah shit now, I see you." Reagan's eyes lit up like a kid on Christmas. "My sister doing big things now. Y'all hiring?"

"Girl, whatever. I know you're not serious about a job."

"Shit, I might be. I know you probably work with some fine-ass educated brothers." Reagan licked her lips dramatically. "Probably can convince me to get a legit job so I can get my *head* together."

Shantae chuckled at the sexual innuendo. "Please, it's not even like that."

"Oh yeah, I forgot. You still with ol' boy, then, huh?"

"Something like that." Shantae pictured the three carat, princess-cut diamond engagement ring nestled in the side pocket of her purse, right next to her compact and hand sanitizer. Slight embarrassment had forced her to take it off any time she wasn't around her fiancé. As much as she hated not wearing it, it was much easier than facing the inquisition.

"Something like that?" Reagan echoed, narrowing her eyes in a questioning glare. "What the hell does that mean? You still with him or not? Which is it?"

"Yes," Shantae said, simply.

"Oh yeah? I'm surprised you still hanging in there. He must have that good ass comatose sex." Her eyes seemed to glint in obvious delight.

Leave it to Reagan. Sex and money. That was all that mattered.

"We are not even about to go there," Shantae said.

Reagan shrugged. "I'm just saying, it must be a reason he's still around. You and I both know he ain't the loyal type. Shit, he's probably worse than me honestly."

Shantae felt the sting of Reagan's accuracy and had to swallow a swell of annoyance at her sister's candor. A damn shame what love would make someone do.

"We need to change the subject."

"Don't be salty, sis. I'm trying to look out for you."

"Well you need to worry less about me and my man and more about getting your life together."

Reagan rolled her eyes. "Here you go with that shit. My life is together."

Shantae glanced around the jail before throwing her sister a pointed look, proving her point. "When do you get out?"

"Two more weeks."

"And then?"

"I don't know. I'll figure something out." A smirk touched her lips. "Maybe I'll do like you and snag me a doctor to take care of me."

A voice blared through the intercom, carrying an agitating wave of static, signaling visiting hours were almost over. "You'll put something on my books?" Reagan asked. "The food here is trash, so I'm trying to get some stuff out of the commissary."

"Yeah, I got you." The words were simple, but a familiar reminder of their unspoken and often one-sided pact. It never failed, and no matter how she hated herself for it, she always had her sister's back. Maybe one day, Reagan would push her selfish tendencies aside and realize that, as sisters, they needed to look out for each other.

Chapter Two

Dorian eyed the scene from his perch at the bar, an assembly of empty Corona bottles and shot glasses at his elbow. Ass and titties were in abundance tonight. They had definitely upgraded since his last visit. Wall-to-wall naked women pranced around the club, the reek of musk and sex all but coming from their pores. Even in the dimly lit room, the strobe lights illuminated the collection of thirsty desperation on their faces as they volleyed between the patrons. Crowded glass high-top tables and barstools peppered the open area, and a T-shaped stage stood center with poles at each corner. Even now, a dancer was up there making her cheeks slap so hard it sounded like she was giving a round of applause. Plush circular booths lined one side of the room, slightly elevated for an unobstructed view of the entertainment from any angle. The whole scene looked like something that should be on the Sin City Strip.

He swallowed a swell of annoyance as he watched his best friend, Roman, use his lips and tongue to place a bill in a dancer's garter.

The atmosphere was magnetic and honestly should've pulled him right in the thick of it, flicking bills at the random bodies along with his boys and indulging in all of the sinful obscenities only appropriate for a strip club environment. Roman was finally getting married, so they certainly had a reason to celebrate. But thanks to yet another argument with his wife, Dorian was now in a fucked-up headspace and really wasn't in the mood. Which was probably Shantae's intent when she started the argument after finding out he was going to the bachelor party.

Dorian watched his boys continue to enjoy the entertainment while he sat pouting in some drunken stupor. The thought had him motioning to the bartender. "Hennessy," he rattled off and the woman flounced away to make him his drink.

"Hey, Big D."

Dorian glanced absently at the woman who slithered onto the stool next to him. Her voice was low and seductive as she leaned in close to purr in his ear. A combination of sweat and some kind of strawberry-flavored perfume emanated from her skin. Instinct had his eyes dropping to the C-cup breasts all but spilling into his lap. She made sure to brush her succulent pearl-size nipples against his arm, and Dorian felt the bulge in his slacks tighten.

"A little birdie told me you needed someone to make you feel better," the woman went on, her pierced tongue licking her lips wet. "Can I make you feel better, Daddy?"

Dorian's eyes cut to Roman, then slid back to the dancer. He had a pretty good idea who the little "birdie" was. She seemed to wait patiently as he accepted the drink from the bartender and took two healthy swallows before setting the glass down. "That's a loaded question," he murmured.

She smiled, showing an erotic gap between her two front teeth. "Is it?" She shifted closer, intentionally turning so her body brushed again his thigh. "I was told to treat you extra special since you're feeling a little down. Why don't you come with me to

VIP so I can give you some . . . cake?" As if to sweeten the pot, the dancer lifted one breast to her mouth and flicked her tongue a few times over her nipple while keeping her eyes trained on his.

The gesture was enough to make Dorian's mouth water. All thoughts of Shantae and that petty-ass argument were flying out the window. "Tempting," he said. "You dangerous, girl."

"I know." Unfazed, the dancer tossed her weave ponytail over her shoulder and sat back on the barstool. "But you still seem a little hesitant," she said with a smirk. "Why don't I just let you get a piece right here?" She propped one six-inch stiletto on Dorian's lap and the other on the top of the bar. Dorian could only watch as she boldly moved her thong to the side, exposing her glistening and completely shaven juicy fruit. The glint of a silver ball from her piercing peeked from the folds. "Is that enough to change your mind?" she whispered.

Dorian snatched his eyes away. Damn, it did look good. That's why he knew Shantae was pissed when he mentioned the little rendezvous with his friends. Because she knew he would be tempted, and she knew he really couldn't be trusted.

Thinking with the head between his legs would surely have him taking this woman up on her offer right there in the middle of the club. As drunk as he was, he was coherent enough to know that this time, sexing a stripper was liable to leave him with enough regret to outweigh the sexual gratification. It was low. And he didn't want to think that was what he needed to resort to. Not when he had a wife. No, he wasn't the happiest in his relationship, but he took his vows seriously. For the most part.

"Ah shit, looka here!" Roman threw his arm around Dorian's neck as he eyed the stripper's open legs. "Looks like my girl YoYo is treating you right. You my boy!" Dorian watched in disgust as Roman leaned over and planted a noisy kiss on YoYo's inner thigh.

YoYo giggled. "Roman, call me later, boo," she said, standing up from the stool. "Your friend here doesn't know how to handle me." She winked and blew Roman a kiss before sauntering off, but not before Roman was able to get a good slap on her ass.

He moaned, taking a seat next to Dorian. His eyes seemed to twinkle behind his glasses as he nudged Dorian's shoulder. "D, what the hell is your problem? I sent YoYo over here to take care of you. She would have had you howling at the moon and shit, boy." His latte complexion was flushed from his own apparent amusement.

Dorian massaged his temples. A combination of alcohol and the bass of the music had the beginnings of a headache throbbing. "You trying to start some shit," he said. "I'm not on that tonight."

"Don't tell me you done went and got soft on me," Roman teased. "Let me find out you one of them down-low jokers now and I swear I'm telling Shantae."

Dorian ignored the joke. "Man, whatever."

"Aw, come on. What's your problem?"

"I'm not feeling it," Dorian reiterated, not bothering to hide his groan. "I'm tired and I ain't in the mood for this."

"Yeah, I know. Your ass ain't never in the mood since you settled down with ol' girl."

It was the truth. Even said in jest, the truth had a pierce of fresh anger rippling through his body intense enough to leave his hands trembling. Roman was right. He had lost himself in his marriage. His jaw tightened and he struggled to hide the internal rage by knocking back the rest of his drink. The liquid stung his throat, but it wasn't enough distraction. He already felt the pin-like prickles of regret stabbing at his heart like an old wound. Time hadn't dulled the ache.

Dorian always had this vision of what marriage was supposed to look like. He remembered how his parents always talked about the "forever honeymoon" stage. It was completely normal to catch them sneaking kisses and flirtatious winks across the table at dinner or groping each other in a dark corner of the house when he would come downstairs for a midnight snack. He knew it should look different, feel different. Raw, bitter emotions of uncertainty came rippling back, and that was what kept constantly nagging him.

Dorian's pocket vibrated and he pulled out his cell phone to eye the incoming call. He felt his lips purse into a frown at Shantae's number. Dorian sighed and swiped his finger to reject the call.

"Was that Shantae?" Roman craned his neck to look at the phone screen.

"Yeah."

"Damn. What next? She going to come up here and get you? What, she got you on a curfew or something?" Roman nudged his friend's shoulder and gestured back to their little party in a section of the club. "Come on, man. Seriously. We trying to have a good time and you over here acting like a female. Cut that shit out."

He was grateful when Roman walked away after that. His friend had always been too damn candid for his own good.

Dorian's phone vibrated again, this time signaling a text. He debated whether to read it or just delete it altogether. Curiosity had him opening the message anyway.

WE NEED TO TALK. WAKE ME WHEN YOU GET HOME

Dorian rolled his eyes and shoved his phone back in his pocket without responding. Like hell he would do that.

"Hey, stranger."

It wasn't even the flirtatious voice that had Dorian turning around. It was her scent. He hadn't seen her in over a year, but he'd always know her by that alluring fragrance. She had once divulged its ingredients, apple and jasmine, but he figured it was the person that could carry the scent so deliciously, yet dangerously sinfully.

He remembered she was short, about a good foot under his

chin. But since he was sitting, he was face-to-face with the juicy cleavage she had busting out of a crop top with bills safety-pinned to the neckline. His medical eye could tell immediately she'd had work done, and whatever MD had blessed her with the extra assets had done a damn good job. Speaking of which, Dorian couldn't stop himself from admiring the rest of her five-two frame. Yes, she was certainly thicker in every place that mattered, and she wasn't thinking twice about showing off every curve.

He saw her dimples next, the sexy impressions in her cheeks present even though she wasn't smiling. Her warm, coconut brown complexion and the natural crinkle curls that fell in a wildly exotic mane. And the deep-set misty gray eyes that seemed to glimmer as she spoke to him. The signature features were all a semblance of Shantae. It was more than clear they were sisters, but this one was the young, carefree, uninhibited version of his much more conservative wife.

Reagan's glossed lips parted in an appreciative grin. "You must like what you see." She did a slow pirouette on the eight-inch heels, showing how the skintight red dress stopped to tease just underneath the succulent flesh of her butt.

Dorian lifted his glass to his lips, almost embarrassed at his blatant lust for his sister-in-law. Damn, the alcohol had hit him with a vengeance.

"Good to see you again, Reagan," he murmured.

"Always good to see you, big brother." Her tone was taunting, and the corners of her lips lifted as if she was trying to hide a smile or a laugh. She slithered onto the stool next to him. "What are you doing here?"

Dorian nodded in the direction of a group of men surrounded by dancers. "It's my boy's bachelor party."

Reagan cringed. "Yikes. Y'all and this marriage shit. Y'all ain't got nothing better to do?"

Dorian had to chuckle. "Well, what are you doing here?"

Reagan gestured toward the bedazzled tiara nearly hidden in the nest of hair on top of her head. The words *Birthday Bitch* were etched in glitter and fake gems. "It's my birthday."

"Oh yeah? Happy birthday. How old now?"

"Old enough to do some things, young enough to get away with it." She winked. "Buy me a birthday drink, Dorian." Not bothering to wait for a response, Reagan lifted her arm to flag the bartender.

"I'll have two shots of Hen and a Midnight Wave." She tossed a casual look in his direction. "What do I owe you?"

Dorian didn't know if it was the liquor, the mood, or just subconscious wishful thinking, but Reagan seemed to be polishing it up just for him. He didn't know why the dangerous thought was turning him on.

"Bruh, you are missing out." Dorian's other friend Myles strolled up, his arm around the waist of a mixed dancer. He reeked of alcohol as he nearly stumbled into the bar. "Oh man, my bad." Myles's grin was wide as he looked between Reagan and Dorian. "I didn't know I was interrupting."

"It's not like that." Dorian didn't know where the guilt was coming from, but he felt compelled to clarify. "This is Shantae's sister."

Myles didn't bother hiding his approving stare as he looked Reagan up and down. "Damn, girl." The rest of his words were inaudible, slurred by one too many drinks. Dorian could only shake his head.

"Aw, you want me and my girls to keep you and your friends company, D?" Reagan licked her lips as she let her finger stroke the collar of Dorian's polo.

He hesitated a second too long, which was enough to have Reagan's grin spreading. His slacks tightened even more, and he felt like she was smothering him, though she'd managed to keep a respectable distance.

"We're good," he said and even surprised himself by how calm his voice was despite his horniness. "Y'all have fun and be safe." And with that he led Myles back to their VIP section.

He felt Reagan's eyes on him, and it wasn't until they made it back to their couches that he risked a look back at the bar. She was gone. He didn't know whether he was relieved or disappointed.

Dorian made himself comfortable in the cushioned VIP bucket chair, a new bottle of Corona in his hand. The sounds of joyful entertainment played around him as dancers gyrated so close, he could smell the musk of their drying sweat and Bath & Body Works spray. Still, his eyes lingered across the room. His mind was full of Reagan.

He managed to scan the room and locate her through the smoky haze and strobe lights. She sat now, perched on the edge of a couch, those toned legs crossed at the knee to expose just enough thigh flesh to make his mouth water. Dorian eyed her little group of friends, all just as young with varying degrees of melanin, ratchet behavior and low-budget clothes with high-budget weave and jewelry. But the way they fanned, flocked, and doted on Reagan made it obvious she was the queen bee of their little tribe. And she was clearly relishing the attention.

Dorian watched her get a lap dance from a curvaceous stripper with a tapestry of tattoos riddling her body. Women were hemorrhaging cash like confetti, and Reagan's sexy laugh lifted over the music.

Funny, Shantae didn't mention it was her sister's birthday. But then again, why would she? After being with Shantae off and on for over ten years, married for nearly one, he could count on one hand how many times he'd met or, hell, even heard his wife mention her estranged sister. And that would've been fine except he knew firsthand how close Shantae was with the rest of her family. The very first time he had met little sis was actually when she'd knocked on the door of Shantae's college apartment. "What are you doing here?" His girl had seemed mortified when she saw the visitor at the door.

Dorian noticed her; he would've been a blind man had he not noticed her. But he hadn't had long to take in the woman. Shantae had made absentminded introductions before ushering him out the door.

The next day, Shantae told him she had asked for money. The girl was trouble, she had made that clear. And now, watching her get up and bounce her ass right along with the crowd of dancers in her section, he could see why.

"You want to try this again, Dorian?" The stripper from earlier had returned. Sure enough, he felt YoYo's hands circling his neck and her tongue stroking the sensitive area right behind his ear. Despite his best judgment, he moaned, welcoming the affection.

Roman sat next to him and couldn't stop the grin that spread. "Here, baby," he said, peeling three twenties from a wad of bills and tucking them into her garter. "Show my boy here why they call you Yo-Yo."

YoYo's eyes danced as she swiveled Dorian around on the stool to face her. "What you say?" she said. "You want to see a trick?"

Dorian started to decline but decided against it. Fuck it. He needed a distraction anyway.

Chapter Three

It was a little past 7:00 in the morning when Roman was drunk enough for Dorian to slip out unnoticed. If it was up to him, he probably would have left hours ago, but he needed to stay long enough to be respectful. After all, Roman had been his boy since residency. Granted, Dorian didn't necessarily agree with him deciding to marry his short-term girlfriend. Hell, hadn't he just been introduced to Bridget four months ago? But with his boy Ro no one could tell him shit. When his mind was made up, it was as good as gospel. Sure, he loved a little eye candy once in a while, but he swore Bridget was the one he wanted to be with long-term.

So as much as he didn't agree with the whole love-at-first-sight and when-you-know-you-know bullshit he was talking when he told Dorian he had proposed, they were still friends.

But now, he had done his friendly deed. After nodding his goodbyes to the group, he worked his way through the haze of weed and cigarette smoke toward the door.

The early morning air was warm for November, but refreshing nonetheless. It had been raining. The pavement was slick drying, and he inhaled the wet, earthy odor that blanketed the air like a quilt. A faint ombre of orange and purple striped the sky, signaling the first pieces of sunrise. Dorian shoved his hands in the pockets of his jacket and headed toward the parking lot.

The party bus Dorian had ordered was parked toward the back amidst a few low-hanging trees. Thanks to Shantae, he had been running late and missed the pre-party shenanigans on the bus, so he had driven instead. Now, though, he was thankful for that convenience. The club didn't close for another couple of hours, and Roman would probably stay there until the lights came on and the dancers left to pick up their kids from daycare.

He heard the angry voices before he even registered what was happening. Women yelling, their curses jumbled on top of each other and only heightened with adrenaline and alcohol. Dorian saw the small crowd that only hours before had been teasing, laughing, and having a great time. Now they were positioned like middleweight boxers in a ring anxiously waiting for the bell so they could go at each other. And right in the middle of it was Reagan, her short frame not deterring her from putting her hands in the face of her much taller female counterpart.

Without thinking, Dorian took off running. Why he was even intervening, he had no idea. It wasn't like he knew this girl like that. Either way, she was still his wife's sister.

"Hey, hey!" He lifted his deep voice above the voices as he stepped through the circle of women and directly between the two who were about to fight. He had to admit, Reagan had a lot of balls. The other woman had a good three inches on her, stopping just short of Dorian's chin. And that was with her heels off, because they had been kicked to the side as she paced completely barefoot.

"Bitch, please," Reagan was taunting, pushing up against Dorian's outstretched arm to burrow her way past. "I ain't got no reason to steal from your broke ass." Clearly the alcohol had taken over. Her speech slurred and she was staggering on shaky legs.

"Who you calling broke, bitch?" Tall girl was taking off her earrings, her eyes cutting like daggers into Reagan.

"Hey, chill out." Dorian spoke again, his voice more forceful and prompting silence. He turned to Reagan. "Go get in the car."

"Fuck you, Dorian, you ain't my damn daddy."

Dorian grabbed her arm, gently but firmly, and nudged her in the opposite direction. "Go, Reagan. Now."

Reagan's eyes never left the other girl, but she relented and hobbled off a little, putting distance between them.

Satisfied, Dorian turned back to the other woman, reaching in his pocket. "Look, I don't know how much you think she took," he said. "But this should cover it. And an Uber." He watched several sets of eyes widen in delight as he peeled off a few hundred-dollar bills.

"Fine," the woman answered, all but snatching the money from Dorian's outstretched hand. She then stooped to pick up her heels and gave her tiny dress a quick tug down from where it had gathered by her waist. "Tell that bitch she better watch herself with her thieving ass," she added before leading the way back toward the club with the other three women in tow.

Reagan was leaning against the hood of Dorian's Range Rover, her arms crossed, a cigarette between her fingers. She rolled her eyes as Dorian walked up to open the passenger door.

"She was lying," she mumbled, clearly still upset about the entire ordeal.

"It doesn't matter." He opened her door and stood back, waiting.

Reagan glanced from him, to the seat, and back to him. "What?"

"Get in. I'm taking you home."

"Get the hell away from me. I don't need you to take me home."

Dorian caught her arm before she could put the cigarette back to her lips. Swiftly, he plucked it from her fingers and dropped it to the ground. "I suggest you get in," he said, his voice calm. "Or we can get Shantae on the phone and you explain to her what's up."

He could tell by her hesitation she didn't like that ultimatum, and it didn't take her long to weigh those options. Smacking her lips, she pushed past him and slid into the passenger seat. Dorian sighed and closed the door. Shantae had been right. Baby sister was certainly a handful.

He felt the tension pulsating as he slid into the driver's seat. She could throw a temper tantrum all she wanted. His protective instinct had kicked into overdrive, and now he felt compelled to make sure she was safe. So what if he was using it as an excuse to keep from going home right at the moment? He wasn't looking forward to whatever the hell Shantae wanted to talk about.

"What's your address?" he asked pulling out of the parking lot. Silence. Reagan sat staring out the window, her lips poked in a pout. "You don't have to tell me," he tried again. "Just put it in the GPS." More silence.

Dorian waited a minute before pulling out his cell phone, making his actions more than clear. If a little manipulation would make her cooperate, so be it.

"Okay, damn," Reagan snapped when he held the phone threateningly between them. "Don't call her because then I'll have to hear her mouth. Just take me home and get the hell on."

"That's what I'm trying to do."

Reagan rattled off her address and Dorian put it in the navigation system though he was familiar with the Ben Hill area. Its reputation of hood, gang violence, and drug-infested complexes superseded its name.

"You always like this?" Reagan broke the silence.

"Like what?"

"This." She gestured wildly in his direction. "This Rescue Rangers shit. You don't have anything better to do?"

"Shantae would kill me if I didn't look out for you."

For some reason, Reagan found that funny. "Oh, I see. You one of those bitch-made men. Your wife really runs shit."

Dorian felt the first flickers of anger and he quickly swallowed it. She was drunk, he had to remind himself. Ignoring the comment, he eased the truck onto the expressway and let the silence linger between them.

"I know one thing," Reagan spoke up again. "Ebony lying ass better not call me no more."

Dorian assumed the woman from the parking lot was Ebony. The one that was about to give Reagan a new face that even his cosmetic surgeon skills wouldn't have been able to fix.

"They say friends and money don't go together," Dorian said.

"Well, if I had to choose one, it'll always be money."

He shook his head at the comment. He didn't know her all that well, but if he had to guess, Ebony was probably right to assume Reagan had stolen her money. Shame.

"How's Tae?"

Dorian frowned. "You haven't talked to your sister?"

Reagan shrugged off his questioning gaze. "She doesn't want to be bothered with me too much." There it was, just under the surface. He could detect a little hurt in the casual words.

"She's good. Why don't you give her a call?"

Reagan shrugged but she didn't comment.

The GPS navigated them into Hamilton Homes, a run-down complex with both apartments and duplexes seemingly dumped on patches of dead grass and pothole-covered streets. Dorian eyed the thugs littering the darkened street between the buildings, their sagging jeans heavy with drugs and money, the stench of weed and Black & Milds wafting in the night air. Someone had their laced-out Cutlass parked on the grass, rap music blasting and overpriced rims spinning.

For the wee hours of the morning, there was a lot of activity, and all eyes turned toward the expensive vehicle riding through.

"Right there." Reagan gestured to building six. Obediently, Dorian pulled the truck to a stop alongside a junk vehicle. He cut the engine off and had Reagan pausing. "You don't have to walk me in," she said quickly.

"I'm not letting you go up there by yourself this time of night."

"What do you mean? I live here."

Dorian placed a hand on her shoulder to stop the argument. "You're drunk, you're tired," he said. "I just want to make sure you get in the house safely. Is that okay?"

Reagan's eyes slid to his hand resting on her bare skin, and when they came back to him, he saw the sudden passion engulfed in the irises. "I'd like that." It was dark, so he couldn't exactly see her smile, but he certainly heard it in her voice.

Just getting her upstairs, he reassured himself. It was the gentlemanly thing to do. He was doing the right thing. So why did he feel so damn uneasy? And guilty.

Dorian made sure to lock his doors and followed Reagan up the walkway to the building. She started up a set of iron stairs, her hips swaying seductively with each step. He tore his eyes from her body and struggled to focus on something, anything else so he didn't have to appreciate the gorgeous view from behind. Instead, he counted two pissy diapers, six roaches, and three cigarette butts on the way up.

They turned the corner and he heard Reagan's sudden gasp at the homeless woman laid out across the stairs, her clothes like shredded rags hanging off her bony frame. Another crackhead, Dorian figured on a shake of his head. The woman looked up and instantly opened her mouth to speak, rotten teeth and blackened gums exposed. She attempted to clutch Dorian's pant leg as he stepped by, her lips moving but no sound coming out. He easily pulled from the woman's weak grip and continued up the stairs. He wondered if Shantae knew, or cared, that her sister was living in these slum conditions.

They made it to apartment 623 and Reagan pivoted on her heel, now facing Dorian. "This is me," she said, holding a set of keys in the air. "Home sweet home. Feel better now?"

"Actually, I do. I just didn't want anything to happen."

Reagan let her eyes fall to the package between his legs and slowly, ever so slowly crawl up his body to meet his gaze again. She didn't even bother trying to hide the blatant flirtation. "Is that so? And what could possibly happen, Dorian?"

Dorian chuckled, passing off the increased sexual tension with humor. "Go to bed, Reagan."

"Come with me."

"Girl, you are acting up."

Reagan stepped close, her body heat causing Dorian to feel like he'd just stepped in a sauna despite the chilled air whipping around them. That signature smell of hers was just as intoxicating, now intensified with the added smell of liquor and cigarette smoke. Her face was only inches from his, close enough that if she dared stick out her tongue it would be all over his lips. She was teasing him, and it was turning him on in all the right ways.

He could have moved, could have told her to back up, could have quickly reminded her he was her brother-in-law, though she probably wouldn't have cared. But he didn't. He lingered, basking in the temptation, almost wishing for her to continue the initiation so he would have an excuse. But he felt the rising sexual tension, and the way she stared, licking her lips, waiting for his response, it was as if they were connecting like two partners simultaneously reaching a point of satisfied bliss.

As if sensing every one of his thoughts and wanting to tease him longer, Reagan stepped back and wordlessly turned to unlock her door. When she got it open, she turned and blew Dorian a kiss before closing the door in his face. He didn't know what would have happened if she had continued, but thankfully things had stopped before they spun out of control. He tried to convince himself that what he felt was relief, even as faint disappointment marred his face.

Chapter Four

Dorian cupped each breast as he studied them with a critical eye. He could feel the woman trembling underneath his palms, and he gave her a comforting smile. "Nervous?"

She let out a quivering breath. "Very."

"I understand. Do you want me to stop?"

"No. I want to do this." She struggled to laugh off her discomfort but sounded way too forced. "It's just . . . no one touches me like this but my husband."

"Well, I'm sure he makes you feel a lot better than this." More laughter, genuine this time, and Dorian felt the woman relax. He went back to work, carefully using his pen to draw on her tender flesh.

"I want to surprise him," Ms. Davis went on, allowing her eyes to close while she waited for him to finish. "Don is such a great husband and father. I just wish he would look at me like he used to."

Dorian's bedside manner kicked in. All of his years of medical training had already prepared him for these types of conversations. Sure, he was a cosmetic surgeon and a damn good one at that. But his reputation extended past his stellar credentials. His patients knew he wasn't just out for money but looking out for their best interest.

Dorian put his pen in the breast pocket of his button-up and wheeled his stool back a bit to create some space between them. "Is this something you want, Mrs. Davis?"

The woman blinked and a red hue colored her caramel cheeks. "Of course I do," she said with an affirmative nod. "I've had four kids and I'm forty years old. My body didn't exactly snap back like it used to."

Dorian heard the damaged self-esteem through her comment, almost like she wasn't speaking her own opinion but someone else's entirely. He begged to disagree. Mrs. Davis looked damn good for her age. Some would argue she wasn't taut and trim, but who the hell expected a grown-ass woman to have a college student's physique? She was still slender, and an in-depth consultation showed Dorian she had just a little jiggle expected of a mother of four. But he certainly saw the fruits of her labors in the gym and vegan diet.

As if afraid he was reading her uneasiness, Mrs. Davis slipped her fingers through her auburn hair, fiddling with the few gray coils that were tangled in her curls. "Sometimes he just looks at me like I'm ugly," she admitted after a moment of silence, blinking back tears. "I just thought if I could get a few nips and tucks, he would love me more like he used to."

The words stung, and his heart went out to the gentle soul. Mrs. Davis was soft-spoken and quite mild-mannered. She had come to him on a referral. But her laundry list of enhancements had well surpassed what she had described as "a few nips and tucks." Breast enlargement, fat transfer, tummy tuck, face-lift, nose job, lip augmentation . . . He would've done less work, it seemed, if he had just built her body straight from scratch. And from the time she stepped in for their consultation an hour ago, it was clear she was afraid of the entire process and was perfectly happy with her natural frame.

A compassionate smile spread on Dorian's face. "Mrs. Davis, you are beautiful," he said. "Inside and out. Don't ever let anyone tell you otherwise. I want you to go home and think about everything. I mean really think on it. Cosmetic surgery is not without its cons, and the recovery time for everything you want should also be considered. Sleep on it, and next week I'll have my nurse follow up with you. I'm willing to do the surgery *only if* it's something you want. And I don't mean to please someone else. I mean you and you only. Understood?"

Mrs. Davis appeared visibly grateful as she nodded and clutched her robe close to her breast. "Funny. You gave me more than my psychiatrist, and I'm paying him $330 an hour."

"Nah, you can pay me in food," he teased as he rose. "Get dressed and see my assistant on your way out. No pressure either way, and this stays between us, I promise." He didn't know if she would actually take his words to heart, but right then and there she looked as if a great weight had been lifted from her shoulders.

Dorian left his patient to get dressed and he crossed the hall back into his office. The blinds had been drawn to reveal an expansive view of the city through his floor-to-ceiling windows. He often found comfort in the scene from twenty-eight floors up, overlooking the tangle of freeways of the East-West Connector. It was still early but by the looks of the congested walkways, people were already trying to get a jump start on lunch.

He took a seat, stifling a heavy yawn. For some reason, he hadn't been able to sleep last night. He couldn't even pinpoint one particular reason why, but he had found himself staying up until this morning, passing the time with social media and sports highlights on ESPN. What really shocked him was when he was watching an auto loan commercial and his mind had wandered to thoughts of Reagan. He didn't know why or where that had even come from, but it had him glancing over to Shantae's sleeping body as if she could read his sordid thoughts. He remembered eventually dozing off around four with fresh thoughts of his wife's sister still on his mind.

Then, when he woke only a couple hours later, the dream was still so vivid he could almost taste her. He had rolled over, intending to act out lingering desires with his wife instead, but she had already left for work. She did leave a text, though, insisting she still wanted to talk to him about something. Part of him did want to know what was bugging her. The other part, the less tolerant part, didn't give a damn.

Again, his mind drifted to Reagan and their little interaction Saturday night. The fantasy was wishful and intense. She was straddling him with nothing on besides the paper-thin hospital gown he gave to his patients during their examinations. She had it open to the front, gently massaging her own breasts and tossing her head back in self-induced ecstasy. Reagan's lips parted, her breath catching in her throat before she released a low, throaty moan that was on another level of euphoria. It was erotic and Dorian could only watch, his eyes capturing snapshots of her every dip, bend, and angle to file away like a Polaroid.

A notification chimed on his cell and had Dorian cursing under his breath at the interruption. He swiped his touchscreen to read the text, expecting to see a message from Shantae. Not her. Better. The two words were indicative of only one person: **HEY STRANGER.**

Dorian sat back; the corners of his lips turned up into the ghost of a smile. He hadn't even spoken to Reagan since taking her home over the weekend. Nor had he expected to. How ironic she had messaged him right when he was . . . what? About to get off on his fantasy, that's what.

His fingers hovered over the keyboard on his cell phone, unsure how to respond. How did she get his number? Thankfully, he didn't have to as her second message popped up on the screen: **CAN WE TALK? YOU GOT A SEC?**

Curiosity piqued, he typed **SURE** and waited, wondering what she wanted to talk about. Hopefully, that Ebony "friend" from the club hadn't come around wanting to finish their little argument. His phone rang not even five seconds later.

"Hi," she greeted. "How you doing, Dorian?"

Damn, it was good to hear her voice. It had this sensual, husky edge to it, like she was auditioning as a phone sex operator. And the way she said his name, like her tongue was licking each letter in her enunciation. Or maybe that was just his imagination. Dorian frowned at the intrusion of his own lustful thoughts. What the hell was wrong with him? *Focus.*

"I know this is weird. I'm sorry. I got your number from your boy Myles the other night at the club."

"Oh, you and Myles were talking?" He hadn't meant to sound so surprised. So . . . interested. Why was he inquiring? So what if she and Myles were talking? He was single and so was she. Good for them.

"I don't know," Reagan answered, not bothering to elaborate. "But anyway, I'm glad you let me call you," she went on. "That meant you weren't mad at me."

"Mad at you for what?" he asked.

"For the way I behaved at the club and even after when you took me home."

He should have been relieved. Why wasn't he relieved? "Oh, don't worry about it," he said. "It's all good."

"No, it's not." She lowered her voice as if ashamed. "I shouldn't have said some of the shit I said. And I sure as hell shouldn't have been flirting with you. I don't do married men anymore." Anymore? Was that supposed to be a good thing?

Dorian paused, not knowing how to respond to that piece of information. As if Reagan realized her brief lapse in judgment, she quickly added, "That's just disrespectful to my sister, you know? You're her husband, so I was really out of line."

"Yeah, for sure. I know what you meant." But did he really? He let out the breath he had been holding and swiveled around in his chair to eye the downtown activity once more. Lord knows he didn't need that complication. A fantasy, nothing more. As erotic as it was, it was just that. Nothing happened, completely harmless, and hadn't they stopped short of crossing those boundaries? And frankly, that was one less headache he needed right now. He hadn't realized Reagan's persistence had him so wound up, but now he felt himself much more relaxed than he had been. "We'll blame it on the alcohol," he teased.

He was met with silence so still he had to look at the phone to make sure the line hadn't disconnected.

"Well, I guess that's all I wanted to say," Reagan said after a pause. "Hopefully next time you see me, I'm acting like I got some sense."

"I'm sure you can handle yourself. Take care."

"Of course. Talk to you soon." *Click.* Dorian glanced at the phone on a frown after she hung up. *Talk to you soon.* Well, that was interesting.

His phone buzzed, this time on his desk, signaling an intercom call from his assistant out front. He pushed the button to answer. "Yes?"

"Dr. Graham, your wife is on line two." Claudia, Dorian's receptionist, was a soft-spoken woman who had more years behind her than in front of her. Dorian hated working her too hard, but she was damn good at what she did, and Claudia claimed the work kept her mind busy.

"Thanks Claudia. Did Pam take care of Mrs. Davis?" Now, he didn't even know why he was asking that. He knew she had handled business. She was an upbeat college student brimming with zealous professionalism. He was glad she had walked into his office with a request for a job in exchange for course credit toward her RN degree. Even though he was only six months young with his own practice, business was thriving, and thanks to both Pam and Claudia, their little team of three had things running like a well-oiled machine.

"She sure did. Mrs. Davis said she felt good after talking to you. She's buying us all lunch after the holidays," Claudia said with a laugh.

Dorian grinned as he clicked over to line two. Now if Mrs. Davis just left that piss-poor excuse for a husband of hers, she would feel even better.

"Hey," he greeted.

"Hey." Shantae's voice carried the same dryness. They had yet to talk after that last argument, and apparently, she was still riding on her little attitude about him going out to the bachelor party the other night. She had even pulled one of her "disappearing stunts" all day Sunday, leaving early in the morning and returning late Sunday night. Usually she would just go to her parents' house when she didn't want to be bothered, which was fine with him. He hadn't been in the mood for that bullshit either. "I'm able to get away for a little. You want to meet for lunch?"

He weighed the offer. The silent treatment was becoming a little aggravating. Plus, they had a vacation coming up. It was planned and paid for while they were on their honeymoon last year. The last thing they needed to do was carry tension with them to Jamaica. And over what? A bachelor party that was over and done with? One thing was for sure, if he let it go on, it would completely ruin his trip because Shantae's stubborn ass could carry a grudge's grudge to the afterlife. "Sure," he agreed. "We need to talk anyway."

＞◦◦＜

Shantae was already waiting when he arrived at their little wing spot. It was a common meeting place for them because it was in short walking distance, a perfect midpoint between Dorian's practice and Shantae's office at the bank.

The restaurant usually had a line spilling out the door, partially because the food was so damn good, partially because it was the size of a bedroom with just enough space to accommodate a handful of wobbly pub tables and some tattered chairs. Behind the cashier counter, a marquee board displayed a simple menu: wings, fish, fries, and Coke products. That's it. Dorian knew the owner, Ben, and the joke *That's it!* had even been added to the marquee board; since their food was so delicious, they kept getting requests for a larger selection of American Deli-esque dishes. "Don't ask 'do we have' or 'are we going to get,'" Ben had said. "Wings, fish, fries. That's it!"

Dorian was glad she had suggested lunch early because they had managed to beat the rush as some of the only patrons there.

Usually they had to take their food to go, but Shantae was seated at one of the tables when he entered, nursing a bottled water. "I ordered your usual," she said as Dorian pecked an absent kiss on her forehead before sliding in the seat across from her.

"I appreciate it." He already could taste the twenty-piece hot wings. The restaurant had perfected some kind of signature sauce that had his mouth burning with flavor but was too good to put down. "You look nice," he complimented, addressing her crisp, navy blue pantsuit and canary yellow blouse. A thin line of pearls paraded across her neck with the matching earrings in each lobe. A few years ago, Shantae had cut her mahogany tresses up above her ears, and now it was growing back into a teased bob she'd enhanced with a few loose curls.

"Thanks," she said with a small smile. "How's work?"

"I played with some breasts this morning. And I'll be looking at thighs and ass this afternoon. You know, the usual."

Shantae snickered at his customary double entendre. "Well, you never could keep your hands off other women," she said and lifted her water to her lips.

Dorian didn't like how Shantae didn't have a trace of humor in her voice.

"I'm kidding," she quickly said and plastered a smile on her face at his prolonged silence. "Damn, D, chill out. You think I would've married you if I still felt like you were up to no good?"

Dorian shrugged off the brief tension. "You lucky I love you," he said. At least she wasn't harboring her anger anymore.

Shantae blew a kiss at him teasingly before getting up to grab their lunches from the counter.

"I'm glad we did this," she said after returning to the table with their meals. "Work has me stressed out with this new merger. And we're having crazy systems issues. We think someone hacked the network."

"Damn, I'm sorry."

"Yeah, it sucks. I'll probably have to stay late a little to get all that shit squared away. I need to have it all done before we leave for Jamaica because I'm not trying to have them calling to ruin our vacation."

Dorian chuckled as he bit into a wing. "Your coworkers not gon' know what to do without you for a week."

"I know, right." She hesitated before she continued. "You never told me how the bachelor party was." There it was. He had been waiting for it.

Dorian shrugged. "It was what is was. Nothing special."

"I figured it was pretty fun. You got home kind of late."

"I had to take your sister home."

Shantae frowned, confusion on her face. "My sister? Reagan was at the club?"

It was an innocent inquiry, he knew. But he couldn't help feeling nervous. Nothing had happened. Well, shit, almost nothing. "Yeah, she was there with some friends or something," he explained.

A beat. "Oh."

Shantae didn't say anything else. Just kept eating. Dorian tried to watch her movements out of the side of his eye. He couldn't tell if she was uncertain, suspicious, or still confused. She had simply ended with an *oh* like it was completely understandable. And why wouldn't it be? It was her sister, after all. No reason to think it was anything more than what he had said. Even still, he felt compelled to give more of the story, if only to ease his own anxiety. "She was about to get into a fight because she was drunk, so she didn't have anyone else to take her. I just thought it was safer, you know?"

Another pause. "Right, I get it. You didn't have to explain." She smiled. "That chick is always getting herself into trouble, I swear. Thank you for seeing about her and making sure she was okay."

Dorian didn't realize he was tense until he felt his muscles relax after her last comment. Glad that was over. Now they could address the elephant in the room. "You wanted to talk to me the other night," he said. "And you've been pissed about something. What's on your mind?"

Shantae sighed and sat back in her chair. "Do you ever think about the twins?"

Dorian winced. It was like a soft blow to his heart. Their miscarriage was still a sore subject for him. He definitely did think about it more often years ago when it first happened, especially considering he had to nurse Shantae through her depression. She took it much harder than he did.

After the miscarriage, Shantae had wanted to do a balloon release in their honor. She had written a note to each of them and placed them in two white balloons. They had driven to the park and set the balloons free, watching them dance in the wind until the streamers disappeared.

Sure, he had pacified himself with a bunch of "things happen for a reason" rationales and Dorian had held on to that as a lifeline to salvage some element of sanity while they grieved and healed. But that still didn't ease the pain. Or the guilt. It was her stressing about his random indiscretions that caused the miscarriage in the first place. At least, that's what she so often threw up in his face. For him, that pill would never get swallowed. Dorian had to admit he didn't think about their babies quite as often anymore. It was so much easier not to.

"Sometimes," he answered, his eyes narrowing in concern. "Why? What's wrong?"

Shantae shook her head to dispel any worry. "No, nothing is wrong. I just know some things haven't been the same between us since we lost them."

"What do you mean, haven't been the same?"

"Are you happy?" she asked, her gaze finally meeting his. "You know, with things how they are now?"

Dorian reached across the table to rest his hand on hers. "Yes," he said, which was for the most part true. "Babe, what are you getting at? Just tell me."

"You don't think anything is missing?" She had this hopeful, expectant look on her face and Dorian sat back on a sigh.

"You want kids," he murmured. It was more of a statement than a question as the realization slowly sank in. "You want kids," he repeated, more to himself. "I mean, *now*, Shantae? Where is this coming from?"

She was fiddling with her fingers, a nervous habit, he knew. "It's just been on my mind lately. I know we never talked about it, especially after . . . you know. But we're not getting any younger . . ." She trailed off, her shoulders lifting in a shrug. "I don't know. I'm not even sure where this is coming from. I guess I just wanted to know is that something you would want again."

Dorian's mind was blank. He opened his mouth and shut it again. "I guess maybe yeah, eventually," he responded. "I don't know. Maybe."

"But not now, huh?" Shantae pushed.

"Where is this coming from, Shantae? This just seems out the blue."

"Maybe for you," she said, biting the words with a twinge of anger. "But I've been thinking about it for a while. I'll be thirty-one my next birthday. Women think about stuff like this because after a certain age, it can get harder and harder to get and stay pregnant."

"I know, I just . . ." Dorian rubbed his temples to keep the brewing headache at bay. "I just started my own practice. Hell you were just talking about how stressful work is with the new merger. We're about to go on vacation. Damn, Shantae, we're just about to hit our one-year anniversary this week."

"Well, whose fault is that?" Shantae snapped. "If it were up to me, we would've *been* married. I kept giving you dates and it was always, 'well, hold up, let's graduate first' or 'not now I'm in medical school' or 'I can't plan a wedding while I'm in residency' then 'oh, sign this pre-nup first.'"

It was true. All completely true. But still . . . "All I'm saying," Dorian said, much gentler this time, "is we have a lot going on right now. How is a baby going to fit into this?" Hell, they couldn't even go a week without arguing.

It was clear she wanted to say something else. He could almost see the words resting on her parted lips. But she didn't speak. Just nodded. "True," she said. "Very true. I didn't think about it like that."

They resumed eating in silence, but Dorian had lost his appetite. The topic had left him uneasy. Yes, she'd agreed, but it was more than evident the conversation was far from over.

Chapter Five

He always dreaded coming back here.

Dorian navigated his black Range Rover through the gentrified streets of McDonough. It certainly had changed since his adolescence. His mom had moved him to the quiet suburbs in elementary school, and at the time, the country back roads and small-town aesthetic had threatened to smother the gritty city lifestyle he had grown accustomed to in College Park. But as he entered middle school, the trees had been cleared, replaced with restaurants, nightlife, and shopping plazas that began to rival other districts. Pretty soon, folks were flocking to the Atlanta outskirts for the best of both worlds: that small-town feel with big city conveniences. Dorian had eventually learned to like the town, but that hadn't stopped him from running back to the metropolitan area before the band stopped playing at his high school graduation.

Speaking of which . . . Dorian braked at a red light, his eyes shifting to the brick building nestled in a thicket of trees and underbrush. A row of trailers flanked the school's left side, and Dorian easily remembered treks in the scorching Georgia heat to sit through Geography, Algebra II, and World History. But seeing his alma mater now brought back a few rough memories, especially considering the pretenses of what brought them to Henry County in the first place.

Dorian's father had been a cop when he'd been killed in the line of duty in a robbery. Or so Dorian had been told. It wasn't until a few years after his death that Dorian found out his dad hadn't been the humble, upstanding gentleman he had led everyone to believe. Apparently, the robbery was just a guise to mask the true reason why he had even been at the convenience store well outside of his jurisdiction in the first place. Though nowhere did the official record mention the prostitute that was in the car with him. The force made sure that the truth had been buried with Officer Lucas Graham, and Dorian and his mom had been financially taken care of because of it.

But Teresa Graham had never been quite the same since, drowning her sorrows in enough liquor and nicotine that the substances had become a staple in their household. It was like she had fallen into some sordid state of delirium after his death, a string of nausea spells and panic attacks forcing her to disconnect from life.

He, on the other hand, had distracted himself with his own comforts: women and sex. Sure, his family now had the materialistic luxuries, but his dad's absence had robbed them both of normalcy, leaving them numb and fractured. And there they were, years later, still trying to pick up the pieces.

He maneuvered his truck into Lake Spivey Estates, a gated community whose homes and amenities were an outward display of the upper echelon. Along both sides of the road were manicured lawns leading up to brick homes in various degrees of majestic. Expensive cars peppered winding driveways, and occasionally, Dorian would spot a neighbor jogging or walking a dog. The entire scene was picturesque, something out of *Lifestyles of the Rich and Famous.* Which was why Dorian had always felt out of place from the time they moved there. They were the only brown-skinned people on this side of the lake. And when word traveled about his mother's addiction, that made it much harder to cope with the changes.

The house looked the same. Every inch of the 4,000 square feet had been tended to with pride. Dorian made sure of that. Even now, Mr. Jimmy, a middle-aged guy who was the all-around lawn-care and maintenance man, stood hunched over a cluster of bushes bordering the three-car garage. He lifted the shears in greeting before returning to the task at hand.

Dorian parked behind a blue Ford Focus, proof that his mother's aide Rochelle was inside. He hefted four bags of gro-ceries to the door and let himself in with his key.

The house smelled of fresh Pine-Sol and vanilla. Glistening marble floors greeted him in the two-story foyer, a chandelier hanging low overhead. Somewhere, an R&B love song wafted through the speakers. Gerald Levert. His mom was a huge fan.

Dorian crossed into the huge gourmet kitchen to unpack the grocery bags before heading down the hallway to the master suite.

His mother was propped up in bed despite the bedside clock reading 2:30 in the afternoon. She had her eyes closed, a hint of a smile on her lips. She almost looked as if she were sleeping, sitting up. Cancer had taken its toll her. She looked frail, broken, her cheeks sunken. A multicolored bandanna added a little life to her otherwise pale complexion. Satin pajamas hung on her thinning frame and she looked too small for the king-sized sleigh bed dom-inating the bedroom. But even still, it was obvious she was just as stunning as she had always been.

Dorian sighed and stepped through the French doors. "Mama—"

Teresa lifted her finger to shush him. Dorian had to chuckle as he realized she was trying to hear the rest of the song. She didn't play about Gerald.

The music gave way into an ad, and only then did she open her eyes and turn in her son's direction. "Boy, you know better, interrupting my concert."

Dorian relaxed, pleased to hear the lace of humor. Today was a good day. "Sorry," he said, crossing to her. "But it's not like you haven't heard that song hundreds of times, Ma."

"Still. Gerald is singing for me, son. I raised you better than that." She lifted her cheek for a kiss. Her skin felt a little colder than usual and paper thin.

"You cold, Ma?" He readjusted her comforter a little tighter around her body.

"I'm fine."

"How you feeling? You look good." He was glad her disease hadn't put a huge damper on her spirits this afternoon.

"I told her that." Rochelle, a heavy-set, middle-aged woman, came from the adjoining bathroom, a pill box in hand. "Ms. Graham said I was lying to her face."

"You both are," Teresa said with a light roll of her eyes. "You lucky I love you, otherwise both of y'all would have to get the hell out."

Dorian couldn't help but laugh as Rochelle eased a hip on the side of the bed, holding out a few pills.

"You would miss me too much," Rochelle teased.

Dorian waited patiently while his mom took her medicine before he spoke again. "Rochelle, I stocked the kitchen."

"Oh good. I'll get dinner started." She turned to Teresa, placing a gentle hand on her leg. "You gon' be okay for a bit?"

Teresa shooed her hand to dismiss the question. "This is my son. Of course I'll be okay. What is he going to do? Kidnap me?"

"If he did, he would bring you right back, I promise you," Rochelle said with a laugh that earned her a swat on the shoulder. Satisfied, she rose and glanced to Dorian. "Can you come see me before you go?" She had lowered her voice.

Dorian nodded. He didn't like the sound of that.

When they were left alone, he took a seat on the bed beside his mom. The suite was the size of three bedrooms, so sitting anywhere else in the room would put him too far away.

"Where's that wife of yours?"

The question was thick with disgust, and Dorian could only shake his head. He never understood why his mom didn't care for Shantae. But then, had she really cared for any of the women he dated?

"She's out running some errands," he answered. "It's our anniversary, so she's putting together a little surprise for us."

The response was met with a grunt. "Anniversary?" She tossed out the word like it was foreign.

"Yes. You know an anniversary, is when two people—"

"Boy don't play with me," she snapped, slapping him upside his head. "I guess she's still hanging around, huh?"

"She is my wife, Ma."

"That don't mean shit these days." Teresa rolled her eyes. "So, I guess your *wife* is too good to come visit your mama too?"

"Ma, stop. You know it's not like that."

"I'm dying, son, not stupid." Her words pierced his heart, but rather than dwell on her truth, he ignored the comment.

"I'll bring her next time, how about that?" Another grunt of disdain, this time accompanying an eye roll. As the only child, especially being the man of the house after his father was killed, Dorian completely understood his mother's disposition. Especially because it mirrored the no-bullshit qualities he also saw in himself.

"You know you're always my number one lady," he added, satisfied when her face cracked with a smirk.

"You damn right, I better be. Now, what's wrong with you, son?"

"What are you talking about?" Dorian was honestly surprised, though he knew he shouldn't have been. It wasn't like he was that obvious. His mother just knew him that well.

He sighed when she just stared at him: The questioning glare had her eyebrow lifted so high it disappeared under the rim of the scarf wrapped around her head. The conversation with Shantae was still fresh on his mind. It felt like he was being blindsided. And maybe he was being a little bit . . . What was the word she had used for him so many times in the past? Selfish? Did that really make him selfish if he didn't want children with his wife? He never told her, or anyone this for that matter, but he wasn't even sure the twins were his. They were constantly breaking up to make up and break up again.

But part of him had to admit that his doubts stemmed from his own infidelity and his repressed feelings against having kids more so than actual suspicion. So, when the miscarriage happened, part of him was upset. The other part, the one that weighed heavier, was actually relieved. Now here they were again, doing the same dance to different music.

"Ooh." His mother's calm voice snapped him out of the temporary trance. "Whatever it is has you really upset." She rubbed his cheek with a small smile. "You look just like Cop when you get mad."

The mention of his father extinguished the little bit of rage he had simmering. His sigh was heavy this time. "I don't want to worry you, Ma," he said instead, which was still just as much the truth. "I'll figure it out."

"Don't let no one stress you out, ya hear me?" Teresa brought her eyes level with Dorian's, and even in her weakened state, they were filled with intensity. "You be strong. You got your father's blood. But greed was his downfall. Had to have his cake and eat it too."

Dorian didn't know why the comment made him uneasy. He was anything but his father in that sense. Sure, he had his fun in the past, but from the moment he'd said "I do," he hadn't dared sleep with another woman. Of course, he looked, touched, appreciated, and at the most had a stripper or two give him some head since a few dollars went a long way, but that was it. He knew his limits.

Dorian lightened the mood with a smile and leaned forward to place a kiss on her forehead. "I got it under control, Ma."

They changed the subject to his upcoming vacation, to which Dorian emphasized she needed to call if anything was wrong, day or night. Teresa mumbled through half-assed consent before she started dozing off. Whether the cancer, the meds, or a combination of both, he caught her head lolling a few times throughout his short visit.

He tucked her in and watched and waited until he heard her faint snore. Then, as customary, he pulled ten $100 bills from his pocket and placed them on the dresser, underneath his parents' wedding picture. He hesitated for the briefest of moments, a wistful smile touching his lips as he stared at his father. It was eerie, looking at a little older version of himself. He had been young, but he remembered the man vividly. A few scattered memories threatened to invade his subconscious, and he quickly pushed those to the side and crept out to the kitchen, leaving his mother to rest.

Rochelle was standing at the stove, an apron tied around her waist. She had water running in the sink and a large stainless-steel pot heating on the open gas flame. She stooped down to open the oven door, and immediately, the smell of cornbread filled the room.

"You got it smelling good in here," Dorian said, leaning a hip on the granite countertop. "What's in the pot?"

"Water." Rochelle chuckled. "But I'm about to make some collard greens to go with this cornbread."

Good Southern cuisine. Dorian remembered she was from Macon, Georgia. Collard greens and cornbread were a staple. No meat necessary.

"Is she asleep?"

"Yeah," Dorian said. "What did you want to talk to me about?"

Rochelle's fingers moved with precision as she turned the cast iron skillet upside down to transfer the cornbread to a plate before moving to finish washing her greens.

"She told you she had to go to the doctor today?"

"She didn't tell me. Everything good?"

Rochelle turned around, using a towel to dry her hands. "She wants to stop chemo."

Dorian dismissed the comment with a shake of his head. "No," he said simply.

"Dorian—"

"I said no."

Rochelle paused. "It's what she wants," she murmured. "Don't you think she knows what's best for her?"

"Hell no. I know what's best for her."

"At least listen to her. It's taking a physical and emotional toll on her—"

"What are you talking about?" Dorian gestured in the direction of his mother's room. "She looked great today. Better than she has in weeks. Like her old self again."

Dorian watched Rochelle's eyes lower briefly before she turned back to the counter. A pregnant pause stretched between them and he couldn't help but feel like she had more to say. He braced himself for the impending argument. He sure as hell didn't feel like going back and forth on this issue, especially with Rochelle, of all people. She had always been so sweet and kind-hearted, and he appreciated how well she treated his mother. It was as if the two ladies were more like sisters than nurse and patient. But thankfully, she remained quiet, the intermittent chops of the knife hitting the cutting board filling the silence between them.

Shantae had rose petals to greet him as soon as he walked through the garage. She had sprinkled a trail on the floor through the kitchen that led straight into the dining room. It was dark, the only light coming from strategically placed candles illuminating his path. She had a slow ballad playing through the surround sound speakers, and a mix of exotic herbs and spices infused the air. She had definitely gone all out to set the mood.

Shantae was seated at the dimly lit dining table, dishes already set with a chilled bottle of wine cooling in the center. As soon as he stepped through the arch, she rose to her feet, a gorgeous red wraparound dress hugging her curves and giving just enough sensual subtlety to get a rise out of him. Damn, she looked good. When was the last time he had really looked at his wife?

"Happy anniversary, sweetie." Shantae rounded the table with two glasses of white wine in hand. She handed one to him before leaning up to plant a delicious kiss on his lips. He moaned into the kiss, drinking in the sweet flavor on her tongue.

"You look amazing," he said, stepping back to admire her. "Happy anniversary." He presented the bouquet of roses he had been holding, and Shantae's smile widened.

"To us." She clinked her glass with his and they both took healthy swigs. Then, she wrapped her arm through his and steered him toward the table.

It looked like she had brought the five-star restaurant to the house. A white linen tablecloth was draped on the glass tabletop, and she had prepped a plate of salmon over a bed of dirty rice and mixed vegetables for each of them. A bowl of salad and a basket of bread rested between two long-stemmed candles, each with a single flame that had shadows dancing on the walls and ceiling.

Dorian was impressed. "This looks great, babe."

"Wait until your surprise." She rested her chin in her hand, her eyes seemingly twinkling with delight.

"Oh, there's more?" Dorian's mind flipped to all the kinky sex stunts she was about to pull out in the bedroom. Shit had him nearly salivating in anticipation. "Well, let's cut right to it, then."

Shantae giggled, amused. "Are you sure? Our food is going to get cold."

"Man, whatever, we have a microwave. Come on."

She tapped a manicured nail on her lip as if she were really contemplating something. Then with a flirtatious smirk, she relented. "Okay, fine."

Dorian was already climbing to his feet when he stopped short at the blue envelope she slid his way.

"Open it," she said. She looked as if she were about to all but burst from some pending excitement.

"This can't wait?"

Shantae smacked her lips. "Babe, come on. Please? I've been holding in the surprise already. I promise, you'll love it."

It looked like the envelope to a standard greeting card, so he was still confused about what could have this woman on the edge of her seat.

He flipped open the flap and pulled out a piece of cardstock. On one side, she had typed three simple words: *Marriage Hall Pass*. Dorian held the paper between his fingers, reading and rereading the inscription. Finally, he glanced up. "What does this mean?" he asked. "I'm lost."

"Read the back," Shantae urged, impatiently waving her hand to speed up the process.

He thought she was being silly, but he obliged, flipping the paper over to read the back. He skimmed the verbiage and looked up to see Shantae still beaming at him, as if proud of herself.

"Girl, you play too much," he said after a pause, giving the card a careless toss on the table.

Shantae laughed at his reaction. "I'm not playing, though."

Dorian fixed his mouth in apparent disbelief. "Yeah, okay. You're going to let me have a night out to do whatever I want, with whoever I want. No questions asked. Yeah right, Shantae."

"I'm serious, babe. This is my gift to you."

Dorian grabbed a piece of bread from the basket. Yeah, he knew she was playing. Or had gone crazy. And since he knew it wasn't the latter, he had to commend her on her acting skills. Anyone else she would have had fooled.

"My coworker told me about it," Shantae explained. "She and her husband do it every year for Christmas, but she said you can do it anytime."

Dorian chewed, still not buying it. "Do what exactly? Like swingers? I need details because this shit is sounding more and more insane."

"She said it's the gift of opportunity. One night only, both of them go do whatever it is they want. Sleep with whoever. Get it out of their system. And then they come home and go back to normal like nothing happened."

"Uh-huh," Dorian said absently. "And why do they do this?"

"It's supposed to bring them closer together." Shantae ran her fingers up and down her wineglass, keeping her eyes on Dorian to gauge his reaction.

He still wasn't buying it. "Oh, okay. Whatever works for them, I guess." Dorian cut into his salmon, the fish falling apart like butter. Warm steam tickled his cheeks as he forked a piece in his mouth.

"You're not even a little interested in this?" Shantae looked shocked at his reaction. "I thought you would like it."

"Did you? Why is that?" Dorian narrowed his eyes, already reading the subtle message in the statement. He knew that she thought his past behaviors made him a serial cheater.

Shantae's eyes ballooned at her mistake, and she shook her head to try and clean it up. "I only meant because, isn't it like every guy's fantasy to have a threesome or something? Isn't this better?"

"Nah, and let me tell you why." Dorian used the end of his fork to count off on his fingers as he continued. "I can have sex or do whatever I want, right?"

"Yes."

"With whoever I want, right?"

"Yep."

"And you're not going to get mad or ask any questions, right?"

"Right."

"That's a damn trap. No thanks." He resumed eating, his head still shaking at the absurdity.

Dorian heard the clink of silverware on china and he lifted his head from his plate as Shantae rose to her feet. He could all but taste the thick tension that suddenly filtered between them.

"Babe, what's wrong?" Her movements were familiarly rigid, and he already knew, even before she spoke, that she was upset. The question was, why? "Babe," he repeated when she didn't answer.

"I'm fine." It was clear she was anything but.

Shocked, Dorian sat back in his chair and watched her begin clearing the table. "You really pissed right now." It was a statement of disbelief rather than an actual question. "I don't want to go cheat on you, and you're mad about that."

"Whatever. You're not interested. Fine. Forget I mentioned it." Shantae carried her plate and glass to the door. "I need to go finish packing. We have an early flight in the morning." She disappeared into the adjoining kitchen, leaving Dorian sitting there in utter shock.

"Un-be-fucking-lievable," he muttered under his breath. His boys were going to have a field day when he told them this one.

Chapter Six

Jamaica was like Atlanta's Freaknik, the scorching heat evidenced with damp foreheads and glistening tanned bodies exposed by cutoff shorts, bikini tops, and flip-flops. Cabs packed the streets in front of Montego Bay's Sangster International, windows down to allow the various reggae beats to intermingle with the airport crowd and city locals. The stifling temperature could have been considered suffocating to some, but to Dorian, it was more than welcome. The arched rooftops and the billowing palm trees accenting the large glass windows coupled with the gorgeous weather were already promising an inviting few days.

Shantae hadn't said too much that morning as they headed to the airport, and she had started dozing shortly after they took off, which was fine with him. It gave him the opportunity to absorb the trip through his first-class window seat, sip his complimentary champagne, assess his current feelings over Shantae's proposal. As he watched her sleep, relaxing in the buzz as the bubbly liquid slid down his throat, he had to admit one thing. He was intrigued. He had tried to put the whole thing out of his mind but after their anniversary dinner went left. But once he realized she had been completely serious about her little Marriage Hall Pass, his thoughts had run rampant.

Part of him also wanted to be angry. Was she just using this as an excuse to sleep with some other man? His mind antagonized him, putting images of his wife in the bed and arms of faceless men. Shit was infuriating the longer he allowed himself to dwell on it.

As they disembarked and grabbed their luggage from baggage claim, she seemed in better spirits. Whether it was the tropical air or the liquor in the Club Mobay Delight drink they'd been given at the gate, Dorian was glad to see she had come up off her little attitude, so it didn't ruin their vacation.

Dorian had called ahead for a car to greet them. As they emerged into the blazing heat, he gestured toward the stocky chauffeur, a polished Jamaican dreadhead with fuzzy locs and a multicolored dashiki, gripping a *Dorian Graham* sign. "Welcome to Montego Bay, Mr. Graham," he greeted, his words thick with his accent. "Mrs. Graham." He nodded to her and she smiled in response. The man took their bags from Dorian and placed them into the trunk of a black Suburban idling among the vehicles that lined the curb.

Dorian opened the car door to let Shantae in first before he followed behind to slide onto the plush leather seats. He tossed his arm around her shoulders as they sped down the island streets, observing the vast array of tropical foliage, listening to some reggae mix blaring through the radio speakers. He could even smell the beach, the scent of saltwater wafting through the open windows. For a moment, all of his problems felt like they were miles away, back in Atlanta, and he planned to enjoy the peace. He sent a quick text to Rochelle to make sure his mom was okay. Satisfied, he gave Shantae's thigh a squeeze.

"You good?" he asked.

She nodded and turned back to the window.

Pulling under the canopy of a gorgeous beachfront hotel, Dorian could see the scene at the entrance was intense, to say the least. There were groups of five here, six there. Eight here, two there. Taxis were pulling up, emptying, loading and pulling off. Bellmen were tossing baggage on carts, handing out tickets, and scurrying inside. Folk were hollering at people they knew and people they wanted to get to know. Guests breezed in and out the sliding glass doors, the hushed lobby music wafting through the breezeway to mingle with the outside activity.

Inside, the check-in line swooped like a snake around the room, tangling with idle guests waiting for elevators or just passing through to the bar. Bodies were piled on cushioned lobby couches and armchairs, the furniture color hidden underneath oversized purses, straw hats, and sun-streaked skin. Laughter and raised voices hung in the air, along with sweat and entirely too much perfume.

Dorian checked in, and as high-paying patrons, they were quickly ushered to one of the expensive villas. Cushioned area rugs were scattered across the gleaming mahogany hardwood floor. Two queen-size beds adorned with red and beige pillows and patchwork linens dominated the airy room. Someone had taken the time to spell out *WELCOME* in carefully arranged rose petals on the bed. Two large, dark wood shutter doors were slid open, revealing the furnished patio overlooking a manicured lawn with hammocks and palm trees. A little farther, but still walking distance, was the white sand and crystal blue water of the beach.

"This place is like heaven," Shantae said after the butler had wheeled their bags in the room and left them alone. "I needed this so much."

Though they both had polished off the complimentary champagne served during check-in in the lobby, Dorian gently tapped his empty glass against hers anyway. "We both did," he said. "So how about we get started enjoying each other?"

Shantae lifted a brow, glanced toward the bed and back at him.

Dorian grinned. "That's not what I meant. But the thought has crossed my mind a few times seeing you in that outfit."

Shantae glanced down at the baby blue bohemian dress, the soft island breeze tickling her exposed back. "I'll take that as a compliment," she said. Dorian opened his mouth to speak, shutting it again when the muffled ring tone of a cell broke the air. Her phone, not his. He stifled a groan when she turned to make her way across the floor to her purse hanging on the door.

"We just got here, Shantae," he said, but she was already digging to retrieve the device.

She glanced at the screen and tossed an apologetic look in his direction. "I'm sorry. One second. It's work."

Dorian could only shake his head as he watched her step out onto the balcony and slide the door shut behind her for privacy.

———⟹•⟸———

One thing was becoming clear.

Dorian sat on the side of the pool with his legs thrown over the edge to cool off in the water. He stared at his wife lounging on a nearby lounge chair, the sun kissing the bits of her skin revealed by the skimpy red bikini, her face hidden behind the shields of her big-frame sunglasses. Something was different between them.

On the surface, it seemed like everything was fine because they were going through the motions of a couple having fun with each other. Jet Skiing that morning with Shantae holding on to his tightened body as the boat pierced the water and the wind slapped his face. They had walked hand in hand toward the boardwalk for a while and when she'd complained her legs were aching, he'd merely scooped her up and carried her on his back until they'd come to one of the many resort pools. Now, as she stretched out letting the sun dry her body, she had claimed to need a nap, popped some earbuds in her ears, and retreated to her own private world.

He figured she had messed around and let work stress her out. That negative energy was contagious, and he hated it was beginning to kill his vibe. He hadn't traveled over a thousand miles to wade through the same tension he lived with every day back in Atlanta, that's for damn sure.

"Leo, stop!"

Dorian glanced over his shoulder at an approaching group. The voice had come from a woman who giggled as a man picked up her slender frame and carried her over his shoulder. Walking alongside them were two other women, one noticeably pregnant in an ivory sundress that flowed to her ankles, the other one with a short pixie cut in a navy-blue halter swimsuit with cutouts at the waist.

The woman now being carried had on a cheetah print bikini and heels, of all things. The man's locs shielded her face from view, but by the subsequent laugh when he slapped her ass, she was enjoying their little friendly engagement.

They stopped at the edge of the pool, and when the man sat the woman down, Dorian saw all three were beautiful in their own individual styles. Cheetah Print looked more glamorous than anything and way too flashy for a day at the pool with her weave ponytail, makeup, and jewelry. But that curvaceous body was definitely her best asset, and she had no problems letting it be known with the string bikini. The pregnant one had a shy aura about her, and with the book she toted, she appeared she would have rather stayed in the hotel room. Ms. Pixie Cut was the youngest-looking, and when she took off her sunglasses to place them on top of her head, her expression carried more boredom and irritation than anything. The man looked like he could have been one of the locals with his chiseled physique, dark complexion, and locs. Dorian couldn't help but wonder what their connection was. Friends? They seemed to have a disjointed relationship, nor did they appear to mesh.

"Hey," he greeted the man and the cheetah print woman as they took their time entering the pool. The other two women had seated themselves at a table under the shade of an umbrella.

"Hey." Only the man responded. The woman just smiled before turning to swim off toward the other end of the pool. Like Dorian, the man lifted himself out of the water to sit on the edge and let his feet dangle in.

As if on cue, a waitress strolled over in a uniform T-shirt and some white shorts. "Mr. Owusu," she said, handing the man a drink from the tray she carried. "Can I get you anything else?" The man reached up to toy with one of the woman's braids, and her smile widened.

"Maybe later, my love," he answered. Then as if remembering, he turned to Dorian. "You want anything?"

"I'm good. I appreciate it," Dorian said.

"No, I insist." The man turned back to the waitress. "Get my man two of your specials. One for him and one for his lady over there." The waitress nodded and flounced off to get their orders. The man exaggerated a groan of appreciation. "Lovely," was all he murmured as he craned his neck to watch the waitress until she disappeared.

"I appreciate it, but you didn't have to do that, man," Dorian said.

"It's no problem. I need to do something to keep that cutie coming around anyway." The man grinned.

Dorian didn't comment. It wasn't like the pint-sized little waitress wasn't pretty. But a quick look across the pool and he saw Shantae's face was now angled toward him, though he still couldn't tell if she was asleep. Better safe than sorry to pretend not to notice the waitress or the other fine-ass women this newcomer had brought with him. If he so much as glanced around a few too many times, he knew her insecurity would kick in full force and intensify an already tense vacation.

"What's your name, man?" Dorian asked instead.

"Leo. You?"

"Dorian."

"You and your lady celebrating something? Or just vacationing?"

"Our one-year anniversary," Dorian answered, though it sure as hell didn't feel like they were celebrating. "What about y'all?"

"Honeymoon."

Dorian risked a quick peek at the woman in the cheetah print bikini as she emerged from the water. She tossed her ponytail over her shoulder before heading to a nearby chair to take a seat.

"Congrats, man," Dorian said, nodding in approval.

"Thanks, but me and Tina over there already had our honeymoon." He gestured toward the two women at the table. "It's my honeymoon with my Kimmy. The one with the short hair."

Dorian's forehead creased in a shock of admiration. "Wait. All of them?"

"My wives," Leo confirmed. "And my baby on the way."

Dorian had to give props to the man. He could barely handle one, let alone three women. Even still, he wouldn't mind so much if he could at least get sex from one of them. He and Shantae were going on day three and she was still on her cycle, which had his sexual frustration building. Especially with all the sexy, scantily clad women this island had to offer.

"Hey, man. Props to you," Dorian said. "My wife wouldn't go for that shit."

Leo shrugged. "You never know. She may surprise you."

Dorian thought again about the Marriage Hall Pass. He had a point.

"You see, women can be complicated creatures," Leo went on. "But I've found that all of those roads lead to two important things." He held up his fingers. "Love and security. You show her enough love and she feels secure financially, she's liable to break her neck trying to please you. Anything extra is a bonus."

Dorian listened intently. Hadn't he showered Shantae with both? Was this really her way of trying to make him happy? "Your girls ever let you live out a fantasy?" he asked.

Leo chuckled as the waitress returned with a tray, handing each of them a drink. "I've got more than a man could ever need or want," he boasted. "Every day is a fantasy. But I'll tell you what. If your girl is willing to give you a little more, why not? Are you really doing something wrong if she allows you to do it?"

At that point, the other woman, who Leo had called Kimmy, strolled up and nudged Leo on his shoulder. "Sweetie, I'm going to take Lena back to the room," she said. "It's hot as hell out here, and the baby's got her feeling sick."

Leo nodded. "Kimmy, this is Dorian. Dorian, my love Kimmy."

"Hi," she greeted.

"Nice to meet you. And congratulations on your wedding."

"Thanks," she said, though she really didn't sound excited.

Dorian turned away from the couple, but out of the corner of his eye, he saw Kimmy lean forward to press her lips against her husband's in a goodbye kiss. For the briefest of moments, he pictured himself like Leo, entertaining both Shantae and Reagan. Not as wives, but with Shantae's consent, it almost seemed like a blessing in disguise. Why cheat when he could have a hall pass?

"We'll be along in a little bit," Leo said, and she nodded before leaving the men alone once more.

"Do what makes you happy," Leo continued with a knowing wink. "Who says you can't have your cake and eat it too? Especially if your wife is the baker." He lifted his glass and Dorian tapped his against it in a mutually understanding toast.

———»•«———

After chatting with Leo, Shantae's offer was now fresh on Dorian's mind, and he hated that he was actually giving it so much thought. She hadn't really gone through the details and he hadn't asked. It was worth digging into, if only to see where her mind was.

They ordered in that night and had dinner on their balcony. The umbrella of the patio table wafted gently in the breeze. The sky was already beginning to color with the impending sunset. Shantae had changed into a cotton short set jumper and a wide-brimmed straw hat that nearly obstructed her face from view. Dorian was also dressed casual in some white khaki shorts and a yellow T-shirt with the Jamaican flag plastered across the front. When the chef had wheeled in the dinner tray, Dorian had taken a deep inhale of the large lobster tail, peas and rice, and baked macaroni and cheese. The distinct island spices peppering the food had his mouth watering.

"That's crazy," Shantae said with a shake of her head as she dug into her macaroni and cheese. "So, he had not one but *three* wives? And they were all friends with each other?"

Dorian had just finished recapping about the polyamorous Leo, Tina, Kimmy, and Lena. Of course, he managed to leave out the little conversation he and Leo had. "Yep," he responded. "Seemed that way. One was pregnant too."

Shantae shook her head. "I could never be cool with something like that."

"Never say never."

"Oh, I can say never on that shit. I would end up killing all of y'all." She giggled into her glass at her comment.

Dorian smirked. "So, I couldn't have another wife," he teased.

Shantae pretended to think about the question. "I guess let me have another husband first and we'll go from there."

They shared a laugh and continued eating. Dorian felt relaxed. More relaxed than he had been this entire time. Whether it was the alcohol or Shantae had finally let go of whatever ill feelings she had been harboring that had put her in a standoffish mood—either way, he was glad. Now he finally felt he could talk to her.

Shantae accepted the glass of wine he poured from the chilled bucket and leaned back, making herself comfortable in the chair.

"You didn't have to go through so much trouble with all this," she said, taking a sip and obviously enjoying the tranquility of the champagne combined with the beachside view. "We could have gone out tonight."

"I thought we would be more comfortable here than in a restaurant," Dorian said. "Plus, I wanted us to talk."

She turned, her eyebrows already creased in a questioning frown. "What's up?"

Dorian paused. "I think I just wanted to see where your mind was about the gift you gave me."

Shantae stared silently, a blur of thoughts playing across her face. "I thought you told me you weren't interested," she said, eventually. "What changed your mind?"

"I'm still not interested. I just don't think I was fair in not hearing you out. I shut you down without giving you the opportunity to explain."

Shantae took another sip from her wineglass. "Well, I hadn't thought it all the way through myself. It's not like I've done it before."

"Okay. Let's start over from the beginning. Where did you say the idea came from again? A coworker?"

She nodded. "Yeah. I don't know if you remember Tiffany. But she said that she and her husband do some kind of marriage hall pass once a year. No strings attached. No questions asked. They pick a day and every year they go out, you know, do their thing and come home and move on like nothing happened."

The whole thing still sounded crazy as hell. And too damn good to be true. Dorian listened, waiting for the catch. "And what is this supposed to prove?"

"I don't think they're trying to prove anything," Shantae clarified. "It just lets them have a little freedom. Get those burning desires out of their system. She swears by it. Says it makes them a stronger couple. Been married twelve years. She says they don't even argue."

"I find that shit hard to believe."

Shantae shrugged. "I'm just telling you what she said."

Dorian sat back in his seat, tossing her words around over and over in his head. "So what? You have some burning desires you need to get out of your system?"

She rolled her eyes. "You're missing the point. If you don't want to do it, just say that. Don't start insinuating shit like I'm trying to sleep around, because I can do that with or without your fucking knowledge."

Her words pierced like a knife. He hated the idea of Shantae out cheating—well, doing everything he had already done to her. It pissed him off even further because her comment was true, and she would be well within her rights.

He blew out a steadying breath, releasing some of the pent-up irritation. "I'm not insinuating that," he said, much calmer than before. "I'm just saying if you're unsatisfied or if there is something I'm not doing, I want you to feel comfortable telling me."

This time, a ghost of a smile flirted around Shantae's lips. "I do," she said. "I would feel comfortable if it was something. But it's nothing. That's not why I think we should do this."

"Okay, then why? Let me hear your thoughts."

Shantae reached across the table to rest her hand on his. Ever so gently, she caressed his knuckles with feather-like strokes. "We're both happy, right," she murmured. "And we trust each other, don't we?"

"Of course."

"Well then, what could go wrong? And who knows, it'll probably be fun," she went on, finally lifting her eyes to meet his. "Just a little experiment. I mean, we don't have to do it every year or anything. And we can always change our minds."

The more she reasoned, the more the idea became more appealing. Thoughts of Reagan played on his subconscious once more. Damn, he wanted that woman. But was that crossing some invisible boundary? He didn't agree or disagree. Not yet. But he sure as hell would be weighing his options.

"And what are the rules?" he asked, just to be sure.

Something glinted in Shantae's eyes. Something dangerous and wildly erotic. "Who said anything about rules?"

Chapter Seven

Dorian never thought he would see the day, that's for damn sure. He stood at the altar alongside his boys, Myles and Neil, in identical charcoal gray tailcoats with gray vests and black bow ties. A single purple handkerchief added a splash of color peeking out of each of their breast pockets. Like the others, Dorian waited patiently, his face stoic, his hands clasped firmly in front as the processional began and Freddie Jackson's "You Are My Lady" blared through the speakers of the event hall.

He didn't dare look over and risk breaking their strict formation, but if he had to guess, Dorian was sure Roman had that big-ass goofy grin on his face. Ever since he had talked to them about proposing to Bridget, and especially after she had said yes, the man had been damn near floating with his head in the clouds. Never had Dorian seen him act that way. Nor did he ever think he would see the day Roman would actually want to go through with this kind of commitment. But one thing he could genuinely say was his friend appeared happy. Damn what anyone else said or thought.

Roman's daughter Maya followed behind the rest of the wedding party, looking just like a mini Roman with the exception of two long plaits with purple ribbons on either side of her head. She tossed a few pink rose petals to her feet before looking up and fiercely waving at her father from the middle of the aisle, which garnered a few chuckles and awws.

Then, the French doors opened and there the bride stood, her arm looped through her father's, a purple and ivory beaded bouquet clutched in her other hand. She did look beautiful, Dorian had to admit. And even the sheer veil couldn't hide the enormous smile plastered on her face.

Dorian chanced cutting his eyes to the side, surprised to see tears sliding down the side of Roman's face. Damn, did he even cry at his own wedding? He didn't think so. He remembered Shantae had been bawling the entire time, her makeup lightly smeared by the time she had made it to him at the altar. She hadn't even been able to get through her vows in one breath. And all the while, he had gone through the ceremonial motions until they'd left as man and wife. Funny how that had only been a year ago when it felt like much, much longer.

He tuned out the couple as they exchanged vows and instead looked to the audience for a slight distraction. Everyone was enthralled by the festivities, some even dabbing their eyes dry with crumpled tissues. He had never been the crying type, so he sure as hell couldn't relate to being so emotional for someone else's marriage. Dorian pegged the last time he had shed a tear was at his father's funeral. And he attributed that to the fact it was his father and he was a kid.

Without thinking, his eyes met Shantae's in the crowd, and she too was watching with a heartfelt, almost envious, look at Roman and Bridget. Strange. Shantae acted as if they had something she didn't. Dorian assessed it for a moment longer before he decided to ignore it. He had long since given up hope of trying to figure out every nuisance that made up Mrs. Shantae Graham. It was less stressful that way.

But when his eyes shifted to the woman beside her, he could only pray no one else had captured that moment of lust. Reagan's eyes were already on him, as if she had been watching and waiting all along until his gaze found its way to hers. Even across the room, he could feel her heated stare as the hint of a smile flirted on her lips. She had tamed her wild mane into a neat bun at the base of her neck to further expose her sexy features. Now as they sat side by side, Dorian saw the striking sisterly resemblance. But still, his eyes lingered on Reagan, perhaps way longer than they should have. Shantae hadn't mentioned her sister would be in attendance while they were getting dressed that morning. Then what was she doing there?

Dorian didn't realize he was still staring until Shantae's head whipped in his direction and he blinked to break the eye contact. He wasn't even sure if Shantae caught him looking at her sister and him quickly turning away. It probably looked guilty as hell. Either way, he directed his gaze back to the altar and resolved to deal with her, and Reagan, later at the reception.

"A toast," Myles said, lifting his glass in the air. "To our boy Roman for finally letting a woman put a leash on his wild ass."

Dorian and the rest of their crew laughed and clinked their glasses together. "Hear, hear," they shouted in unison, the reception activity buzzing around them.

"Y'all crazy," Roman said, chuckling at their brotherly banter. "But you know what, I don't even care. I love that girl."

"Yeah, we know," Dorian teased, nudging his arm. "I ain't never seen your nose so wide open."

"Hey, hold up. At least my woman didn't punk me into a marriage, Dr. Graham," Roman shot back with a shrug and lifted his glass to his lips to down the rest of his alcohol.

Dorian narrowed his eyes. There was that candor again, whether he wanted to hear it or not. He ignored the twinge of agitation. "Wait, what you mean? Shantae ain't punked me into shit." He watched as all three of his friends exchanged knowing looks before bursting out into another round of drunken laughter.

"Man, please, we already know if Shantae hadn't gotten pregnant you wasn't thinking about no damn marriage," Myles said.

"Especially not with her," Roman added. "But he thinks we're stupid."

"Truer words have never been spoken, my friend." It was Neil's cosign this time. He pushed his glasses up farther on his nose. "She does have you on lock and key."

Dorian laughed, partially to ease his discomfort. "Man, whatever," he said. "If my girl punked me and has me on lock and key, why is she trying to give me a hall pass?"

Neil frowned. "The hell is that?"

"Nigga, you need a hall pass to use the bathroom in your own house?" Myles howled in laughter at his comment.

Dorian rolled his eyes. "Y'all know our anniversary was the other day," he explained. "So, she gives me a Marriage Hall Pass, which is basically permission to cheat for one night." All three stared, apparently waiting for him to laugh at the joke he had just made.

"Man, quit lying." Roman was the first to speak.

Dorian took another drink. "I'm serious."

"Well damn, let me ask Bridget for some shit like that."

"And watch she divorce your ass before y'all get to the honeymoon," Myles retorted.

"Well? You gon' do it?" Neil's questioning look was back on Dorian.

"I haven't decided," he admitted. Something was still holding him back. What, he didn't know.

"What's there to decide?" Roman nudged Dorian's shoulder. "Other than which ass you want first and in what order."

"Does that mean Shantae gets to have a hall pass?" Neil asked, apparently trying to make logical sense of the whole arrangement. "Or does it only work one way?"

"Nah, her too I believe."

"And you cool with that?" It was Myles this time, shaking his head. "Hell no, ain't nobody sleeping with my girl but me."

Roman snorted. "What girl? You ain't got no damn girl."

Myles's grin was smug. "Yeah, okay. If I ain't got no girl, who did I bring with me then?" He nodded toward the buffet table where Reagan and Shantae stood in line chatting, plates in hand. Dorian's heart dropped. Damn, they were dating. Why did that piss him off?

"Isn't that Shantae's sister?" Neil spoke up as they all continued to stare.

"Hell yeah, it is," Roman pretended to lick his lips in appreciation. "And she fine as hell like Shantae too." He glanced in Dorian's direction. "But you better watch out, though. Big brother Dorian gon' beat your ass you fuck over his baby sister."

Dorian cringed. He definitely wasn't trying to think of Reagan as his baby sister. Not when he was trying to get between her legs himself. His throat suddenly felt dry, so he poured himself another glass from the Crown Royal bottle they all were passing around between them. "Man, I don't care about that," he murmured with a little too much attitude. It was a bald-face lie and he hoped no one could tell.

"When y'all start talking, my friend?"

"The bachelor party," Myles said. "Yeah, she was all up on your boy. Just throwing it at me all night."

Dorian felt his fingers tighten on the glass. He knew that had to be a lie. Not when Reagan had been pushing up on him all night. He didn't know why this story was bothering him so much. Myles was notorious for embellishing the truth when it came to his sexual exploits, so Dorian was sure this was no different.

He tried to tune Myles out as he began to detail their many

dates and late-night rendezvous, the way she would sex him down with all the tricks and flexibility of a regular porn star. Yeah, shit was infuriating because not only should that have been him, but Shantae had been ducking and dodging sex for the last three weeks. And to hear baby sis was giving it up so quickly, and let Myles tell it, so frequently, had Dorian itching to punch that little complacent look off his friend's face.

Dorian knocked back the rest of his liquor and set his glass on the table. He needed air. Even he couldn't believe how badly this girl had gotten to him. Never had he ever wanted to fight Myles. Roman, yes. All the damn time. But Myles was generally their little group's jokester and all-around happy-go-lucky guy. Dorian had never even gotten in an argument with the man in their five-year friendship.

"You good, D?" Myles broke through his concentration. Dorian glanced around at all three of them watching him. He hadn't noticed he had risen and was now just standing there in a daze. His vision blurred a little and he blinked a few times before he dared move. God forbid he take a step and tumble face first right there in the middle of the reception hall.

When he was sure he was steady, Dorian nodded. "Yeah, I'm good," he said, surprised when his words didn't slur. "I'll be right back."

"You need to go find some ass for that hall pass, bro," Roman said, and again they all snickered as Dorian stumbled away.

The DJ had the Black People's National Anthem "Before I Let Go" blasting, and a terrible harmony of voices lifted over the music to blend together as everyone crowded on the dance floor. Dorian found his way through and headed for the front door.

It was chilly tonight, as expected for winter. He didn't know why Roman had opted for a wedding so close to the Christmas holiday season anyway. A few folks were leaving the party early, but other than some stragglers, he was alone to enjoy the night air.

The music and joyous celebratory noises were slightly muffled but could still be heard from his perch right outside the foyer. Roman had told them Bridget was the youngest of seven, so her family had been waiting to throw the wedding of all weddings for their baby girl. Dorian didn't know for sure, but he could bet their guest list was somewhere in the ballpark of three hundred folks.

He sucked in a greedy breath of air and found his way to a nearby bench. At least he felt better. It was just the mix of heat, liquor, and people, he reasoned. No way anything else could substantiate him wanting to fight one of his best friends over his sister-in-law.

"Dorian?" Damn, speak of the devil. Reagan strolled up the sidewalk, the end of a lit cigarette clasped between her fingers. Dorian couldn't help but eye her jungle green lace dress. The neckline was low enough to have a little cleavage peeking through, and the hemline easily brushed her knees. It wasn't even too overtly revealing. So why then, did he want to rip it off right then and there?

"You okay?" Reagan asked, her lips turned in a concerned frown. "You don't look too good."

Dorian stifled a groan as she took a step closer, bringing with her that delicious-smelling perfume that had his mouth watering. He would be just fine if she stayed back. Any closer and he would likely lose it.

"I'm good," he said. "What you are doing out here?"

Reagan held up her fingers and put the cigarette to her lips. Was it just him or was she exaggerating wrapping those luscious lips of hers around the butt of that cigarette? She inhaled deeply, then lifted her face to blow a steady stream of smoke in the air.

"They ran out of food in there," she said. "I just stepped out for a smoke. Trying to decide if it would be rude of me to go get some McDonald's." She giggled, and the sound was so low and sultry. Like music to his ears.

"Tell your boyfriend Myles to get it for you," he said. Immediately he cursed himself. He hadn't meant for the suggestion to sound so bitter. He didn't even recognize his own tone.

Reagan cocked her head to the side and lifted an eyebrow. It was dark but it also looked as if her eyes were dancing in subtle amusement. "Yeah, maybe," she said simply. She tossed what was left of the cigarette in a nearby patch of grass and used the toe of her stiletto to extinguish any remaining flame. She started back toward the entrance to return to the reception.

"I thought you said you weren't dating him." Dorian didn't even know he had said it until the words left his lips.

Reagan's shrug was one of nonchalance. "Shit changes," she said. "Why? Is it a problem?" She waited, keeping her eyes level with his.

Now it was Dorian's turn to shrug. "I mean, you're grown. You can do whatever you want to."

Reagan nodded. She reached to pull the door open before he stopped her again.

"I just didn't think he was your type. That's all."

She turned again, this time an entertaining smirk on her face. "Oh yeah?" She closed the distance between them and leaned over to Dorian, her face only inches from his. "And what's my type," she whispered, her breath tickling Dorian's lips, "you?"

He didn't bother thinking. Fuck trying to be rational.

His hand circled the back of her neck, his fingers tangling in her hair and dragging her toward him. She could've stopped it. He was moving slow enough to see if she would. He had time to catch her eyes for a split second, saw the desire reflected in her pupils before her heavy lids fluttered closed and she sucked in a sharp breath as his mouth crushed hers.

He wasn't prepared for the hunger that erupted from the contact. Nor was he prepared for her compliancy, the ease with which she matched his need. He felt her shudder, but he was aroused when he tasted the sweet urgency mixed with nicotine on her tongue, her lips parted both to give and to receive. He swallowed her moan and, on a muffled curse, tugged her hair back and snatched his lips from hers to press against the delicious column of her throat.

Dorian heard her suck in a desperate breath when her mouth was free, soaked in the sheer pleasure as he explored her neck. On a startled gasp, she stepped back and glanced around the empty parking lot to be sure no one had seen them going at it in the moonlight. Adrenaline had him completely sober now, and he too glanced around. Though he, on the other hand, didn't give a damn about spectators. Not at the moment.

She lowered her eyes to the pavement, and he continued to watch her, willing her to look at him. On a sigh, she looked up to finally meet his eyes. "How long are we going to play this game, Dorian?" she asked.

He wanted to smile when he heard her voice had thickened with desire. At least he wasn't the only one. But still, he didn't answer. Instead, he took one of those leisurely full-body gazes, as if he were committing each piece of her to memory. The saying was true. Forbidden fruit always tasted the sweetest.

"Let's cut the bullshit," Reagan continued, licking her lips. "You're my sister's husband. I don't give a damn. I'm your friend's girlfriend. And I still don't give a damn. If you want me, I'm all yours. Just come get me, Doctor." She turned and disappeared back into the foyer, and Dorian could only watch. Say less. He fully intended to have her. Because at this point, he frankly didn't give a damn either.

Chapter Eight

"I just don't get her sometimes, babe." Shantae's voice lifted over the water as she ranted.

Dorian was half listening as he showered. He had caught snatches of the story—at least, he thought he could figure out the gist of it. Apparently, she and her sister had an argument at the wedding after Reagan had asked for money. *Again.* According to Shantae, she was pissed because this was the second time this week. Something about her baby's dad Terrell being behind on child support and her son TJ needing a better role model.

Dorian mumbled some words of acknowledgment, but he knew Shantae wasn't expecting him to do more than listen. Not that he was trying to. He was thinking about when and where he was going to turn the girl out. He was all but smiling as his wife continued to fuss, but his mind was elsewhere. What would she feel like? Would she taste as good as she looked? He didn't know his body had been aching for this woman until they kissed, and now he couldn't shake it. The more he thought about it, the more excited he became. He felt himself rising, and the shit was getting painful. He quickly flipped the handle to send the cold spray blasting and damn near threw his body into an epileptic shock with the sudden drop in temperature.

"Shit," he yelled, gritting his teeth at the pressure. Shantae ignored him and just kept right on talking.

"I guess I'm just supposed to take care of her and my nephew, right," she was saying. "Like I don't have my own shit and my own bills to worry about."

Dorian cut off the water and snatched his towel from over the frosted glass door. He had calmed himself down, that's for sure. Now he was feeling the remnants of the alcohol in a pounding headache.

"Well, she is family, babe," he mumbled since it sounded like a nice, neutral response.

Shantae was in their mirror massaging some sort of green paste on her face. "I guess family doesn't take advantage of family, right," she snapped, clearly frustrated.

"I didn't mean it like that." Dorian's voice was weary. He had enough trying to deal with the hangover. He sure as hell wouldn't be able to handle Hurricane Shantae 2.7 also. He kept his tone gentle. "I just meant that right or wrong, she has no one but you. Hell, I don't have any siblings—"

"I know, baby, I'm sorry." Shantae turned and wrapped her arms around Dorian's waist, careful she didn't smudge her facial mask on his arm. She sighed. "I didn't mean to snap at you. It just . . . frustrates me because she has the potential to do so much better, you know? Make something of herself for her and her son. But it's like she doesn't care. Do you know she can do hair? Like really do hair. She never went to school for it or anything. Just taught herself, and she's better than a lot of beauticians I've seen. But while she could be trying to get a job or open a salon, she's dropping TJ off at my parents' while she's out drinking and clubbing."

Dorian listened intently. Damn he didn't know half the stuff Shantae was saying about Reagan. "All you can do is keep being there for her," he said when she paused a moment. "And leading by example."

Shantae leaned up and planted a friendly peck on his lips. "I appreciate you, babe. I really do. How do you put up with me?"

Good question. Shantae gave Dorian's naked butt a squeeze and turned back to the mirror.

Dorian wrapped the ivory plush towel around his waist and waited for a moment, not sure how to broach the subject. Best to just come right out and say it. He cleared his throat. Why was he nervous? It had been her idea. Maybe she was calling his bluff. Wanting to see if he would go for it so she could revert to her old ways because she suspected he was cheating. Dorian pondered that possibility a little longer before he shrugged it off. Oh well, he decided. She shouldn't have offered. And even if she reneged, he sure as hell wouldn't let her forget it. But at this point, the prospect of sexing Reagan was worth the chance.

"I was thinking again," he started, joining his wife at the granite countertop of their double vanity. "If we opted to do the hall pass, when would you want to do it?"

He caught something flicker in Shantae's eyes. Very brief, and very subtle. So much so he had to wonder if he saw anything at all because she was now turning to face him, a wide smile that had her dimple winking in her cheek.

"You keep asking," she said. "So you must be really interested."

"I'm just trying to make sure we both have a clear understanding and we're on the same page. That's all."

"Well, I'm clear," Shantae agreed. "More than clear. I really think this will be good for us as a couple. Just as long as we can come home the following day with a clean slate. Like it never even happened. Agreed?"

Hell yeah, he could. He just hoped she was as understanding at that time as she was right now. "Of course," he said. Then for good measure he added, "No strings. No questions. And we're coming out on the other side of this a stronger, closer couple."

Shantae nodded, and as if she were completing a business transaction, she held out her hand. Dorian felt silly but he accepted it and gave it a gentle squeeze.

"And no takebacks," Shantae said quickly as they stood there in mid-handshake. "Not fair to get each other's hopes up and then the day of, one of us backs out. Might as well see it all the way through at this point."

Dorian shook her hand. Like hell he was backing out now. He and Reagan had been playing around for the past few weeks. And now he was going to have her. He was nearly tempted to call her right then and there to set things in motion, but that would have seemed way too eager.

"So, when were you thinking?" he asked as Shantae turned back to the mirror to continue wrapping her hair under a black satin bonnet.

"Well, do you have plans or anything this weekend?"

"Nope."

Shantae grinned at his reflection in the mirror. "I guess now we do," she said and patted Dorian on the chest. "Night, baby. Love you," she said and crossed into the adjoining bedroom.

He should have been more excited. Why wasn't he more excited? Dorian yawned and chalked it up to an eventful day. He knew once he spoke to Reagan and they got their plans finalized, he would be looking forward to the weekend. In the meantime . . .

Dorian saw that Shantae had used the last bit of toothpaste. He looked under his cabinet first, then hers. Hopefully one of them had remembered to grab some during the last store run.

The bright pink box caught his attention as soon as he sifted through Shantae's makeup and hair care products. It was pushed toward the back, but the label was bold enough to have him frowning as he reached to pull it into view. But he already knew. Even as his fingers touched the cardboard, he already knew what the contents were. A quick peek inside the open flap only further confirmed it. Now the question was, what was his wife doing with a pregnancy test? And what were the results?

<hr />

"Did you ask her about it?"

Roman sat back in his executive office chair and stared at Dorian from across the desk. At first glance, no one would guess the educated, well-spoken emergency room physician was the same raw best friend Dorian and scraped up off many a college dorm parking lot back when they met. Everyone knew Roman was the wild party animal of the bunch. So it even shocked Dorian that, except for his bachelor party, Roman had really scaled back on his weekly turn-ups. Bridget had certainly done a number on him.

Dorian rose to pace his friend's office, his mind still racing over the recent findings he had divulged to Roman. "No, I didn't ask her about it," he answered. "Hell, I didn't know what to say. Or how to say it."

"Nah, don't play. You scared of those results."

Dorian winced at the accuracy. Was that why Shantae had asked him about a baby that day at lunch? She was trying to get pregnant? Or was she already pregnant? Dorian tried to rack his brain for the last time they had sex, which, in and of itself was a damn shame, it had been so long. Somewhere around mid-October. With Thanksgiving coming up, wouldn't that make her about . . . five or six weeks? He didn't know how that worked.

"I'm thinking if it were true, she would've told me by now," Dorian reasoned more to himself.

Roman nodded. "True. So maybe she isn't, then. Or maybe she is and just wants to be a hundred percent sure. Or maybe she got rid of it. Shit, I don't know, D. Just ask her. See what she says. But look, we need to get to the real shit." Roman winked and he sat forward again, his elbows resting on his wood desk. "What are you going to do about your hall pass? You're doing it, right?"

Dorian smirked. "Yeah."

"I was about to say you a fool if you don't, man. You decide who yet?"

Dorian already knew he wasn't divulging that information. He didn't even know how true it was that Reagan was in a relationship with their friend Myles. But the fact that she was Shantae's sister alone was giving him enough anxiety.

"Still weighing my options," he lied after a brief pause.

"Okay, man. It just better be somebody good. Don't waste it." He stood and snatched his lab coat from a nearby hook. "I got rounds and then I'm out. You know we're headed to Bali this weekend for the honeymoon. You gon' have to keep Myles posted until I get back."

Dorian chuckled but didn't respond. That sure as hell wasn't happening.

"And hey," Roman added as they reached the door. "Remember, you're not just doing this for you. This is for all of us. If things go smoothly, I'm putting Shantae in Bridget's ear." He slapped Dorian's back. "So don't fuck it up for me, man."

He was right. Dorian didn't bother delaying the inevitable any longer. As soon as he left Roman's office, he was already pulling out his cell phone.

Reagan answered on the first ring, as if she had been waiting for him. "Hey, stranger," she greeted, a smile in her voice.

Dorian licked his lips. There it was. That excitement he had been waiting for. "Hey, sexy," he said. "What are you doing this weekend?"

Chapter Nine

Dorian couldn't help but feel nervous as he stared at the Christmas tree dominating their formal living room. For as long as they had been together, Christmas was always Shantae's favorite time of year, one of the reasons she had insisted on a wedding during the holiday season. It was also why she just had to have that damn tree up in the middle of November as opposed to waiting until after Thanksgiving like normal folks. The tree's white branches were adorned in teal, gold, and bronze ornaments of varying sizes. Strands of gold beads and lights draped across the lush foliage and twinkled against the night sky's backdrop of the bay window.

Dorian took another deep breath as his eyes landed on the few wrapped presents stacked on the white tree skirt. He felt silly as hell being nervous like some shy teenager. He knew what he was getting himself into, and he was far too experienced in the sexual arena to have cause for concern. But this was different. And that alone was enough to cause him to harden in his crisp Polo slacks.

Suddenly uncomfortable with the bulge, Dorian got up and

crossed to the kitchen. His hands busied themselves with pouring a shot of Hennessy, even as his mind wandered to the delicious events that would take place in a few hours. She had sounded so damn sexy on the phone earlier. He figured she would be naked and ready for him when he came over. But it was her idea that they meet for dinner and drinks first. Then they could get a hotel room, and how did she describe it? Let him devour her. Dorian lifted the glass to his lips as they turned up in a pleased smirk. Yeah, he planned to devour her, all right. Every inch of her.

Heels clicked down the hardwood stairs and Dorian turned just in time to see Shantae enter the living room. Damn, she looked good. The fire red bandage dress hugged her slim figure and dipped provocatively low to expose her cleavage. It was short as hell, nearly riding up under the bottom of her ass and showing off those honey brown legs, toned with her weekly workout regimen. Her black tresses lay feathered against her cheeks, while the back tapered against her neck. It looked like she had taken extra care with her makeup, putting it on with the precision of an artist painting a canvas. And though gorgeous, she had gone minimal to further enhance her natural beauty.

Her doe eyes met Dorian's and her nude-colored lips peeled back into a wicked grin. He had to admit, his wife had pulled out all the stops tonight. When was the last time she had gone to such great lengths for him? With the exception of their recent anniversary, he honestly couldn't remember. For a brief moment, Dorian was tempted to call off their little arrangement, take her upstairs, and make her remember one reason why she had married him in the first place.

"Look at you, handsome," Shantae purred. The scent of her perfume was exotic and greeted him before she joined him in the kitchen.

Dorian glanced down at his simple attire, the Polo slacks and button-up casual enough for what he had in mind. "Definitely not compared to you," he said, with a nod toward her dress. "You look amazing."

He saw the hint of a blush at the compliment. "Thank you," she said. "Pour me some of that too, please."

Dorian obliged, pulling down another glass and pouring her some of the brown liquor. Shantae took a seat at the island and accepted the glass he handed her. "What are we toasting to?" Dorian asked, refilling his own glass.

"To new experiences," she answered with a smirk.

Dorian nodded and bumped his glass against hers before taking a deep swig.

Shantae polished off her drink and turned on the swivel stool to stand up. Dorian watched his wife sashay toward the front door, and he groaned inwardly.

"Damn, baby, can I at least get some before you go?"

Shantae tossed a smile over her shoulder. "I got you tomorrow, baby," she said, snatching her coat from the back of the couch. "All day if you want. But you know what tonight is."

Dorian nodded and tried not to focus on Shantae's body jiggling as she shimmied into her coat. Yeah, he knew. He would just have to take his sexual frustration out on someone else. He could hold off on lusting for his wife. Her sister was waiting for him, and dammit, thanks to his wife, he was about to take full and complete advantage of this once-in-a-while opportunity.

<hr />

But Dorian had to continually coach himself as he made the short drive to Reagan's hotel. Never had he crossed the line to this extent. Not even when he was cheating on Shantae with every upperclassman in college. It was always classmates, coworkers, friends that he had met, a few one-night stands, even an adjunct professor one semester. But never any relation to his girl. He couldn't help feeling uneasy at the decision, like he was slowly taking himself to the top of a roller coaster and was teetering on the edge, waiting for it to catapult him into a whirlwind of dips and twists. Or maybe he was just overreacting.

Now here he was. Sitting in the parking lot of the premium St. Regis Hotel in Buckhead, a hard-on penetrating the crotch area of his slacks, he thought about what waited for him in the hotel. He checked the time: 8:17. They had reservations for dinner in the restaurant at eight.

Dorian sat a moment longer, taking in the cool night breeze through his cracked window. Again, he pictured his wife in her tight dress, and his jaw clenched at the possible things she was doing. Or letting someone do to her. He had been going back and forth with these visions all afternoon, so he knew it was only a matter of time before the sordid thoughts faded and he could focus on his own impending actions.

His phone rang and Dorian swiped the screen to answer. "Yeah?"

"Are you coming?" Her voice was sultry with a slight slur, evidence of the alcohol in her system. "Or did you change your mind?" Her voice was nearly drowned out by the background noises of the restaurant.

"I'm coming in now," he said and hung up. He killed the engine and emerged from the truck, taking his time across the parking lot. As he headed toward the hotel, he knew his gait was slightly off, no thanks to the swollen meat bouncing off his thigh.

He had made a point to get a room at the most upscale hotel in Atlanta. Yes, it could seem foul since he had brought Shantae here a few times. And yes, it was costing him a shit-ton of money for the night. But he wasn't about to cheapen this experience. Plus, he knew even with all of Reagan's conniving and mooching, she wasn't used to the finer things in life. Dorian knew she would appreciate the indulgence.

The five-star hotel had been decorated for Christmas. A huge tree dominated the lobby, nearly invisible under the numerous ornaments and garland. Lights, wreaths, and red ribbon bows hung on walls and wrapped around columns to add festive color and charm. Even the front desk attendant tipped his Santa hat in Dorian's direction as he breezed by.

The restaurant had an elegant yet inviting atmosphere, and Dorian felt slightly underdressed among the suited patrons dripping in jewelry and money. The ambience was candle-lit with chandeliers dimmed for intimacy and fine-dressed waitstaff carrying an array of gourmet delicacies.

Reagan was already seated in a quaint two-seater booth by a huge glass window overlooking the cityscape. Though she didn't stand up, she held out her arm for an embrace as he walked up.

Obediently, Dorian obliged and leaned into her hug, inhaling that seductive scent she always carried along. And just because it felt equally appropriate, he went ahead and followed it up with a gentle kiss. The gesture seemed so natural and fluid. Someone could have easily mistaken the pair for long-lost lovers.

"You look good," he said as he eased into the seat across from her. Her simple black dress dipped invitingly low both in the front and the back. Diamonds, well more than what she could afford, glittered at her ears and the slim column of her neck. She too had taken care with applying makeup, though her smoky eyes and deep purple lipstick were far more dramatic than Shantae's. She had left her hair to do its own thing, and it draped thick and loose around her face.

"Thank you. So do you."

"You haven't been waiting long, have you?"

Shadows from the flickering candlelight played on Reagan's face. "Yes," she said. "But I know you'll make the wait worth my while."

Dorian licked his lips. He planned to.

A waiter brought a vintage wine to the table and poured each of them a glass.

"This place is insane," Reagan commented, glancing around at her surroundings. "You ever been here?"

"Mm-hmm, a couple times. The food is great, and they have one of the best wine collections in the city. Are you a wine drinker?"

Reagan's scrunched up her nose. "Not really. I need something stronger to give me a buzz."

Dorian laughed. "Well, we know what happened the last time you got a buzz."

The flashback to the club had Reagan rolling her eyes.

"Whatever," she said, dismissing his joke with a wave of her hand. "I'm just saying. I like what I like and if it works, why change it? But," she added, lifting her glass in the air, "I am always open to trying something new."

Dorian raised his glass as well. "To something new, then," he said, clinking his glass to hers. How ironic that he and his wife had just toasted to the same thing. He watched her take a ginger sip and smack her lips together as if trying to assess the taste.

"Well, what do you think?"

"About the wine?" she asked. "Or the company?"

"Both."

Reagan pursed her lips, running a finger up and down the stem of her glass as she pretended to give the question some serious consideration. "Not as bad as I thought," she admitted. "It's making an impression. Enough to leave me wanting more."

Her grin spread with the eloquent play on words.

The waiter returned to take their orders and left them alone once more. Reagan took another sip and cleared her throat. "So, Dr. Graham, what made you finally take me up on my offer?"

Dorian didn't know why, but at that moment, he felt compelled to be honest. He owed her that much. "Shantae gave me a hall pass," he admitted. "A little experiment, you could say."

Reagan sat forward, her face resting on her hands. "Is that so? I'm intrigued. Do tell."

"Basically, we have a night to be free from marriage."

Reagan chuckled. "And you chose to spend it with me. Why is that?"

Dorian continued to keep it completely real with her. "Because I want you," he said simply.

"Fair enough. But does it bother you I'm Myles's girlfriend?"

"It should," Dorian admitted on a shrug. "But no. You have however long you want with Myles. I just have you for tonight."

"Well then. I guess I better make this a night you will always remember."

———※◇※———

Dorian hadn't meant for them to stay down in the restaurant so long. He had expected to be lapping on to round three by now. But the drinks and conversation were flowing, and they were both having a great time. Reagan's personality was infectious. Of course, she was brazen and said exactly what was on her mind, and he sure as hell didn't mind her constant flirting. But she was also inquisitive and attentive, genuinely interested in what he had to say.

He had asked about her passion for styling hair. It seemed like he had dampened her mood a little with the question before she had rambled on about not having the time or the money to pursue that since it wasn't making any real money. But she had commented she had never had anyone take such an interest in her passion and it was wildly turning her on. That was when he had called for the check and instructed her to go on up to the room and wait for him.

An instrumental version of "Jingle Bells" wafted through the elevator speakers as the he rode it up to the grand deluxe suite. She had pulled the flip lock between the door and the wall so he could just push it open.

The room was spacious, embraced in hues of cream with jewel

tone accents. The five-star hotel's luxury was evident in the custom furnished interiors and artistic decorations. Dorian had called in his requests ahead of time and the staff had not disappointed. Rose petals trailed from the door and were sprinkled on the plush comforter. The curtains had been drawn on the French doors to reveal a panoramic view of the city skyline.

He heard the water running and what sounded like jazz and humming coming from the bathroom. The succulent smell of vanilla grew stronger the closer he got. Dorian pushed the door open and smiled at the provocative sight.

Reagan was soaking neck-deep in the jetted tub. Her body was completely hidden under bubbles, and lit candles surrounded the lip of the tub, causing flicks of light to bounce off the water. Her hair was now piled high into a messy bun on top of her head, and either beads of water or sweat glistened off her rich chocolate complexion.

When she turned to eye him, a mischievous smile spread on her lips. For a split second, an eerie feeling sent a shudder down Dorian's spine. Damn, she looked just like Shantae. Same complexion, same eyes, same dimple winking at the left cheek. Not twins by any means, but the sibling resemblance couldn't be mistaken.

He struggled to shake away the thoughts of his wife. The moment was here, and this was most certainly not Shantae.

"So, you just gon' stand there?" Reagan said, her voice low in seduction. "Or are you going to join me, Dr. Graham?"

Pushing all doubts out of his mind, Dorian came out of his clothes. He crossed the bathroom and dipped his foot in the water. He cursed as the liquid scorched his skin. Reagan chuckled.

"Be careful," she teased. "You might get burned." The candlelight cast a slight shadow across the smile planted on her face.

"You think you funny, little girl." Dorian hissed as he submerged the rest of his body in the tub. He leaned back against the side as Reagan quickly got to her knees and positioned herself between his legs. Suds trailed down the shape of her breasts.

"Oh, trust me," she said, massaging his thighs. "I'm not little by any means anymore." She laughed when Dorian continued to stare. She lifted one breast to her lips and flicked her tongue across her erect nipple. "Touch them," she demanded, arching her back so her titties stood high and proud in his face.

Dorian had to admit, being dominated was erotic. Shantae never took command in the bedroom. That was one thing he had requested on numerous occasions, but she had yet to oblige. Sometimes, it did feel humiliating to have to ask for sexual favors.

He lifted his hands and cupped her breasts, surprised at how soft her flesh felt between his fingers.

"That feels so good," Reagan moaned.

Anxious to feel them in his mouth, Dorian leaned forward and took one nipple between his lips. Reagan wrapped her arms around his neck, urging him to continue. He twirled the delicate pearl around in his mouth and sucked on it.

Dorian had moved on to the other one when Reagan pulled back and rose to her feet. Water continued to trickle down her body.

"I promise you, it's like nothing you ever tasted," she hinted, twirling her hips in his face. "Not even my sister's." She smelled of strawberries. Dorian licked his lips and groaned at the flavor. Forbidden fruit. As much as he wanted, in all his cheating ways, he had never indulged in oral after he and Shantae were married. That was something reserved exclusively for his wife.

But the temptation was overpowering—or maybe it was just because it was Reagan—and Dorian closed the distance between them, his tongue immediately darting out to lick the remaining flavor off her juicy fruit. She was right. She tasted nothing like Shantae.

"Damn," she whispered, bracing herself on the marble wall.

The insinuation was clear, and that turned him on even more. Oh, how the tables kept seeming to turn between them, as if each was vying for control of the other but kept losing the battle. The mounting pressure was leaving them both weak.

Dorian grinned. He could still feel her wetness soaking his beard and mustache. "You liked that?" he asked.

"Hell yeah," she said. "You're going to have to do that more often. I'm spoiled now."

Dorian frowned. Reagan knew this was a one-time thing. He had made that clear on the phone. But thankfully he didn't have to ruin the mood with clarification of their arrangement. She was already kneeling in front of him to return the favor.

Dorian's head fell back, and the way she was working her mouth and hands on him, he thought his knees were going to give out. Again, his mind wandered to his wife. Shantae had age to her advantage when it came to her sexual experience, but baby sis had damn sure sharpened her skills. Of that, he was certain.

Dorian couldn't take it, and in an instant, he snatched himself from her lips, pulled her up, and hoisted her in the air, her legs instinctively locking around his sweaty waist. She had already assured him she was on birth control, and stopping now to fumble for a condom was out of the question. He couldn't even think about the consequences of breaking yet another unspoken rule.

"Tell me you love me, Dorian," Reagan was panting, and her voice came out in a breathless whisper.

Dorian felt himself swell with the impending euphoria and he concentrated on quickening his pace. Not on Reagan's ridiculous words.

"Please," she murmured at his silence. "You don't have to mean it. Just tell me." Dorian felt her legs begin to tremble, prompting him to penetrate deeper and harder. His breathing was labored as he stroked her walls already slick with the prior orgasm she had barely gotten over. Her nails dug into the muscles bunched in his shoulders and her own ragged breaths roared in his ears. "It's yours," she whispered, her voice like silk, and that was all it took. He cursed, pulling out just in time to empty his load on her back. Weak, he leaned on her, trapping her body against the wall.

Reagan moaned and smiled. "That was good, babe."

Dorian nodded. It sure was. He hadn't expected that. His mind lingered on the odd request only moments before. She had wanted him to tell her he loved her? Crazy. No need to bring it up. The moment was over. And Reagan must've known damn well he wouldn't comply because she didn't bother repeating it herself, now that they both were relaxing in contentment.

The water had chilled on his legs, so Dorian stepped out of the tub. He grabbed one of the plush hotel towels from the rack and wrapped it around his waist.

"Where are you going?" Reagan threw a leg over the edge of the tub as well and slid her body up against his. Her arms circled around to massage his chest. "I thought we could order some dessert."

"Yeah, that sounds good."

"And after," Reagan stood to her tiptoes to lick his ear, "we can go for round two."

The thought of slipping back between Reagan's thighs had Dorian's body springing to life once more. He could only grin as she sidestepped him, not bothering to wait for a response. She strolled back into the bedroom, naked and still dripping wet, and Dorian watched the movement, nodding his approval.

Yeah, she knew the effect she had on him. He had to appreciate Reagan because the woman knew how to please a man in all the right ways. Damn, Myles hadn't been lying after all. If only, they . . . The thought had a disappointed frown touching his lips. If only a lot of things. If only.

Dorian stepped into his slacks and half listened to Reagan call down for room service. When she was done, she lay naked on the bed and patted the space beside her. Dorian took the hint and sat down. She scooted closer, letting her body brush up against his.

"So, tell me something, Dr. Graham." Reagan traced his abs with a lazy finger. "Who is *Mrs.* Graham doing tonight?"

A slither of anger had Dorian's jaw clenching. He remembered Shantae prancing out of the house in her tight-ass dress and couldn't even stomach the thought of what, or *who*, as Reagan put it, she was doing. Truth be told, he still wasn't 100 percent comfortable with their little arrangement. But to him, the pros outweighed the cons. He never would have said "once a cheat, always a cheat" because he had certainly proved that theory wrong. He had changed. But if his wife permitted one night off from marriage, what kind of fool was he not to accept such an opportunity? Even if it meant affording her the same liberty. And Shantae was probably right. He could almost feel his love strengthening even now, and yes, he was missing his wife. Absence was making his heart grow fonder. Dorian just had to continue battling the uncertainties, because that did nothing but piss him off.

He glanced down at Reagan, and she seemed to be struggling to swallow a grin. "Don't talk about my wife," he said with a frown.

Reagan sat up on her elbows, her breasts bouncing with the movement. "I don't see why not," she said. "She's my sister, and that is the agreement, right? Wouldn't you want to know who was in her guts while you were in mine?"

It took all of Dorian's strength not to slap Reagan. No, he had never hit a woman, but the urge had never been stronger to, either.

Needing something to do with his hands, Dorian reached for his shirt and slid it over his head. He rose and began searching for his shoes. Mere seconds before, he was gearing himself up for night-long sex sessions. But whether intentionally or unintentionally, Reagan had known exactly what to say to cool the sexual tension down several hundred degrees.

"I know you're not leaving," Reagan said, recognizing his brisk movements. "Really, Dorian?"

"Nah, you tripping," he said, his voice laced with restrained anger.

"You might as well stay," Reagan taunted. "I'm sure Shantae isn't even done letting whoever eat her out like a Golden Corral buffet."

Dorian didn't even realize he had moved until he felt Reagan beneath him on the bed. For a brief moment, the thought invaded his senses. Shantae with her hands on the back of some man's neck as he feasted on her. Shantae with her lips around the other man as she pleased him in ways he had to damn near plead from her. His beautiful, innocent wife being licked and dicked down by some nameless, faceless man who could only feel victorious the moment he saw Shantae come over and over because he had discovered that sensitive spot.

Then the haze cleared, and Dorian saw Reagan's flushed face as she lay on the mattress still pinned underneath his heavy frame. He let her go and could only stare at her as he willed his anger to subside. *What have I done?* He looked down at his own trembling hands. They no longer felt like his.

Turning, he headed for the door, listening to her coughing and sputtering as she struggled to drag oxygen into her throat. If he had looked back, he would have seen Reagan's lips turning up in a satisfied smirk as he made his panicked retreat.

Chapter Ten

Dorian woke up with a migraine and a guilty conscience. He knew he had fucked up last night. Bad. He sat up and leaned on the leather headboard, squinting against the harsh morning sun spilling through the blinds. He had caught snatches of sleep, but every time he dozed off, he pictured Reagan. Damn, he had enjoyed the sex way too much, and it seemed like his body had been awake all night, itching for hers. But it was now the next day, the hall pass was expired, and he would just have to put all thoughts of Reagan out of his mind. At the end of the day, he still had love for his wife. But he had to admit, he did feel bad for the way things had ended the night before.

Dorian reached for his phone on the nightstand. He opened a new text message, and his thumbs breezed over the keyboard to compose an apology.

GM. SORRY FOR WHAT HAPPENED LAST NIGHT. I DIDN'T MEAN TO HURT YOU. I THINK I WAS JUST ANGRY. IT STILL DOESN'T MAKE IT RIGHT AND I FEEL LIKE SHIT ABOUT IT. I HOPE WE CAN MOVE PAST IT WITH NO ILL FEELINGS.

Dorian hit Send and then, remembering, he added **THANK YOU FOR A GREAT TIME** and sent that message as well. He set his phone back down and turned to cuddle with his wife.

To his surprise, her side was empty. In fact, it was still neatly made with only a few wrinkles from his apparent tossing and turning. Dorian listened and frowned when he was met with silence. *Where the hell is she?*

He tossed his legs over the side of the bed and made his way across the hardwood. They hadn't really set ground rules for the morning after, but still, Dorian thought it strange that Shantae had stayed out all night.

Dorian trotted down the stairs and paused to listen again, slightly relieved when he heard running water coming from the guest bathroom. The water shut off and Shantae emerged, wrapped in a thigh-length red terrycloth robe and a shower cap on her head. She trickled drops of water across the floor as she walked into the kitchen.

"Hey," Dorian greeted, his eyebrows still drawn together in confusion.

Shantae glanced up and a warm smile brightened her face. "Good morning, babe," she said. "Do you want some coffee?"

He didn't like it. She sounded too damn chipper. He was tempted to ask what had her ass floating on cloud nine. But then he knew he couldn't. Those were the rules. Besides, he already knew if she had revealed even a fraction of a detail, it would piss him off. He thought again about his reaction to Reagan, and that extinguished a little of the anger that was threatening to build.

Instead, Dorian took a seat at the island, his eyes on the open bathroom door. Steam was still emanating from it. "Why did you take a shower in the guest bathroom?" he asked, his eyes now on Shantae's back as she busied herself with the Keurig.

Shantae lifted a shoulder in nonchalance. "Just didn't want to disturb you," she said.

Dorian waited, half expecting her to elaborate or at least explain where she had slept, but Shantae did neither. Just turned with two mugs of coffee in hand and slid one across the granite countertop to him.

"After breakfast, we probably need to head on over to my parents' house," she was saying after taking a sip.

His mind drew a blank. He was still watching and waiting, trying to see if he noticed any visible changes. He was almost willing her skin to show some evidence of where the man had kissed her or touched her. Of course, there was none. *Like it never happened.* Hadn't she said that when they shook on the agreement?

He glanced up to see Shantae giving him a curious frown. "You okay, babe?" she asked.

Hell no, he wasn't. But it wasn't like he could voice that. "I'm good," he answered instead. "What were you saying about your parents' house?"

"Remember? She asked us all to come over for dinner to celebrate my dad's retirement," Shantae reminded him. "We agreed to this the other week." He didn't remember. She noticed and added, "Before the bachelor party." Now he did. "You know how my mom gets when we're late. Plus, I can help her out so I don't have to hear her mouth. And we might as well take the Christmas presents over there while we're at it."

Dorian nodded absently. He watched his wife as she moved about the kitchen, still talking lightly about that evening's dinner. Her ass jiggled under her robe and her skin was still damp from her shower. He could almost smell the fresh body scrub seeping from her pores. He thought again of what Reagan mentioned the night before. He had tried his best not to focus on what his wife was doing during the hall pass, but for some reason, Reagan bringing it up was really digging at his heart. Was that jealousy? Was he, the recovering serial cheater, actually jealous? That was a new one.

"Let's not do this anymore," Dorian blurted out. He noticed Shantae's confused stare and he realized he must have interrupted her, right in the middle of whatever the hell she was talking about. Which was now even more validation that he hadn't been listening to a word she said.

"Not do what anymore?" she asked.

Dorian stood up and rounded the island, pulled his wife into his arms. He was right. She smelled fresh, all evidence of the previous night completely scrubbed away. Still feeling the rakes of guilt on the recesses of his subconscious, Dorian lowered his lips to hers. For a moment, he held the kiss, feeling her receptive tongue welcoming the contact. He swallowed her moan as her arms circled around his neck. Breaking the kiss, Dorian could only sigh in frustration as he lowered his forehead to hers.

"What's wrong, babe?" Shantae asked, lifting her hand to his face to stroke his cheek.

"Shantae, let's not do this anymore," he said. "The hall pass thing. I think I'm done."

Shantae pulled back to meet his gaze. "Why? Is something wrong?"

"I'm not saying that. I'm just saying I don't think we need to do it anymore."

Shantae turned back to the counter to resume stirring the pancake batter. "I would think you, of all men, would appreciate the opportunity," she said.

"What do you mean, 'me of all men?' " Anger began to rise as he waited for her response.

Shantae ignored him. "Look, we'll talk about this another time," she said instead. "I'm not trying to argue."

"I thought you said this was an experiment anyway," he said, unable to control the irritation seeping through. "That if we didn't want to do it anymore, we didn't have to."

She kept her back to him, but he saw her body beginning to

tense. Good, let her get mad. He didn't care. "Why don't you go ahead and pack the gifts in the car so we can be ready to go to my parents' after breakfast?" Her tone was level. "We can talk about this later, Dorian." His whole name. Not babe, or even D.

Anger had Dorian turning and heading back upstairs. Something was wrong. It wasn't supposed to be like this the day after their hall pass. They were supposed to be in bed, fucking like rabbits to re-stake their claim on each other. At least, that was what he figured was supposed to happen anyway. He snatched his pants from the chair and pulled out a pack of Black & Milds. He lit one up and took a deep drag, filling his lungs with the smoke.

Exhaling, he remembered his earlier text to Reagan and grabbed his phone to see if she had responded. She hadn't. Dorian opened another text message and used his thumb to type. **SO YOU NOT GOING TO RESPOND? AT LEAST JUST LET ME KNOW YOU'RE OK. I AM SORRY.**

The flying envelope icon swooped across the screen, indicating the message had been sent. He sat his phone down and took another puff of the Black, listening to the distant clink of pots and pans drifting up from the kitchen. A thought crossed his mind and Dorian suddenly felt a mix of excitement and fear. He would see Reagan in just a few hours anyway at the dinner. He didn't know what to expect, but he hoped like hell evidence of last night's actions wouldn't reveal themselves today.

———⋙◦⋘———

Shantae's parents had downsized after their daughters left the house and had recently moved into a newer, Craftsman-style bungalow outside of Tyrone. The neighborhood was reminiscent of a picturesque Pleasantville, complete with wide front porches and tapering pillars.

Dorian wheeled Shantae's Jeep Cherokee against the curb and parked beside the mailbox. He watched as Shantae put on the last little bit of her makeup. It had been a quiet ride over, and the air was clearly thick with repressed tension he hadn't even realized had heightened.

With a sigh, Dorian laid a hand on Shantae's arm, pausing her movements. "We good, babe?" he asked.

Shantae didn't even look his way, but he caught her lips turn up into a little smile. "Of course. Why wouldn't we be?"

"I just didn't want us to fall out about the conversation from earlier."

Shantae's shoulder rose and fell in a nonchalant shrug. "It's cool. You said what you had to say, Dorian. I said what I had to say. As far as I'm concerned, the conversation is over."

Dorian frowned. In his mind, the shit was far from over. But rather than voice that thought and risk sparking another argument, he leaned across the console and placed a kiss on Shantae's cheek.

They gathered the two shopping bags of wrapped presents and walked up the short driveway, entering the house through the side garage. Immediately, the delicious aroma of soul food assaulted Dorian's nostrils, and he inhaled deeply. The instrumentals to what sounded like Earth, Wind & Fire's "September" wafted through the speakers of a small radio on the counter. Shantae's mom, Barbara, was humming along to the tune while she busied herself at the sink, wrist-deep in fresh collard greens. She turned at the sound of the door and her smile bloomed before quickly being replaced by a frown. Dorian could only chuckle at how much the expression mirrored Shantae's, from the full pouty lips to the slight slant of her hooded eyes as they narrowed in annoyance. She looked festive in her knee-length red quarter-sleeve turtleneck dress, black tights, and flats with barely an inch of heel. At sixty-four, Shantae's mother looked damn good with merely a few wrinkles to enhance her distinguished look.

"About damn time," Barbara said, removing her hands from

the water long enough to dry them on the dish towel. "Shantae, get over here and finish cleaning these collards while I work on the sweet potato pie."

"Good afternoon to you too, Mama," Shantae said, even as she moved to the sink to do as instructed.

Dorian set the bags of gifts on the floor and shrugged out of his coat. A quick survey of the kitchen showed covered dishes and trays littering the laminate countertop and breakfast table. Pot roast, macaroni and cheese, rice, cornbread, deviled eggs . . . Apparently, Barbara had gone all out for her husband's celebratory dinner, whipping up all of his favorites. But no Reagan. He didn't realize he was holding his breath until he felt the exhale releasing pressure from his chest.

"How are you, Mama?" he greeted, crossing to give Barbara a peck on the cheek.

"I'm good, Dorian," she said. "So glad y'all came."

"Mama, you know we weren't missing Daddy's dinner," Shantae chimed in.

"I know that. It's not you I'm concerned so much about. It's that sister of yours."

The mention of Reagan had Dorian freezing.

"Why you say that?" Shantae said, rolling up the sleeves of her burgundy sweater.

Barbara shook her head and clucked her tongue, as if chastising the woman in her head. "She claims she is working, so she just drops that baby of hers off over here and leaves. All times of the day and night. She won't answer calls, and you never know when you'll see her again. Like TJ is in there with Papa right now because she came over here and left him. No clean clothes, no nothing. That was two days ago. Haven't even heard from her."

"Are you really surprised, Mama?" Shantae's voice elevated with the rhetorical question. "She doesn't even call me unless she wants some money. You told her to come today, though, right?"

Dorian waited and watched Barbara shrug. "I did. Now *if* she'll come is the real question," she said with a sigh. "You know how that girl does. Just here, there, and everywhere and shuffling my grandbaby with her as she *finds herself.*" She bent her fingers in air quotes as she said the last part.

The conversation was making him uncomfortable. Of course, he hadn't told Shantae any of what he and Reagan discussed last night. Hell, she didn't even know they had been communicating at all. And to make matters worse, Reagan had apparently just dumped her son off this weekend, why? So she could lay up with him. That made him feel disgusting.

"Dorian, baby, can you take those gifts to the living room and put them under the tree?" Shantae asked.

"And put the coats in the guest bedroom," Barbara added. "Charles is around here somewhere with TJ if you want to find him."

Dorian nodded at the mention of Shantae's father. Charles was a kindred spirit, so a little conversation and maybe a drink before dinner with him sounded like just what the doctor ordered. Lord knows he needed it.

He found Charles in the living room, lounging in his recliner while a little boy fiddled with Legos at his feet. Both sets of eyes turned in Dorian's direction as he entered through the barn-style sliding doors. Shantae's father smiled in greeting, while TJ turned his attention back to the task at hand.

"Hey!" Charles said, standing to engulf Dorian in a warm hug. "You're early. Didn't expect you until later."

"You know how mother and daughter are," Dorian teased.

"Got that right." Charles shook his head in mock disbelief. "Barbara had me up at four this morning cutting the grass. Couldn't do it yesterday because she wanted it fresh." He murmured something inaudible, further emphasizing his disdain for the morning task, before glancing down at his grandson. "TJ, what do you say to your uncle?"

The little boy didn't so much as spare him a glance. "Hi," he muttered, still completely engrossed in his project.

"Hey, TJ," Dorian greeted anyway. "How old are you now?"

"Four," he answered simply, his little voice carrying a touch of childlike annoyance at the disturbance. Right at that moment, his entire world rested on making a dinosaur out of those brightly colored blocks.

Dorian could only stare in awe as his tiny fingers worked to put the pieces together. Since Reagan didn't come around often, the last time he had seen TJ, he was in a soiled Pampers with a pacifier in his mouth. Now it felt strange watching how much he had grown, decked out in a plaid Polo button-up and khakis, no doubt a recent purchase by his grandparents. Dorian remembered TJ used to have a head full of baby doll curls but those were gone too, replaced by a faded haircut with a front part that brought out his boyish features. Even more so, he remembered Reagan's body from the previous night, and it damn sure hadn't looked like she had popped out any children. Dorian frowned at how quickly his thoughts had turned and shook his head at his lack of self-control. He was going to have to do better.

"I hear congratulations are in order," Dorian said, crossing to the Christmas tree to begin unloading the presents. The topic was safe, the maneuver a welcome distraction. "How does retirement feel?"

"Like a damn breath of fresh air," Charles admitted on a laugh. "It has only been a few days but boy, have they been a relaxing few days."

For as long as he had known Shantae, he had known her father as one of the hardest working men in the state. He had put in forty-plus years with the federal government, working his way up the GS pay scale until he was able to retire comfortably with a nice nest egg. Since Shantae's mom had retired herself as a hospital food service cook two years ago, Dorian figured it was a welcome change as they stepped into this new journey. But knowing them, they weren't able to sit still too long. Charles had already mentioned he was trying to talk Barbara into buying a boat and traveling the world. But she would never, not when Reagan was so needy and her grandson didn't have any kind of stability except when he was with them.

"About time for you and Shantae to have babies," Charles commented. "That would give an old man something to do so Barbara won't have to find stuff to keep me busy."

Dorian forced a light chuckle, though he didn't comment. He knew Shantae's parents had treaded carefully on the subject of kids given when happened when they were in college. They were one of the ones calling what happened a blessing in disguise. Interesting how far he and her father had come, because Lord knows Charles was ready to lynch him and burn him at the stake after Dorian got his baby girl pregnant. But that was then, and this was now. Shantae's parents were right. Enough time had passed for healing. And like Shantae had echoed, they weren't getting any younger.

Dorian thought again about the pregnancy test that he shouldn't have known about. She never brought it up and neither did he. It must have been handled, in whatever way that meant. Sometimes ignorance was bliss.

"So where is Reagan anyway?" Dorian asked, ashamed he had to struggle to make the question sound innocent.

"Not sure," Charles answered. "Said she was going to be here later. Who knows when 'later' is in Reagan's terms."

Dorian kneeled down to begin arranging the wrapped gifts under the tree. The logical part of him didn't want Reagan to come and would be counting down the minutes until "later" became "not at all." The other part, the part that had him throbbing, wouldn't have minded catching another glimpse of her and that sexy-ass body. That was what worried him. The little lingering piece of desire.

Since a child was in the room, Dorian decided against the

drink and instead, went back to the kitchen to see if there was something else Shantae needed him to do. He walked in on what appeared to be the tail end of the women's conversation.

"Just tell him," Barbara was saying.

Shantae's sigh was heavy as she leaned against the counter. "But what if he gets upset? I already know how he feels about it."

The squeak of Dorian's shoes on the waxed linoleum had their eyes darting in his direction. The subsequent silence was deafening, evidence they had indeed been talking about him.

"Tell me what?" he coaxed, when neither woman made a move to speak.

Shantae glanced at her mother before rounding the island and wrapping her arms around his waist. "It's not important, sweetie," she lied, pecking him on the lips.

"Dorian, can you do me a favor?" Barbara gestured toward the two twelve-pack boxes of Sprite on the breakfast table. "Can you go ahead and put those in the refrigerator for me?"

Dorian nodded and walked to the table. He surely hoped Shantae didn't think she had weaseled out of whatever it was she needed to tell him. He thought again about the pregnancy test, his mind unsettled by the mystery.

His back was turned to the door, so he didn't even realize Reagan had entered the kitchen until he heard her speak. The sudden sultry voice wafting in the kitchen was enough to have him fumbling over the soda cans. He turned as Reagan peeled out of her coat, revealing a skintight jungle green dress, with her cleavage spilling out of the deep V-neckline. The hemline hugged her thighs and easily met the thigh-high black boots, with only a peep of skin showing between. Dorian didn't even realize he was staring until he felt his tongue roll over his bottom lip. He snatched his eyes off her and the way her body jiggled with her movements, despite the clingy material.

"Why don't you answer your damn phone?" Shantae said.

Reagan rolled her eyes. "I didn't know I needed to," she snapped.

"Well, yeah, when you're leaving Mama and Dad to raise TJ, that would be considerate of you to answer your phone when they call."

"Damn, let me get in the door before you grill me, sis."

"Watch that language in my house, Reagan," Barbara said with a frown.

"Mercy, people, really?" Reagan didn't bother to stifle her groan. "Good fucking afternoon to y'all too."

"Reagan!"

"Where is my kid?" Reagan said, ignoring the reprimand. Her heels were already clicking across the floor as she headed toward the hallway.

"With Daddy."

"Fine." Reagan paused long enough to pinch the sides of her dress and tug the hem down a bit. She glanced in Dorian's direction, but to his surprise, she didn't even acknowledge him.

The words had left Dorian's lips before he even had time to register he wanted to ask a question. "Oh, you not gon' speak?"

"Hey," Reagan said dryly, before disappearing into the hall.

Shantae sucked her teeth. "That girl is a trip," she murmured, before resuming her place at the stove.

Dorian wanted to agree, but he could only shake his head. He knew what her problem was, and he wanted to kick himself for how out of control he had gotten the previous night. He owed Reagan an apology, and since she didn't answer his messages, he would have to speak to her before the day was over. It was the least he could do.

Chapter Eleven

Dorian let the conversation play around him while he ate his dinner in silence. He didn't know why he felt so nervous. Reagan hadn't said more than two words to him, and she acted just as casual as everyone else. So damn casual that he had to replay the previous night just to make sure he wasn't going crazy and hadn't imagined the entire thing. He should've been relieved, he knew. But the more cordial her manner, the more it felt like she was intentionally baiting him. And that was racking his nerves and, much to his surprise, causing a swell of disappointment.

Though he sat beside his beautiful wife, all thoughts were consumed by the woman who sat across from him, licking her lips after every morsel, with her titties damn near resting on the table as she leaned over to take in another forkful of food. Guilt was beginning to set in. One, because he knew he wanted nothing more than to hike that tight-ass dress up and have her right there over the pot roast. Two, because he knew his thoughts were wrong. And three, because he didn't give a damn. Dorian took another sip of wine and struggled to focus on the conversation.

"So, you didn't tell us what was so pressing you had to drop TJ over here all weekend and not answer your phone."

Reagan didn't bother to hide her irritation at her sister's comment. She glared at her across the dining room table. "Oh, I didn't?" she said, feigning innocence. "Just had some important business to handle."

"Well, just call and let us know, sweetie," Barbara said. "You know we love the baby and never mind keeping him, but just in case we have plans."

"Mama said you were working," Shantae said. "But that's probably doubtful since you always need money."

Reagan's laughter was somewhere between hurt and condescending. "Well damn, you never seemed to mind before."

"You really should get yourself together," Barbara said. "You're grown. You make all these choices and it ends up affecting TJ in the long run."

"Barbie, let it go," Charles interjected. He used Barbara's nickname when he was trying to calm her down. This time, it didn't seem to be working.

Reagan sucked her teeth. "No, it's fine, Daddy. Let her chastise me for the awful daughter I am and praise Shantae as her favorite."

"Well, maybe if you acted more like a daughter, then you would get treated like one," Shantae snapped. "You act like you don't even have a family until you need something. Or to get bailed out of some kind of trouble. Hell, you pull those disappearing stunts so much and expect people to run behind you."

Reagan's eyes flicked to Dorian before meeting her sister's angry gaze. "Oh, trust me. The ones who needed to know where I was, knew."

"And what is that supposed to mean?"

When Reagan simply rolled her eyes, Dorian let out a shaky

breath. "Baby, calm down," he said to Shantae, giving her hand a squeeze.

"No, Dorian. Let her answer," Shantae said, not bothering to look in his direction. "Let her tell us why she keeps taking advantage of this family."

"Family?" Reagan spat the word with so much venom. "What family? All Mom and Dad care about is you, Shantae. And hell, you? I don't even like you. You ain't never gave a damn about me, so excuse me, dear sister, if I'm not kissing your ass like your *family.*" With that, she pushed back from the table and stormed out of the dining room.

The silence was heavy, and for a moment, all that could be heard were utensils scraping plates and quiet gulps as someone downed the rest of their wine.

Dorian didn't know why he felt so bad. They had always treated Reagan like some black sheep and glorified Shantae. He had witnessed it on countless occasions, and though he didn't necessarily agree, he had never felt it was his place to speak on it. Reagan had always been rebellious, wild, and too damn sneaky. No one had even known she was pregnant until she had called from the hospital, saying she was in labor. Even then, she was hush-hush about the father, insisting her son didn't have one. Compared to her older, successful sister, Reagan was a stain on the household. A statistic. And she had never fully recovered from the negative association.

"You about ready to go?" Shantae asked, breaking the silence.

Dorian frowned. "Now? We haven't even finished dinner."

"We don't want you to go, baby," Charles said from the other end of the table. "Don't let Reagan spoil our celebration."

In response, Shantae pushed back from the table, her chair scraping the hardwood floor. "It's not Reagan," she said. "I'm just not feeling well, Daddy. I think I just need to go home and lie down." She grabbed her plate and glass and headed for the kitchen.

Reluctantly, Dorian rose to his feet and grabbed his own plate. "I'm sorry, Mama. Charles."

"It's not your fault," Barbara said. Her eyes landed on TJ, quietly watching TV in the adjoining living room, and she could only sigh. "We have never been the closest family. I just hate this happened today. I was wanting to do something nice for Charles. I suppose we'll try again at Christmas."

Dorian nodded and followed his wife into the kitchen. He watched her at the sink. Her movements were brisk as she began rinsing dishes before loading them into the dishwasher. He leaned against the counter. "Shantae—"

"Dorian, don't," she snapped, throwing up a hand to stop his words. "I don't really want to hear it right now."

"Don't you think you're overreacting just a bit? She's your sister."

Shantae whirled around, her eyes blazing, her forehead creased in an appalled frown. "I'm overreacting? What the hell do you know, Dorian? You didn't have to grow up feeling like your sister hated you for just being alive. Anytime I got an award or a word of praise, that just drove us further and further apart. And I've done nothing but try and bend over backward to befriend Reagan. I would do anything for that girl, but the more I try, the more she hates me. And I haven't even done anything. How is that supposed to make me feel?"

She was damn near in tears now, and Dorian crossed to her. She stepped out of his attempted embrace and ran her hands over her damp cheeks. "Can you just go pack up the car or something?" she murmured, turning back to the sink. "Just give me a minute. Please."

Dorian rested his hand on her trembling shoulder, not surprised when she shook it off. He knew when she got like this, she shut off and it was best to just leave her alone until she opened up once again.

He walked down the hallway and turned the knob to enter the

bathroom. To his surprise, Reagan was hunched over the vanity, seemingly frozen as she stared at her reflection. Her puffy eyes met his in the mirror and it was more than obvious that she too had been crying.

Dorian shut the door behind him and leaned against it, shoving his hands in his pockets. He was at a loss for words as Reagan watched him, as if willing him to say something. "How you feeling?" he asked.

Reagan shrugged and forced a smile. "Never better."

"Your sister loves you, you know," Dorian said. "Your parents too. I think everyone just wishes y'all were closer."

"No, that's not it." Reagan shook her head as if refusing to believe his words. "My parents hate me. Ever since I was about twelve, everything just . . . changed. And then when I got pregnant . . ." Reagan rolled her eyes and turned to face him. "Lord, you would think the world had ended. They haven't treated me the same ever since. And Shantae, it's like she rubs it in my face, Dorian. No, I'm not some big-shot banker or whatever, with a few fancy degrees and a rich, sexy-ass husband. But damn, I'm trying."

Dorian had to chuckle at the summation. "First off, I'm not rich," he said, wagging a finger in her face. "Sexy yes, but not rich."

That seemed to lighten the mood a little. Reagan's lips turned up in an amused smirk. "Whatever. Aren't you a doctor?"

"Cosmetic surgeon."

"Like I said. Rich."

Dorian relaxed into a laugh. "I don't know who told you that, little girl," he teased. Reagan always hated when he called her that.

The mood shifted again. He felt it as if someone had turned on a light switch. He didn't know whether it was the look she gave him, or the way she licked her lips, but the sexual tension had become thick and suffocating.

"Little girl, huh?" Reagan let her eyes graze over his body. "You didn't think I was such a little girl last night." She took a step in his direction and Dorian lifted his hands.

"Wait a minute." He lowered his voice and glanced to the door. He was praying no one was in earshot. His in-laws' home had walls as thin as paper. "Now look, we talked about this. You know that was just a one-time thing."

Reagan shrugged and took another step. "I know. So, what's one more?" She began lifting her dress, revealing more and more of her thighs. Dorian swallowed, willing his eyes to look away even as he felt his inches rising.

"One time only," he repeated. This time, he placed his hands on Reagan's shoulders to stop her pursuit. "I'm married."

"So? You were married last night."

"That shit was different, Reagan. You know it. I told you the rules. You agreed, remember?"

"You also said no questions asked. Remember?" Reagan lifted her hands to rest them on his and began guiding them down to her breasts. Dorian again shook his head but didn't stop her. He was now cupping her breasts, her hands on top of his, her nipples straining against his palms. "She doesn't ask any questions, remember?" she whispered. Reagan squeezed his hands, coaxing them to begin kneading the supple flesh of her breasts. Damn, he just wanted to suck them. Just once more. As if reading his mind, Reagan removed her hands from his and lowered them to her hemline.

"You need . . ." He trailed off as she hooked her fingers in the straps and slowly began to peel off the dress she wore. The fabric fell to pool at her feet and she stood, completely naked, her brown skin like milk chocolate against the stark white bathroom.

"Fuck." Dorian tore his eyes from her body and turned to face the shower curtain. He couldn't do this. Not to Shantae. He had already tried it, pushing the limits with her sister in the first place. But he had permission, to an extent. Now it would just be all-out cheating. And he had never cheated on Shantae since she'd become his wife.

Dorian didn't hear her come closer, but he suddenly felt Reagan's breasts pressing against his back. Her hands circled his waist, trailed down to rub his thighs, before moving to massage him through his pants. "You don't have to put it in," she whispered. "Just let me lick it."

Dorian didn't respond, nor did he have the strength to stop her as she unzipped his pants and dipped her hand inside. Somehow, she managed to maneuver her fingers inside the waistline of his boxer briefs, and he could've come right there when her hand grabbed him. The sudden skin-on-skin contact sent a guilty shiver down his spine. He grabbed Reagan's wrist. "We can't do this," he murmured, struggling to keep from moaning. To his surprise, and disappointment, he felt Reagan pull her hand from his pants and step back. He figured she was upset, but it was for the best.

When he heard her moaning, Dorian turned around. Reagan was now seated on the vanity, her knees pulled up to her chest. Her legs were spread as she began to play with herself. Dorian kept his eyes trained on her fingers. "You can watch me," she invited, resting her head behind her on the mirror. "But I'm going to satisfy myself right here, with or without you, Dorian."

She moaned again and bit her lip as her fingers continued to explore her delicate flower. Dorian felt his mouth watering. He didn't even realize he had grabbed his own manhood until he felt it throbbing in his hand.

"Yes," Reagan cooed. "Go ahead. Imagine it's me. It's ready for you, baby."

The encouragement was enough to have Dorian complying,

stroking and squeezing, listening to Reagan's murmurs of self-gratification. She was using her other hand to pinch and fondle her nipple. The sight was beautiful, watching her spread-eagle with his name dripping from her lips.

Reagan came first. She threw her head back, her eyes squeezed shut, her legs trembling so hard it was a wonder she didn't shake her right off the counter. He was right behind her, his vision blurred to the point he didn't notice she had situated herself in front of him to finish the job herself.

Reagan smiled, licking her lips in satisfaction. "Thank you," she whispered.

Dorian didn't say anything as she climbed to her feet. He watched her body as she worked it back into the tight dress.

"You feel better?" she asked, tossing a wink over her shoulder. "I know I do."

"Reagan, we can't do this anymore."

Reagan fluffed her hair, eyeing his package still clutched in his hand. "Do what? We didn't have sex. This time."

Dorian shook his head. "That's it, Reagan," he said, shoving himself back into his pants. "I'm serious. This shit has to stop."

Reagan turned on the water and bent down to angle her face under the faucet. She took in some water, gargled, and spit it back out. When she turned around, Dorian tried his best to read her expression, but her face remained neutral.

"I understand," she said. Her voice was just as calm. "And you're right. I apologize if I'm overstepping my boundaries."

Dorian nodded. "We still cool, right?" he asked, just to be sure.

"Of course." Reagan's genuine smile blossomed. "You'll always be my brother-in-law, so you're kind of stuck with me. I don't want our relationship to be awkward."

Dorian relaxed a little. He needed to hear that. Lord knows it was getting more and more complicated.

Reagan opened the bathroom door, gasping when she saw Shantae standing on the other side.

"What are y'all doing?" Shantae asked, her eyes darting from her sister to her husband.

Dorian's eyes ballooned and he quickly shifted his body a bit to hide the fact that he hadn't even zipped up his pants. Panic had the words sticking in his throat.

"He was just talking to me, sis," Reagan said, lowering her eyes. "He just mentioned that maybe I was a little out of line back at the table. And I'm sorry for that."

Shantae sighed. "Maybe some of that was my fault," she said, and Dorian held his sigh of relief. Good thinking. He had to give Reagan her props for that rescue. "I really don't want us to hate each other, Reagan. You're my sister and I love you."

Dorian watched them embrace and cringed when Reagan pecked Shantae on the cheek. Those same lips that had been on him only a few moments before.

When they pulled away, Shantae turned to Dorian and smiled. "Thanks, babe."

"For what?" Dorian was still fixated on Reagan. A peculiar look now rested on her face.

"For talking to Reagan. And me," she added. "I know I can be a little stubborn sometimes."

"No problem, sweetie."

"You ready?"

Dorian nodded and watched Shantae head back down the hallway. He let out the breath he had been holding. "Damn, good looking out, Reagan," he said. "And I'm glad you two are cool again."

Reagan stepped toward him and smiled when she felt him tense up. "Relax," she whispered and in one swoop, zipped up his pants. She then stood on her tiptoes, so her lips were nearly touching his ear. "Control your bitch," she whispered. "She needs to stay out of our way." With that, she licked his earlobe and stepped back.

Dorian froze, watching her switch her hips out of the bathroom, and he felt his panic rising. What the hell had he gotten himself into?

Chapter Twelve

Dorian didn't know what he was doing. He just knew he'd left the office, claimed he was going for a drive, and ended up in front of Elegant Perfections Hair Salon. Reagan had mentioned she worked there part-time a few days a week, just to have a little extra cash.

He sat in the truck, his hands on the steering wheel, and debated if he should go in. He shouldn't be so involved, he knew. Reagan hadn't bothered him, but Shantae had mentioned Reagan had needed to stay at their parents' house one night because her baby dad, Terrell, was on the warpath, whatever that meant. Either way, it was enough that she felt a little unsafe, and honestly, Dorian was concerned. He just felt compelled to check on her. Make sure she was holding up okay. Why he cared, he had yet to find the answer to that one. Either way, he did. And he didn't think there was anything wrong with that.

Dorian saw her as soon as she walked out of the building. Her hair shielded her face as it reflected a royal auburn in the sunlight. The grin had spread before he'd even realized it, watching her trot down the stairs, her purse bouncing against her hip. She glanced around, and he studied her face. Though she squinted through the harsh stream of sun, he saw her eyes downcast, her lips drooped to a saddened pout. She pulled a pair of sunglasses from the collar of her T-shirt and sat them on her face, the large tinted frames shielding most of it from view. As she turned and started walking the opposite way, he stepped from the car and jogged to catch up.

"Reagan," he called. She turned, her lips still pursed in a frown.

"You stalking me too?" She winced when her attempt at a joke came out snappy and sarcastically rude. "I'm sorry. That was uncalled for. You caught me at a bad time." Dorian nodded, hooked his thumbs in his pockets.

"It's too early in the day to be pissed."

"Yeah, well, you haven't had a pissy morning like I have."

"That explains the winning attitude." Even though the tint was a rich black, he saw her roll her eyes.

"I'm not in the mood, okay?"

Dorian shrugged, turned, and headed back toward his car. "Fine." Her attitude had rubbed off on him, and he felt the edges of anger prickling his nerves. He could've kicked himself for coming out to see her.

Reagan watched his retreating back and sighed.

"Dorian," she called and had him pausing by the door of his truck. "Walk with me?" He turned, didn't answer as she walked toward him, stopping an inch away. "I'm pissed, so I have an attitude. But it's nothing you can't handle, right?" She had a point.

"Where you headed?"

"Does it matter?"

He grinned. "Checkmate."

Reagan started walking and he fell into step beside her.

"What does that mean anyway?" she asked. "Checkmate. It feels like you're making fun of me in my face or something."

"You have to understand chess."

"Teach me."

"Maybe one day. So, what happened?"

She kept her eyes trained on the congested street ahead, frowning again.

"Just . . . stuff with Terrell," she admitted on a careless shrug. "And with this bullshit job that doesn't pay shit. And some other stuff, but it's really a long story."

On an understanding nod, Dorian gestured toward the upcoming hot dog stand. "Hungry?"

She glanced at him on a surprised laugh. "Seriously, Dorian? It's ten in the morning." He shrugged, stepped under the awning of the stand, and fished for his wallet.

"Do you want one or not?" She shrugged and he turned to the attendant. "Two. Ketchup, mustard, relish."

Reagan shook her head, watched him pay the man, take the hot dogs dripping with dressing, and pass one to her. She bit in, moaned at the delicious taste.

They polished off the meal and started back on the sidewalk, headed toward the downtown area. He sensed she was back in her zone again and he remained quiet, listening to their shoes hit the pavement in a harmonic unison. They came to a bench and without warning, she stopped to sit. He looked down at her as she took off her sunglasses and pushed the sweaty strands of hair from her forehead. "I quit," she started after a moment of silence. "I'm sure you're not surprised, though."

He sat down, leaned forward propping his elbows on his knees. "Why would you say that?"

"Oh, please, Dorian. Don't act like you don't believe that shit my parents and Shantae have said about me. I can't keep a job, I'm unstable, yada yada." She sighed, fiddling with the arm of the sunglasses. "Well, apparently I'm doing something wrong. It seems like I always get the shitty end of the stick."

Dorian nodded and sat back, draping his arm companionably on the bench behind her shoulders. "That's not true. You don't have to work for someone else. You know you can always start your own salon."

She sighed in reluctance. "Maybe one day when I get the money, I will."

They sat in silence, idle eyes watching people hurry by. Reagan zeroed in on a woman in an all-black business suit, watched her swinging her briefcase as she walked by, and grinned. She gently elbowed Dorian, nodding to the woman.

"What do you think she's thinking?" she asked him.

He frowned at the woman. "What?"

"It's a game Shantae and I used to play when we were kids. Someone picks a person that looks interesting and you make up things about them based on how they are dressed or their expressions or just how you perceive them."

Dorian looked again to the woman, noted the determined frown on her face, the hurried steps in the high heels. He shrugged. "I'm late for a meeting," he tossed out and had Reagan rolling her eyes.

"You're so boring. You're supposed to say something funny like . . ." She glanced at the woman, narrowed her eyes in consideration. "Like, 'I can't believe all this money I got, and I still can't get a man,' or 'I've been holding this gas in for the past half hour. I thought the guy said there was a bathroom on this block.'" He chuckled, watching Reagan look around again. "Okay." She gestured toward a shirtless man jogging by, his muscles rippling with the swing of his arms. "What does he keep in his wallet?"

Dorian looked at the guy, lifted a brow. "Besides a picture of himself?"

Reagan burst into laughter. "Very good. You're getting the hang of it."

"You say you and your sister used to play that?"

"Yeah. When we couldn't get to a table to play chess." She tossed a playful wink at him and he grinned, staring into her eyes as if he were searching for something. She glanced away and, even though it was an obvious evasion, cleared her throat. "Thanks."

"For what?"

"For making me feel better. For the hot dog. For everything." He nodded. "No problem."

"So we ate, we talked, we laughed. I guess this was kind of like our second date," she teased. "What would my sister think?"

"I told you, the hall pass was a one-time thing."

"Okay. What was this?"

Dorian studied her face, lingering on each physical feature. He lifted a hand to twirl a few strands of her hair around his finger. He honestly wished he knew. For some reason, Reagan was magnetic. "This is us, doing what friends do," he answered finally. It was a weak response but the best he could come up with.

"Friends, huh?" Reagan chuckled and shook her head. "Okay, *friend*." She opened her mouth to say something else, then shut it again when her cell phone vibrated in her purse. Dorian watched her stand and walk forward a bit, at the same time bringing the phone to her ear.

Dorian waited, watching her as she paced a bit, her words muffled by her lowered tone. He couldn't help but take the opportunity to admire her body as she turned her back to him, giving him a full view of those thick curves.

Reagan hung up the phone and approached him on a sigh. "I have to go," she said. "But I appreciate this, I do."

Dorian hid his disappointment with an understanding nod. "I'm glad I stopped by. It seemed like you really needed someone to talk to."

"Yes, I needed you," she said.

He heard her play on words but decided it best to ignore it. Instead, he rose.

"You need to walk back?"

"No, I'm fine. I'm meeting a friend around the corner." Was it just him, or had her whole mood changed in the span of that short phone call?

"Okay. I'll see you later. Just call me if you need anything."

Something flickered in Reagan's eyes. He couldn't be sure what, but her smile widened at his comment. "I sure will."

Chapter Thirteen

"Dr. Graham, you have a visitor."

Claudia stood in his doorway, her fingers fiddling with the waistline of her floral print dress. Her huge glasses nearly hid her face, but he could easily detect the frown creases embedded in the side of her mouth.

"What's wrong?" Dorian asked, leaning back in his chair.

She opened her mouth to respond but stopped short when Dorian's friend Kenny appeared at her side. "Oh, excuse me, Ms. Claudia," he said.

Claudia sat her hands on her hips and shook her head. "Boy, don't you see grown folks in here talking?" she teased.

Kenny laughed. "I just need to have a quick word with my boy," he said.

"Hmph," Claudia grunted and waved off the statement. "Don't you ever work? Seems like you always up here bothering him." She nodded her head in Dorian's direction.

He had to laugh at the truth of the comment. Kenny worked in the IT department of a company on the eighteenth floor of the building, but he *was* always finding a reason to trek it up to his office. Dorian had had to put him out numerous times so he could get some work done. They'd met six months ago in the cafeteria the day Dorian had rented a suite on the twenty-eighth floor for his practice. A lifetime of knowing each other couldn't have made him closer. Dorian used to tease that Kenny just hung around trying to get glimpses of the fine-ass women that paraded through his office for body work. Kenny had never confirmed nor denied that assumption.

Claudia left them alone, and Kenny immediately shut the door and plopped down in one of the box arm guest chairs across from Dorian's desk. "Man, that lady . . . I tell ya," he said, shaking his head.

"Stop it. You know Ms. Claudia just likes to make fun of your crazy ass," Dorian said, saving the files he had been working on. "Besides, you can't get mad when she tells the truth. You don't work."

"Shit, I work enough," Kenny countered. "Within my forty-hour work week, my projects get done."

Dorian swiveled around in his office chair to gaze out at the Atlanta high-rises. He always marveled at this magnificent view and its calming effect. Right now, the sky had darkened with the projected rain, but the forecast did nothing to stop the traffic and congested sidewalks.

"I came in to see what we're doing for lunch," Kenny said. "You know Becca and all them folks over in Human Resources having that retirement party thing, but I don't want none of that nasty-ass food."

Dorian chuckled and glanced at the digital clock on his desk. "It's only a quarter till eleven. I wasn't trying to go to lunch right now. It's too damn early."

"Oh, for real? What time do stomachs usually open?" Dorian laughed as Kenny rubbed his midsection for emphasis. "You know my girl can't cook," he went on. "Sending her man out in the mornings on Frosted Flakes and shit."

The knock had Dorian turning to eye the closed office door. "Come in," he said.

She would come to his job looking edible. Reagan's tight blue jean jumpsuit hugged every curve, and she had the zipper down just enough to tease wandering eyes with the outline of her breasts. Her hair had been pulled up into a ponytail, and large gold hoop earrings dangled low enough to brush her shoulders. The camel-colored snow boots only came up to her calves, which really drew the eye upward to the thick thighs straining against the fabric.

"I hope I'm not interrupting," Reagan said, her eyes focused on Dorian. "Your assistant told me to come on back."

"Um . . ." Dorian licked his lips and, after feeling his hormones beginning to wake up, decided to remain seated. "No, it's no problem. You're not interrupting."

"Damn, how you doing, beautiful?" Kenny rose and held out his hand. He didn't bother hiding how his eyes lingered over the woman's body.

Reagan accepted the hand. "I'm good."

"Kenny, this is my sister-in-law, Reagan," Dorian introduced. "Reagan, this is my boy, Kenny."

Kenny lifted Reagan's hand to his lips and kissed it. "A pleasure to meet you."

Reagan giggled and removed her hand from his. "Dorian, I came to tell you goodbye."

"Goodbye?" Dorian asked in confusion.

"Yeah, TJ and I are leaving. I got a job out of state, though I sure hate to leave my family." Sarcasm dripped from the last statement. Between the hall pass and the fiasco that happened at the retirement dinner the previous week, it was a wonder she hadn't left sooner.

"Well, how you getting to the airport? You need a ride or something?"

"I definitely don't mind taking you." Kenny jumped in, licking his lips.

"Thanks, but I have a ride," Reagan said, readjusting the strap on her purse. "I'm about to go get TJ from my parents' first."

Dorian didn't know why he felt the need to ask, but the words were out before he could stop them. "Well, let me take you to lunch. The least I can do, since there's no telling when I'm gon' see you again." He didn't look at Kenny, but he could feel the man throwing a questioning stare in his direction.

"I appreciate that," Reagan said with a smile. "Can I just go use the bathroom really quick and we can go?"

"Yeah, back down the hall on the other side of the waiting room," Dorian said, motioning in the general direction. "Claudia or Pam can show you if you need them to. I'll meet you by the elevators."

Kenny waited until Reagan was gone before he spoke up. "Um, what was that?"

Needing something to do with his hands, Dorian began to stack and restack the papers on his desk. "What was what?" he asked innocently.

"Don't play." Kenny leaned back so he could angle his head out of the door and look down the hall. "That's your sister-in-law? Why you ain't never mentioned her before?"

"What you want me to say? 'Ken, guess what. I have a sister-in-law?'"

"Yes!"

"She's dating a friend of mine," Dorian informed him, though he wasn't entirely sure of that anymore. Especially with her leaving.

"Uh-huh." Kenny gave a knowing smirk. "And you going to lunch now? I thought you just said it was too early. Guess it ain't too early for her, huh?"

Dorian rounded his desk and pushed Kenny toward the door. "Man, that's my wife's sister," he said. It was pissing him off how right his friend was, but he obviously couldn't let on to that fact. "She just said she was leaving. Hell, I haven't seen her in some years. May be another five or six before she finds her way back to Georgia. Who knows."

Claudia glanced up as both men made their way in her direction. "Taking lunch, Dr. Graham?" she asked.

"Yes, ma'am," Dorian said. "Taking my little sister to lunch." He felt compelled to establish the sexy woman's relationship with him. Especially after seeing Claudia's eyebrows creased in a disapproving frown. He wondered if the reiteration made him seem guilty, or if that was just how he was feeling at the moment.

Claudia seemed to relax at the statement, and she smiled. "Oh, okay, then. Well, enjoy."

Kenny followed Dorian to the elevators. "You need to hook me up," he said, while they waited for Reagan to emerge from the restroom. "I mean, chick is young and fine."

"One, didn't she just say she about to leave," Dorian reminded him. "Two, I told you she got somebody. And three, what happened to your lady? You know, the one you living with who can't cook for shit?"

"Man, I ain't trying to hear all that." Kenny dismissed the question. "I'm trying to get with baby sis."

Reagan came out of the restroom and headed their way, her hips swaying with each step. She had let her hair down and had apparently applied a little more makeup, judging by the glossy lips that stood out in a rich purple hue.

"Damn," Kenny murmured, and Dorian could only stare as his friend verbalized his own thoughts. "Yeah, hook me up, man. Put in a good word. You got me?"

"Yeah," Dorian lied. Call it territorial or just plain selfish, but there was no way in hell he was going to give Kenny the opportunity to enjoy Reagan. Not when he still wanted her for himself.

⸻⸻

"So, what's up with your boy?" Reagan asked, after they had sat down and ordered. She had chosen a little pizzeria around the corner and they had apparently beat the lunch rush. They were the only ones in the restaurant, perched at a high-top pub table with a checkered tablecloth.

Dorian took a sip of his Coke. "What you mean? Nothing's up with him," he answered with a nonchalant shrug.

"Whatever. Ol' boy was all up my ass," Reagan shook her head in disgust. "And I can tell he was one of those cocky ones."

"Why you say that?"

"He's light-skinned. All them Shemar Moore–looking dudes think they shit don't stank. Or they can pull any chick."

Dorian started to rebut the stereotype, but he had to admit, Kenny did act like that. "Would you give him a chance?" He didn't know why he was curious. When she hesitated, he recognized the slight twinge of jealousy and had to take another swallow of his drink to wash down the annoyance.

"Nope," she answered, finally, resting her elbows on the table. "He's really not my type." It was clear, she was baiting him to ask more, especially by the desire flickering in her eyes.

"Yeah I know. Myles is more like it."

Reagan gave him a "you don't get it" look but didn't bother commenting.

"So, where you headed anyway?" Dorian asked instead at her continued silence.

"Dallas. A friend out there hooked me up with a job and a place to stay."

"A friend, huh?"

The question had Reagan smirking. "No, not *that* kind of

friend," she clarified. "*She* is just a homegirl of mine and she had a spare bedroom. So we can just crash with her until I get myself situated."

Dorian frowned. "You and TJ in one bedroom?"

"Yeah, he sleeps with me anyway," Reagan said with a shrug. "Besides, it's just temporary. I'm looking for another place now."

"What's the job?"

"I'll do shampoo at this salon she works at."

Dorian shook his head. The girl seemed like a lost soul. "You moving all the way to Dallas for that kind of job?"

"It's better than having nothing going on here."

"Shit, you can do that here too," he said. "There are plenty of hair places in Atlanta. Why don't you just stay with your parents or something?" he suggested. "It's safer than where you are now and it'll save you a few dollars. I'm sure they'll love having you and TJ around. Plus, if they see you're serious, they can help you get on your feet." He already knew she wasn't even entertaining the idea, so he tried a different approach. "Let me ask you this. Even if you don't stay with your parents, why not stay here in Atlanta? Why go all the way to Dallas? At least here, you'll be closer to family so we can help you."

Reagan grinned and sat her chin in her hand. "You want to help me, Dorian?" she asked with a hint of seduction.

"I want to make sure you and TJ are taken care of," Dorian clarified, curbing the innuendo. "You don't have anybody in Dallas."

"I don't have anybody, period."

"I wish you would stop saying that."

Reagan shrugged but kept her mouth shut as the server brought the wood-grilled pizza to the table. They ate in silence. Dorian was tempted to bring the topic up again, but he knew it was a dead conversation. Reagan always had been a free spirit. He just wished she would ground herself more. Especially considering she had a kid.

By the time they had finished and boxed up the last few slices, it had started to drizzle. The wind bit through his coat as he held the umbrella out for Reagan to huddle under, and he didn't object when she wrapped her arms around his waist.

Dorian opened the door for her and then skirted the hood to dash into the driver's side just as the sky opened up. "What time is your flight?" he asked, watching the rain pelt the windshield in sheets. "Weather may be a little bad to fly out today."

Reagan fiddled with the heat knobs. "Yeah, maybe you're right," she murmured. "I have to see. We'll probably be okay, though."

"Please, just be careful. You sure you don't want me to take you to your mom's?"

He didn't notice Reagan had slid her zipper down a bit lower to allow her breasts to peek through the opening. "No, but you know what I do want you to do?" she whispered, brushing her damp hair from her forehead. "I want you to make love to me, Dorian."

Dorian paused with his key hovering over the ignition. His body seemed to spring to life at the loaded request. He kept his eyes trained on the glass ahead, afraid of what he would see when he looked over to the passenger side. "Reagan, you know I can't."

"I know." Reagan inched closer to the middle console. "But you want to, don't you?"

"That's not the point." He eyed the diamond-encrusted white gold wedding band on his finger and sighed.

"Listen, I'm not trying to make this uncomfortable for you," she said. "I just like you, Dorian. I always have. So when you called me about the hall pass thing, I was thrilled that I could finally have you, if only once. I thought I would be satisfied with just that. But I just want you so bad. All the time. And the shit won't go away." Dorian didn't respond, so she rushed on. "I know this is wrong and I promise, this stays between us. You and

I both know when I leave Atlanta, I'm probably not coming back for a while. Let's just have this one last time, Dorian. Please. I need you."

She leaned forward and Dorian willed himself to pull back. But he didn't move. Even after she pressed her mouth against his, he could only hold his breath and relish how good it felt to have her tongue coax his lips apart. He swallowed her moan and she pulled away just long enough to whisper, "Touch me, Dorian." She then grabbed his hand and slid it inside her zipper to rest on her breasts. All rational thoughts dissolved at the feel of her soft skin, and this time, it was Dorian who pulled her back to devour.

The rain provided a sensual ambience as the two wrestled with their clothes. As soon as Reagan had peeled out of her jumpsuit, she threw her leg over the driver seat and straddled Dorian's lap. Dorian bent over to suck her nipples, at the same time reaching for the glove compartment.

"What are you doing?" Reagan's voice came out breathless.

"Condom," he murmured against her flesh.

"No, I want to feel you, Dorian." She teased him further, massaging him until all his logic seemed to disappear. "Don't you want to feel me?"

He didn't bother weighing the decision. He gripped her hips and slid her on him, cursing when he felt her clenching against him. Damn, she felt good. They began moving, as if entangled in some slow dance, Reagan's hands balancing on his shoulders.

"You feel so good, baby," Reagan was nearly whimpering. "Is this all mine?"

"Yeah," Dorian grunted, urging her to quicken her pace. He could feel the sensation building, and the anticipation was making his toes curl in his shoes.

"Tell me you love me," Reagan whispered, leaning forward to lick his ear. She had now elongated her strokes, taking in every inch of him and coating his skin with her nectar. She ignored the tightened grip on her hips and moved faster. "Tell me you love me, Dorian. Please. You don't have to mean it."

He felt the pressure continuing to build and he pulled her body closer to his, wrapping his arms around her waist. "I love you," he shouted as he released inside her. At the same time, he felt her reach her peak, and her body began to quiver.

For a moment, they sat there, each breathing heavy as they came down from the high. Finally, he felt Reagan pull away and climb back over into the passenger seat. She reached into the glove compartment, shuffled past the papers and box of condoms until she found the napkins.

"Thanks," she said, holding a wad out in his direction. Dorian nodded and began cleaning himself. Reagan managed to put her jumpsuit back on, and she flipped down the mirror and ran her fingers through her damp hair.

"It stopped raining," she observed.

Dorian hadn't noticed. All he could think about was sex with Reagan, what they had just done, but also, he was aching to do it again. He should have felt guilty now. Why didn't he feel guilty? He remained immersed in his thoughts, even after they had made the short drive back to the office.

Reagan turned to him and smiled. "It was good seeing you again, Dorian."

He nodded, not really sure how to respond. "You get where you're going safely," he said. "And . . . I guess we'll be seeing you around."

Reagan watched him as if she expected him to say something else. When he didn't, she got out, nearly slamming the door behind her. Dorian watched her stomp down the sidewalk and cross the street at the intersection. He debated following her and once again offering her a ride, but something told him that wasn't a good idea. Instead, he wheeled into the parking garage and hoped she made it wherever she was going. He knew she was leaving, and they had managed to get away with their little fiasco, but he couldn't help the uneasy feeling that settled over him.

"Your wife came looking for you," Claudia said, as soon as Dorian stepped off the elevator. Dorian stopped dead in his tracks. *Since when does Shantae just show up at my office before calling?*

"Oh? She still here?"

"No, sir. I told her you were out to lunch with her sister."

Dorian nodded and hurried into his office. He didn't know why it looked suspicious, but something just didn't sit right with Shantae knowing he was out with Reagan. And considering he was still warm from having her, his paranoia was riding on level twenty.

He punched in Shantae's number and held his breath, listening to the ringing.

"Hello?"

Dorian tried to analyze her tone through the one-word greeting but he couldn't really tell. *Is she mad? Does she know something is up?* "Hey, babe. I just got back from lunch and Claudia told me you came by."

"Yeah. I was actually at an off-site meeting in the area and I just wanted to stop in and take you to lunch or something. But Claudia said you were with Reagan?" She had inflected the statement like a question, and Dorian knew that meant she was waiting on an explanation. His mind was cluttered with thoughts, so he tried his best to sound as nonchalant as possible.

"Oh, yeah, she just dropped by on her way to the airport."

"Airport? Where is she going? She didn't tell me she was leaving."

Dorian barreled on, not knowing if he was helping the situation or making it worse. "Well, I guess she's going to call you in a bit. She was on her way to Mama's to get TJ. Something about a job in Dallas."

"Dallas?" she echoed.

"Uh-huh." He held his breath, waiting.

"Oh." Shantae paused as if she were processing the information. "And y'all just went to lunch?"

"Well, I was on my way out anyway," he lied, swiping at the sweat beginning to form on his brow. "And she was hungry, and I figured it was cool, since there's no telling when we'll see her again. You know how your sister is."

Shantae chuckled. "Tell me about it," she said. "Can't keep up with that girl. I'll probably give her a call in a minute, if she doesn't call me. So, what do you want for dinner?"

Dorian wanted to sigh in relief. He could feel his muscles relaxing bunch by excruciating bunch. He had definitely dodged a bullet. It was a good thing Reagan was leaving. He didn't know if he would be so lucky if there happened to be a next time.

Chapter Fourteen

She was acting different. Dorian couldn't really put his finger on it, but lately, Shantae was more reclusive. He didn't know if he should be nervous, but the short answers and silent treatments were enough to heighten his panic.

It had only been a few days since Reagan had left, and despite missing her conversation and the bomb-ass sex, he was honestly glad she was gone. It was safer that way. Easier to resist temptation when there was none. But with Shantae not giving him any attention or affection, he had even toyed with the idea of texting Reagan, but he knew he would be doing nothing but opening another can of worms.

After yet another morning of silent tension and strained conversation, Dorian knew he had to do something to put the excitement back into his marriage. The only way to get his mind off Reagan was to make sure he and Shantae were focused only on each other. He informed Claudia he was taking the rest of the afternoon off and went to the grocery store. Shantae loved his teriyaki salmon so he made sure to pick up some, as well as vegetables, rice, and the ingredients for a red velvet cake. The tulips in the floral department caught his eye, so he grabbed a bouquet, as well as some red wine.

Dorian didn't cook often because Shantae had always deemed the kitchen her territory. But when he did, he damn sure knew how to throw down. Before long, the delicious aromas were wafting throughout the downstairs and had his mouth watering. The cake was almost done, the vegetables had been sautéed, and the salmon was seared to perfection. He went ahead and set the table with their wineglasses and the beautiful arrangement front and center in a crystal vase.

Dorian checked the stove clock, mildly surprised when he realized his wife still wasn't home. It was well after six and she was usually home by five thirty. But then, she tended to stay over at work sometimes, especially if it was a really heavy season. Or maybe she had stopped by the store to grab some dinner or gone to her parents' house. He cursed when he realized he probably should've given her a heads-up about the food waiting at home and he picked up his phone to call her. It went straight to voice mail.

Dorian sighed and glanced around the kitchen. Everything was ready and smelled delicious. He hoped she was on her way. Just in case, he dialed his mother-in-law and rested a hip on the counter while listening to the phone ring.

"Hey, Mama," he greeted when Barbara answered. "Is Shantae over there with you?"

"No, sweetie. Why? Is everything okay?"

Dorian rubbed his face. "Yes, ma'am. I just hadn't heard from her, and now she's not picking up the phone. I'm sure she probably stopped somewhere after she got off work, though. No biggie."

"Okay, well you tell her to call me when she gets home. Let me know she's all right."

"Will do." Dorian paused when he heard the garage door open. "In fact, that's her coming in now."

"Okay, good. Still have her call me, though."

"Yes, ma'am." Dorian hung up as Shantae entered the kitchen from the garage. She jumped, startled when she noticed Dorian waiting by the counter.

"Baby, you scared me," she said with a small smile. She sniffed, her eyes glancing at the grill and the pans on the stove. "You cooked dinner?"

"Yep," Dorian answered.

"Aww, how sweet. I'm really not that hungry, though, but I'll still eat a little something, since you went through so much trouble." Shantae tossed her blazer on the back of the barstool and crossed to peck Dorian on the lips. Then she turned and plucked a roll from the basket on the counter.

"I tried to call you," Dorian prompted when Shantae made no move to divulge her whereabouts. "You were a little late, so I didn't know if you had stopped at the store or stayed late at work. Your phone went straight to voice mail."

Shantae nodded as she chewed. "Yeah, it's completely dead. In fact, let me put it on the charger now." She reached into her purse and pulled out the cell phone.

"By the way, your mom said to call her."

"My mom?"

"Yeah, I called her to see if you had gone over there."

Shantae sucked her teeth. "Damn, Dorian, why would you do that? Worrying my mother."

"I didn't mean to worry her. I was just looking for you."

"Well, thanks a lot." Shantae rolled her eyes and carried her phone, purse, and jacket up the stairs.

Dorian waited to see if Shantae would return and groaned when he heard the shower running from their bedroom. He made himself comfortable at the table, sipping his wine to pass the time.

Long after the water had stopped, his wife still had not come back downstairs. The food was cold, he knew, and even his own appetite had diminished.

He went upstairs into the bedroom they shared, and frowned. Shantae was done with her shower all right. She had changed into her silk pajama set and even wrapped her hair under a bonnet. She sat up in bed, the glow from her cell phone illuminating her features in the dark as her fingers scrolled on the screen. She was close to the edge of the bed so the cord from the charger could reach the socket.

"Well, damn, you could've at least told me you weren't eating at all," Dorian said, struggling to contain his anger.

Shantae didn't even bother looking up. "I told you I wasn't very hungry."

Her nonchalant attitude only heightened his frustration and he began to undress, snatching his T-shirt over his head.

"What is your problem, Shantae?" he asked. "I get off early to cook for you, bought you flowers. Hell, I even baked a cake. And you can't even eat, much less say thank you. What kind of inconsiderate shit is that?"

Shantae sighed and placed her phone on the nightstand. She folded her hands in her lap and finally lifted her eyes to meet his. "Baby, what's going on with us?"

"Hell, that's what I want to know." Dorian sat on the edge of the bed. "That's why I wanted us to have a little date night. To try and talk or deal with whatever is going on."

Shantae nodded. "Maybe it's work," she suggested. "I've just been so stressed out lately."

"I told you, you didn't have to work if you didn't want to," Dorian said, reaching for her hand. "I told you I make enough money for the both of us. You know that."

Shantae laughed. "Yeah, but your money is your money, and my money is my money. You made that clear when you had me sign that damn pre-nup."

"Oh, here we go." Dorian rose and headed toward the bathroom. "We not about to argue over something that happened when we first got married. It's been a year, Shantae. Damn. Don't I take care of you? Don't I give you whatever you need and want? What difference does a pre-nup make if we are not about to get divorced?"

Shantae climbed from the bed and crossed to wrap her arms around Dorian. "I know, babe. That's not what I meant. I just don't want to feel like I'm depending on you, you know? My job makes sure I pull my fair share. We got us, remember?"

"Yeah." Their saying had always held weight, but for some reason, it didn't really feel the same. Maybe it was the tension of the evening, maybe it was the way she said it. Maybe he was just off since the whole Reagan issue. He didn't know. And the shit was aggravating the hell out of him.

Dorian turned to kiss Shantae, and she parted her lips to receive him. Their kiss was passionate and for a brief moment, it felt genuine. Then she pulled back.

"I love you," she said.

"Love you too." He eyed her a moment longer. She looked as if she wanted to say something else but didn't. Instead she climbed back in the sheets and picked up her phone once more.

"Babe," Dorian said, remembering. "What was it you and your mother were talking about at dinner that day? When I walked into the kitchen?"

Shantae glanced up as if she were having to remember.

"Don't do that. You know what I'm talking about," Dorian pushed and Shantae sighed.

"It's nothing," she murmured. "I just had a little pregnancy scare, that's all."

He nodded but kept quiet. So, he was right to be concerned about the pregnancy test he found.

Shantae quickly dismissed the idea by shaking her head. "I was just having a little case of baby fever, but trust me, it's gone now. That's not something we need to worry about. And I'm not pregnant anyway, thank God." She forced a smile that didn't reach her eyes.

That alone told Dorian it was indeed something he needed to worry about. But rather than say all of that, Dorian kept his mouth shut and went into their adjoining bathroom.

For some reason, he didn't feel like they had accomplished anything.

When he came out from his shower, Shantae had her back to him and was snuggled under a pillow, snoring lightly. He debated waking her for sex, but he didn't feel like dealing with the attitude. So instead, he climbed in beside her and picked up his cell to see what porn he could please himself to. *Damn shame a grown man with a fine wife sleeping next to him still has to gratify himself.*

Dorian had just settled on one of his old faithful videos when the notification icon appeared at the top of his toolbar. He opened his texts and was pleasantly surprised to see the one-word message from Reagan.

HEY STRANGER.

He glanced at his wife still sleeping beside him before deciding to respond. It wasn't like he had to worry about Reagan anymore. She was laid up in Texas somewhere. What difference did a little text message make?

WHAT'S UP LIL SIS?

He had to laugh when he saw her eye-rolling emoji.

LIL SIS, HUH? SO, WE DOING IT LIKE THAT NOW, BIG BRO?

HEY, I'M JUST TRYING TO ESTABLISH BOUNDARIES.

I DON'T DO BOUNDARIES.

APPARENTLY, YOU DON'T EITHER.

NAH. BESIDES, YOU LIKE ME DOMINATING YOU. IT'S FUN. NOT LIKE YOU HAVE FUN WITH MY BORING ASS SISTER.

Dorian cringed before responding.

LET'S NOT TALK ABOUT SHANTAE. WHY ARE YOU TEXTING ME SO LATE?

I MISS YOU.

Dorian's fingers hovered over the keys. How was he supposed to respond to that? Reagan's next message came through, as if she had sensed his hesitation.

YOU DON'T HAVE TO SAY ANYTHING. I KNOW YOU MISS ME TOO BABY. HEY, WANT TO SEE SOMETHING?

Again, Dorian hesitated. Damn right he wanted to see something, but did he need to? He typed *yes*, then erased it to type *no*. Then erased that and thought a moment. Thankfully, he didn't need to respond, because a multimedia message came through. He hit Download and waited while the picture digitized on his screen.

It was a close-up between her thighs. Reagan's legs were spread wide, revealing an erotic new piercing. It was red and swollen, but he had to admit, the silver bauble looked sexy.

WOW. DID IT HURT?

NOT AT ALL. IN FACT, IT TURNED ME ON. I'M INTO KINKY STUFF.

Dorian was getting more and more turned on himself. Shantae was pretty routine when it came to sex—whenever she found time to give it to him—and though it was still great, it was refreshing to change it up a bit. One reason he had begun to look forward to the hall pass.

He flipped back to the picture again and used his thumb and index finger to enlarge it so he could see the details of her delicate pink folds. He wanted her. That much was clear. The frustration had his body aching.

Dorian put his phone down and, without a second thought, eased Shantae over. He dipped his hand inside her pants and began stroking her body until he felt it humming to life. She moaned, still on the edges of consciousness.

When he was satisfied she was ready, Dorian entered her from behind, bracing her upper body down into the mattress.

"Ooh," Shantae murmured. "Babe, what are you doing?"

Dorian shushed her and squeezed his eyes shut. Shantae felt nothing like Reagan, but it was better than his hand. So he began working against her, visualizing the picture Reagan had sent. He then remembered her playing with herself in the bathroom and sped up. Below him, Shantae was moaning and moving in sync to his rhythm, but his mind was consumed by Reagan.

When he felt Shantae's body convulse, he felt his own building and had to bite his lip to keep from yelling out Reagan's name.

"Damn, babe." Shantae collapsed in exhaustion. "You always know just what I need."

Dorian rolled to his side and eased his briefs back over his hips. His body was soaked, but he would deal with it in the morning.

Dorian waited until Shantae had drifted off back to sleep. It never took her long afterward, and sure enough, he soon heard her heavy breathing once more. Dorian used the opportunity to grab his phone and saw Reagan had sent two more messages.

HEY WHAT HAPPENED?

YOU STILL THERE OR YOU FELL ASLEEP ON ME?

Dorian responded to the latter.

NAH, I DIDN'T FALL ASLEEP. I'M ABOUT TO THOUGH. HAD TO PUT YOUR SISTER TO SLEEP FIRST.

He added the laughing emoji and hit Send. He really didn't know why he had told Reagan that, but part of him felt it was reestablishing their boundaries even though Reagan had already made it clear she didn't care.

Dorian gave it twenty minutes before deciding she wasn't going to respond. He texted her good night before setting his phone on the nightstand and turning to pull his wife into him. Instinctively, Shantae's body folded into his, her head resting on his chest.

He didn't realize he had drifted off to sleep until he heard Shantae's phone vibrating on the nightstand. It stopped and then immediately started back up again. Dorian nudged her awake, at the same time glancing at the clock. "Shantae, get your phone," he said, not bothering to hide his annoyance. "Who the hell is calling you like that this time of night anyway?"

Shantae sat up, wiping her eyes. "What?"

"Your phone, Shantae," Dorian said again, nodding in the phone's direction.

Frowning, Shantae leaned over and pulling out the charger, swiped the screen to answer. "Hello?" Her voice was still clogged with sleep.

Dorian waited, his frustration immediately turning to concern when he saw Shantae's eyes widen.

"Oh, my God. Okay, Mom. Which hospital?" She was already tossing the covers back. "We are on the way."

Dorian jumped up. "What is it, baby?"

"That was Mama. Reagan's in the hospital."

Dorian paused in confusion as Shantae began snatching clothes out of her drawers. "Wait, hospital? Where is she?"

"Southern Regional."

Dorian pulled on a pair of sweats. What had happened? He was just talking to her. And more importantly, why the hell was she still in town?

Chapter Fifteen

They had been at the hospital for hours, it seemed. Dorian shifted in the uncomfortable waiting room chair and eyed the emergency room's occupants.

It was fairly crowded for a Tuesday night, with a compilation of men, women, and children dozing on the various pieces of hospital furniture. A few coughs or sneezes here and there and the lobby was quiet, with the occasional roll call from the triage nurse. The stench of antiseptics was strong enough to make his eyes water.

Shantae had dozed off next to him, and Barbara was there beside with Charles holding a sleeping TJ in his lap. "Attempted suicide," Charles revealed, as soon as Dorian and Shantae had arrived.

Apparently, Reagan had never left town. She had been at her parents' and she had called her father. Charles said she was crying and apologizing for being an awful mother and an awful person before hanging up. He had gone upstairs and realized she had locked herself in the bathroom. He broke the door down and found her body in the tub, the water already stained red with the blood oozing from slits in her wrists.

Shantae had cried while Barbara insisted her daughter had done it for attention. Which had Dorian wondering why. Whose attention was she seeking?

For now, he just had to sit and wait, consumed with questions until he could address them with the only person with answers. And since Roman was her on-call physician, he'd last provided an update that Reagan was restrained and heavily sedated.

Shantae stirred and Dorian reached over to pat her thigh. "Babe, why don't you go home and get some rest," he suggested as she yawned. "Or go back to your parents' house with your nephew. I can stay here until the doctors have more information."

Shantae shook her head. "No, you can go. I need to be here with my sister."

As exhausted as Dorian was, he felt he needed to be there too. Not just for the moral support, but because it was Reagan. And his gut was telling him he was somehow more involved than he realized.

A few moments longer and Roman pushed through the doors and headed their way. Dorian was glad his friend had been the one to see Reagan when she first arrived by ambulance and had been the one to update the family a few hours before.

All of them stood when he approached, a professional smile in place and clipboard in hand. "Good news," he said. "She has stabilized, and we did not need to do the blood transfusion after all."

"Oh, thank God," Shantae murmured.

"We are going to admit her for a few days, just to monitor her, but I don't see where she struck any arteries or caused any permanent damage." Roman paused, his eyes glancing toward Dorian for a brief moment. "Now I'm not trying to insinuate anything, but it's my job to ask." His brows furrowed in worry.

Shantae spoke up. "Roman, what is it? What's wrong?"

Roman sighed. "Has Ms. Reynolds been previously treated for any . . . psychological issues?"

Dorian looked to Barbara and Charles, who immediately shook their heads.

Roman nodded but Dorian could see he didn't necessarily believe them. "Just have to ask. Suicide attempts are often referred for psychological evaluations, since that's typically where it stems from. So, no depression, no bipolar or any type of mental diagnosis that you are aware of?"

"Roman." Barbara's tone was clipped. "There is nothing wrong with Reagan, I assure you. Now can we see her?"

Roman let a defeated sigh fall from his lips. It was apparent this was something he witnessed all too often. "Absolutely," he said. "Just let me get her moved and checked in and I'll be out to escort you." His eyes lingered for a second on Dorian before he strolled off, and he already knew what that meant. They needed to talk. Understanding, Dorian excused himself and rushed to catch up with him.

"What's up, man," Roman said as soon as they were alone. "For real. Does Reagan have some mental issues or not? I know she didn't just wake up this morning and say she wanted to kill herself."

Dorian shrugged. "Not that I know of," he said. Truthfully, he really didn't know. He thought about Reagan, their recent conversations, and even how she acted in the time he was dating Shantae. Flighty, yes. Unstable, absolutely. But for Roman to mention it, it had to have some shreds of truth.

"Is she gon' be all right?" Dorian asked again, just to be sure.

Roman sighed, the night's events showing in visible lines of fatigue across his face. "Yeah, man," he said. "But y'all need to get her checked out. For real." He paused, then added, "You know your boy blowing me up."

Dorian wondered how Myles knew about Reagan. Had she

called him too? "Don't tell him anything," he said. "Let the family deal with this first."

"You know I can't tell him nothing anyway," Roman reminded him. "But you need to. Or somebody, because he's about to go crazy trying to figure out what happened to her."

Dorian nodded, though he really didn't want to be the one to tell Myles. Was it even his place? That was his friend, but Reagan was . . . hell, he didn't even know. But for some reason, he felt like he would be breaking some invisible code. Especially considering she just might be in that hospital bed because of him.

"I'm just glad she's all right," Shantae was saying when Dorian rejoined the group and put his arm around her shoulders. She leaned into his embrace. "Why would she do some shit like this? She knew she could've talked to me about anything she was going through."

"Has she ever attempted something like this before?" Dorian asked, and Shantae shook her head.

"I was thinking. Do you mind me asking her if she wants to come stay with us for a while, Dorian?"

Dorian swallowed, struggling to keep his face casual. "Do you think she can just stay at your parents'?" he asked, avoiding the question.

Shantae's eyes slid to Barbara and Charles, who were whispering between themselves. "That's where she was when she did this shit, Dorian. I don't want her over there giving my parents a damn heart attack. And in front of TJ." She sighed, massaging her temples. "I think I would just feel better if she was at the house and I could keep an eye on her myself."

"But I know you work late a lot," Dorian pointed out. "Especially lately with the merger."

"Well, she'll have you there too."

Dorian didn't want to express how worried he was about that little arrangement. Not so much worried about Reagan, but about his damn self. How the hell could he resist this woman when she roamed where he ate, slept, and showered?

A nurse returned this time and ushered them back into another waiting room. This one was not as crowded and even had a little children's play area. "You will have to go in one at a time," the nurse, a young Hispanic woman, was saying as she handed each of them a visitor's badge. "She is awake and somewhat responsive."

"Can one of us spend the night so she doesn't have to be alone?" Shantae asked.

The nurse nodded. "That would be a good idea. I'll confirm with the doctor if it's okay."

They each took turns going back to see Reagan. Shantae went first, then Barbara. While each of them rotated in, Dorian sat in the play area, putting together puzzles with TJ. He seemed too preoccupied to know or even care what was going on with his mother down the hall. One of the joys of childhood: ignorance.

Dorian waited until Charles had returned from Reagan's room before standing up to stretch. "I'm just going to show my face," he told Shantae. "Then we can go."

"I'll probably just stay here for the night and have you come back and get me tomorrow."

Dorian nodded before turning to walk down the hall. He didn't know why he was nervous. A nauseated feeling settled in his gut, and part of him felt he should've skipped the visitation altogether. The other part had him still moving forward, his sneakers squeaking on the polished floor.

He paused outside her room. He really didn't know what to expect, but he felt compelled to see her, if only just to make sure she was all right. That's what he kept telling himself as he pushed the door open.

Reagan looked frail under the hospital sheets. Bandages were wrapped around each wrist and an IV dripped what Dorian assumed was pain medicine into her arm. The quiet hum and whir of machines buzzed from monitors on the side of the bed, in tune with the steady rise and fall of Reagan's breasts.

At the sound of the door opening, Reagan's head turned in Dorian's direction. She forced a thin smile. "I wondered if you were going to make it back here to see me," she said.

Dorian's movements were slow as he walked toward the side of the bed. He wasn't used to seeing her so . . . weak. Not the strong, dominating Reagan he knew. "How you feeling?" he asked, stopping a few steps away from the bed.

Reagan sighed and closed her eyes. "Sore. But better now that you're here."

Dorian ignored the comment. "Your sister said she wanted to stay with you tonight." He figured she would appreciate the news, but he was surprised when Reagan sucked her teeth.

"Whatever," she mumbled, opening her eyes again. She reached in his direction. "You can come closer. I promise I won't bite you, Dorian."

Dorian hesitated but took her hand and took a step closer, allowing his hip to rest on the side of the railing.

"Just ask me," Reagan said, when he just continued to stare. "Go ahead."

"Why did you do it?"

"The truth? Because of you."

Dorian frowned. He had honestly expected the confession, but that didn't make it any less shocking. "You don't mean that," he murmured at a loss for words.

Reagan laced her fingers with his and kept her gaze steady. All traces of humor had completely faded. "Dorian, I have loved you for years. Ever since Shantae started bringing you around. I know I was just a teenager then, but I'm grown now, and I've never been more sure about anything in my life." Dorian tried to pull his hand away, but Reagan held tighter. "I know it's wrong and I know there is no way we can be together, but please, Dorian. After what we've shared, I can't just go back to being your 'lil sis.' I'm not asking for much. Just a little time every once in a while. I promise it stays between us, and we don't have to do anything you don't want to."

This time, Dorian did pull his hand away and ran a hand over his face. If it wasn't for the fact that he was in a hospital surrounded by machines and patients needing oxygen, he would have pulled out a cigarette.

"I thought you were leaving the other day. What happened?" He was partially stalling, but also genuinely curious.

"I couldn't leave you," Reagan admitted. "I wanted to, but I just couldn't get on that plane. You were right. I have nothing to go to in Dallas. Everything I want, everything I need, is right here."

"Is that why you did this?" Dorian asked, tossing a frustrated gesture toward her bandaged arm. "You slit your fucking wrists because, what? You remembered I'm married to your sister?"

Reagan lowered her eyes as tears seeped from her lids and glistened on her cheeks. "I'm sorry," she whispered. "Please don't be mad at me, baby. I just . . . I don't know. When you told me you had just had sex with her when we were texting, something in me snapped and I just got so sad. I can't explain it. I promise it won't happen again. Please," she added, when Dorian remained quiet. "Just promise me you'll think about it."

Dorian shook his head. "No, Reagan, I can't agree to this. I'm not doing this to my wife. I love her."

"But you told me you loved me too."

"Reagan." Dorian struggled to remain calm, but he could feel his irritation increasing with each passing second. Maybe Roman was right. She did have some mental issues. "You know that was in the heat of the moment. And you told me to."

"So, you really didn't mean it?"

"You know I didn't."

"Yeah. I know." Reagan's sigh was heavy. "I understand. I guess I just don't see what there is for me to live for, then."

Dorian's blood chilled at the subtle threat. "What do you mean you don't see what there is for you to live for? What about your family? What about TJ? You're his mother."

Reagan remained quiet, her eyes focused on the tiled ceiling above her head. Her face seemed glazed over like she was in some kind of trance.

Dorian stepped to her side again, his tone softer. "Reagan, please, just . . . don't do anything stupid again. Promise me."

Now she did look at him. "Can I have a kiss goodbye?"

"Reagan, please . . . just stop it."

"Promise me you'll think about what I said, and you have my word. I won't do anything stupid."

Dorian swallowed. If it meant keeping her safe, he didn't see the harm in promising to consider her absurd proposition. It didn't mean he had to act on it. His nod was slight, but Reagan's smile deepened, letting him know he had apparently appeased her. For now.

Chapter Sixteen

"What's all this?" Dorian entered the break room and spotted the catered lunch from a local BBQ food truck. Claudia had already laid out the spread of pulled pork, chicken, potato salad, baked beans, and Texas toast.

Claudia grinned, handing him a paper plate. "Remember I told you Ms. Davis said she would buy us lunch after you did your consultation with her?"

Dorian's frown was replaced with a light chuckle. "I thought she was joking. She really didn't have to do this. Can you please send her a thank-you card?"

"Will do. And," she added, "she told me to tell you she left her *unappreciative-ass husband*. Her words, not mine."

Dorian couldn't help but laugh. "Good for her. In that case, send her a congratulatory card too with a little gift card so she can treat herself."

Claudia pulled a two-liter of Coke from the refrigerator. "You okay?" she asked at her boss's continued silence. "You seem a bit distracted lately. Anything I can do?"

It was true. Even still, Dorian shook his head. "Just family is-sues," he admitted. Reagan's attempted suicide was still heavy on his heart. Nor did he know what to make of her little request. So far, she hadn't brought it up again. But he would've been a fool to believe she would just drop it. Not after he had seen the great lengths she had gone in order to get his attention.

"Your mom okay?" Claudia's eyes rounded in concern. She knew about his mother's prognosis just like everyone else.

"Yes, she's fine. Doing as well as can be expected." He hated he hadn't been back to McDonough to visit her in a while, so he was really just quoting Rochelle's words at that point. Even with the Reagan situation sucking all of his time and energy, he knew it was no excuse. He needed to remember his priorities and stop letting that girl get him off his game.

"Well you need to *un*-distract yourself," Claudia said. "Don't you have surgery this afternoon?"

He did. A tummy tuck. He'd done the procedure so many times he was sure he could so it with his eyes closed. But still.

"I'm focused," Dorian assured her. "Just need to get some food in my system and then I'm heading over to the hospital. I'll be fine."

Claudia nodded and gave his arm a light pat. "By the way, your sister called this morning. You were in a post-op visit."

Dorian grimaced and struggled to keep from rolling his eyes. Yeah, he knew she had called. He had three missed calls on his cell phone too. "Thanks," he said. "Why don't you go get Pam so we can all dig in before this food gets cold."

"And before Kenny brings his greedy tail up here," she added.

A bell chimed, signaling someone had entered the office. Clau-dia sighed and rolled her eyes. "Too late," she whispered. As if on cue, Pam poked her head in the break room.

"If that's Kenny, you can send him on back," Dorian said fork-ing some potato salad onto his plate. "I figured he could smell this food all the way down in his office."

Pam giggled. "No, sir, it's a Myles Washington here to see you. He's not on the appointment calendar."

Funny how quickly he could lose his appetite. Dorian felt a bubbling feeling in the pit of his stomach. He hadn't been avoiding Myles so much as he had been "conveniently" busy every time his number flashed on the phone. But he had never come to the office before.

"Um, okay. You can send him back to my office. I'm coming."

He didn't mean to stall, but he purposely took his time collecting more food on his plate, even washing a few of the serving utensils that had collected in the sink. Dorian knew this wasn't a social call, so he was anxious to hear what Myles had to say. Chances are it was all about Reagan. Even though Roman had told him to, Dorian still hadn't mentioned to Myles just why Reagan was in the hospital. He figured he would leave that up to her.

By the time he made it back to his office, Myles was already waiting staring out at the magnificent Atlanta view outside his window. By the looks of the dusty jeans, Timberland boots, and hard hat, it was clear he had just come from one of his work sites. Myles owned a construction company, so it was not unlike him to be dressed down.

Dorian hesitated for the briefest of moments at the door before he entered. Might as well get it over with. "Hey, Myles," he greeted, circling his desk with his lunch in hand.

Myles turned around, his face neutral. "What's up?" He noticed the food. "Oh, my bad. I didn't mean to interrupt your lunch."

"You're fine. A patient brought it in. You're welcome to some if you're hungry. There's enough."

Myles shook his head. "I'm good."

"So, what brings you over here?"

Myles gestured to the window. "I'm working right across the street at that SunTrust building," he said. "And I wanted to stop by to see had you talked to Reagan."

Dorian took a bite of his chicken sandwich, chewing to delay while he thought of an appropriate answer. "You haven't talked to her?" he asked.

"Nah, man. I've called a few times. She keeps sending me to voice mail. I've been trying to check on her because she called with some bullshit about she didn't think she deserved to live anymore. I'm worried as hell. And I've been calling Roman to see what he could find out, but you know he ain't saying shit."

Dorian relaxed. Of course, he was just concerned. That was to be expected. He wondered why Reagan wouldn't just tell him instead of stringing him along. But again, that wasn't his place either.

"She's fine," he assured her. "She's at the house with me and Shantae until she finds her own spot."

Myles seemed visibly relieved by the news. "Well, shit, why didn't she just tell me that? She could've come to stay with me."

Dorian shrugged. Yeah, he would've liked that better too.

"Well, what happened? Did she say?" Myles pressed.

"Nah," Dorian lied without even thinking about it. "But you know that's family stuff. The main thing is that she's fine. Shantae is going to look out for her sister."

Myles nodded. He looked as if he wanted to say something else but didn't quite know how.

Dorian noticed the conflicting emotions playing on his face. "What?" he questioned.

"And you haven't talked to her?" Myles asked. "She ain't saying nothing to you about me?"

Dorian didn't like how strangely he posed the question. *What is he getting at?* "I mean, we talk in passing," he said, carefully. "I told you she lives at the house, so it's not like I don't see her. But other than that, you know I've been working . . ." He trailed off, still unsure if that was what Myles wanted to know.

Myles's eyes dropped to Dorian's cell phone resting on his

desk. "I just don't get why she's not answering my calls," he murmured almost to himself. He angled his wrist to glance at his watch and then turned to head for the door. "Can you tell her to call me when you see her this evening?" he asked.

"Yeah. No problem."

"I appreciate it." Then he was gone.

Dorian frowned after him, not really sure what to make of the visit. Something was definitely on Myles's mind. He acted as if he were fishing for something. But what?

Dorian looked at his phone and saw he had another missed call. And it was Reagan's number and picture displayed on his lock screen.

Chapter Seventeen

Dorian sighed, watching his wife's head bobbing under the sheet. She felt good. Damn good actually. But for some reason, he just wasn't feeling it. He never thought there would be a time that a woman, especially his wife, couldn't please him. Maybe it was because Reagan was in the next room. Maybe it was because he wasn't sure if she could hear their sexual trysts.

How messed up was his life? He couldn't enjoy sex with his wife because he didn't want to make her sister jealous.

"Babe, it's cool," Dorian said, resting his hand on Shantae's head. "I think I'm just tired."

Shantae looked up, her face creased in irritation. "Tired?" she echoed, doubtfully.

"Yeah. It's been a long week." It wasn't really a lie. Work had been stressful enough, but it had damn sure been an exhausting week, trying to keep his distance from Reagan.

Of course she had taken Shantae up on her offer to move in after she was discharged from the hospital. She hadn't gotten in Dorian's way too much, except for the occasional body rub when they passed in the hall or the skimpy-ass clothes she wore around the house.

Dorian had caught himself watching her getting dressed once when she had left her door cracked. Thankfully, Shantae had come home from work and he had rushed back into his bedroom before either of them caught him.

Dorian hated having Reagan in the house. Mainly because he knew now more than before that it was only a matter of time before he was sexing her down again.

More than anything, she was always dialing his phone even though she never wanted anything. "I just wanted to hear your voice," she would coo in the phone. "You act like you're ignoring me at home." Thing is, she was right. And though the numerous calls could be misconstrued, she had managed to keep them clean and platonic for now.

Shantae rose from Dorian's lap, letting the sheets pool at her legs. She hadn't bothered changing out of her work clothes, so her white silk blouse was disheveled and her pin-striped slacks were around her knees, exposing the lace thong Dorian loved. Her hair was now standing over her head where Dorian had been running desperate fingers through it, guiding her pace.

"Well, I don't know what the problem is," she said. "What? You don't find me attractive anymore or something, Dorian?" She got to her feet and began undressing.

"Baby, you know that's not true." And it wasn't. Shantae still was as beautiful as ever, with her slim frame. But she was no Reagan. And he hated himself every time he compared the two.

"Yeah, whatever." Shantae was now completely naked and she strutted into the bathroom. "I'm going to take a shower," she announced. "Can you order a pizza or something, because I don't feel like cooking."

"Sure."

"Just get enough for us," she added. "Reagan said something about going out tonight."

Dorian was glad Shantae was in the bathroom so she couldn't see his instinctive frown. "Out?" he echoed.

Shantae's voice was drowned out by the running water, so whatever she said, he didn't hear. Dorian got up and slid on some sweats and a T-shirt before making his way to the bedroom down the hall. It was closed, so he knocked lightly.

"Come in," Reagan called from the other side.

He opened the door and caught her standing in the full-length mirror. She was certainly going out, judging by the cream turtleneck sweater dress she wore. Like all of her garments, it hugged her curves just right and stopped at her knees to give way to the camel knee-length heeled boots. She had accessorized with gold hoops, bangles, and a pendant, and she had let her curls hang wild and untamed at her shoulders. She looked damn good, and the smile at Dorian's expression was evidence that she knew it too.

"What do you think?" she asked, turning to face him and sitting her hands on her hips. The question was a tease.

Dorian nodded. "Nice," he said. "Going out?"

"I have a date."

He didn't know why he felt some kind of way. She needed to go out. Anything to get her claws out of him. "Okay, that's cool. Myles?" He kept his voice nonchalant.

"Nah, someone else."

"You know he came by the office the other day."

Reagan picked up the matching cream blazer from the bed that Dorian recognized as Shantae's.

"He asked me to tell you to call him."

"Okay." She appeared completely disinterested.

Dorian leaned on the doorjamb. "Changed your mind about him?"

"I didn't say that." Shantae used her manicured nails to fluff her curls once more. She was intentionally being evasive, he could tell. And it was beginning to frustrate him.

"Don't wait up for me," she said with a smirk and squeezed by him in the doorway. Dorian had expected her to rub up against him, was almost wanting her to, but she managed to get by without so much as a touch.

The doorbell rang and Dorian decided to follow her down, just so he could see who the hell she was going out with. Not that it was any of his business, but she had the man coming to the house, so he had every right to know.

"You wanna get that for me?" Reagan asked, stopping at the bottom of the steps.

"Why you say that?"

"I mean, you're following me like you my daddy, trying to check out my date for prom so get the door, boo." She leaned on the back of the couch and crossed her arms over her breasts. Dorian noticed that mischievous grin as if reflecting on some inside joke.

"You a trip, girl," he said, shaking his head and walking to the door.

He wanted to be angry, but all he could do was stare at the man standing on his porch, basking in the glow of the porch light. "What the hell are you doing here?" He hadn't meant for the question to sound so harsh.

Kenny chuckled as he stepped into the foyer. "Damn, man, why you say it like that? Nice to see you too."

Dorian covered his jealousy with a grin. "Nah, man, you know that's not how I meant it," he said. "Just didn't expect to see you. Why you ain't tell me you were coming by?"

"Because he didn't come for you," Reagan chided, stepping between them. To throw salt on the wound, she wrapped her arm around Kenny's waist and tossed another grin in Dorian's direction.

Dorian wanted to remind her of what she had said about his friend not being her type but figured that would be a little inappropriate. She clearly read the thoughts on his facial expression because Reagan rattled on. "I know what I said, but after Shantae did her little matchmaker thing, I just had to get to know this man."

Dorian glanced to the stairs. "Shantae, huh?"

"Yeah, when she came by the office that day looking for you, I asked her about her sister," Kenny said, throwing an arm around Reagan's shoulders. "I figured she could slide me ol' girl's number, and she did. Tell her I said good looking out." He looked down at Reagan. "You ready?"

"Yeah, here I come. Let me grab my purse and I'll meet you outside." Reagan waited until Kenny had left before she turned back to face Dorian. "What's the matter, sweetie? Jealous?"

Hell yeah. "No, you grown, girl," Dorian answered with a nonchalant shrug. "Do your thing."

Reagan's eyes narrowed and disappointment had her lip poking out a bit. "What if I told you I plan on having sex? Would you be mad?"

She was digging the knife in deeper. Dorian grabbed her arm and navigated her to the kitchen out of earshot of the stairs. He assumed his wife was still in the shower, but he couldn't be sure.

"Why are you doing this?" he asked in a hushed tone.

"What am I supposed to do, Dorian? Just sit idly by and listen to you and Shantae with y'all boring-ass sex? I have to sit in my room lonely as hell and please my damn self, listening to her and wishing it was me. So, I'm going to find somebody who will tighten me up. I have needs too."

Dorian didn't have a response, so he just watched her.

Reagan blew out a breath, and changing her tone, she reached out to caress his arm. "I won't do it, baby, if you don't want me to," she whispered seductively. "Promise me you'll make love to me tonight and I won't even go. He means nothing to me."

Dorian watched her reach for the pack of cigarettes she kept on the counter and fire one up. She knew he didn't allow smoking in the house but at that point, he didn't even care to address it. She took a deep drag on the stick and he could only watch Reagan through the smoke.

He knew he needed to let her go with Kenny, but he didn't want her to have sex with him. He wanted to do it, but he couldn't. He just couldn't. Not again. Especially now knowing where her head was. Reagan was on some true love shit, making oogly eyes at him every chance she got. She had even tried to kill herself a week ago. She was dangerous. And a small piece of him was honestly flattered.

Dorian still hadn't answered when he heard footsteps on the stairs. Though he and Reagan were leaning casually over the island, guilty instinct had him snatching back and turning to the cabinet to pour himself a drink. Reagan stabbed out her cigarette in a nearby ashtray.

"Oh, Reagan, you're still here," Shantae said, entering the kitchen. She was in a long T-shirt that brushed her knees and the same red terrycloth robe that had apparently become her favorite.

Dorian's back was to them, so he didn't see Reagan look his way, but he felt her staring. He pretended to be engrossed with selecting the liquor he wanted from the various bottles lining the bar.

"Yeah," Reagan said, rising to her feet. "But I'm about to go, so I guess I'll see y'all later?" A question explicitly directed at Dorian. She waited, expecting him to answer. He didn't.

"Probably not," Shantae said. "I know how late you come in, and my ass is about to crash."

Reagan nodded. "Okay, well, see y'all in the morning."

Dorian remained silent as she walked away, and he didn't turn around until the front door had shut behind her. "So, Kenny, huh?" he asked, attempting to be as casual as possible.

Shantae shrugged. "Yeah. I didn't think you would mind. He asked me for her number, so I gave it to him. Kenny has always seemed like a nice guy."

"He has a girl."

"Well, they're just going to a movie, I think. She's not going to marry him." Shantae circled the island and leaned up to peck Dorian on the cheek. "Good night, sweetie. You about to order food?"

Dorian nodded, deciding against that drink. There was only one thing on his mind, and she had just strolled off with his friend. His second friend at that, since she had stuck her claws in Myles from the beginning. But unlike Shantae, he would be waiting up for her ass to return that night.

Only two kinds of men sat waiting up for a woman. Either the woman's father, or the woman's significant other. And since he was neither, it seemed childish for him to be watching the clock from his perch on the top of the landing, especially when he was sleepy as hell and kept nodding off. Still, he forced himself to stay awake and continued to wait as the time crept by. He was embarrassed and ashamed, but he damn sure didn't move.

At a little after 2:00 in the morning, Dorian heard the front door open and the heavy dragging steps of feet in excessive inebriation. He rose from his position and paused when he heard another set of footsteps. Reagan's giggle was giddy and flirtatious, followed by the sound of sloppy kissing.

On a last thought, Dorian peered into his bedroom to make sure Shantae was still asleep. She was. Had even gone as far as to put on her satin eye mask, so she was pretty much comatose until morning. Just to be sure, he pulled the door closed before tiptoeing down the stairs to confront the drunk couple. No way in hell were they about to have sex in his house.

The two had made it to the couch and were now tonguing the hell out of each other. Dorian stopped short and had to squint hard before he realized the man wasn't Kenny but some dark-skin guy with muscles bulging from underneath a plain white T-shirt. By now, he had hiked Reagan's dress up around her waist and laid her back against the leather cushions. Then, like a hungry man indulging in his first meal, his mouth was all over her, slurping and sucking on her beautiful folds while her legs wrapped around his neck. A delicious moan slipped from her lips as she arched against him.

Dorian felt his basketball shorts tighten as he recognized the rapid succession of euphoric expressions that played on Reagan's face. He remained in the shadows, enraptured by the scene and figuring both of them were way too engaged and too drunk to notice he was there. That's when Reagan's eyes opened and met his in a direct gaze. He froze. Then her lips turned up in a smile, and she lifted one hand and beckoned for Dorian to come over.

What the hell am I doing? He didn't know. But at the moment, he really didn't care to rationalize his actions. All he knew was he was hard and felt like lead between his legs and the way Reagan was licking her lips, he knew she was willing to satisfy him.

Dorian pulled it out of the waistband of his shorts and Reagan wasted no time taking it between her lips from her upside-down position. She moaned, either from the taste of him or the vicious beating the man was putting on her, but she sure as hell didn't let the discomfort of the position stop her. Dorian had to bite his lip to keep from moaning his damn self.

She let go of him long enough to catch her wave, her legs shivering in the aftershock of her orgasmic bliss. Turning, she bent over in the direction of nameless man, and Dorian quickly flipped her around. He would be damned if this man got the pleasure of Reagan first. "You need to leave," Dorian told the man. All the while his hungry eyes were ravishing Reagan's body. Obediently, the man cleaned himself up and left them alone.

Reagan arched her back in Dorian's direction, encouraging him to take everything she had to offer. He obliged, entering her roughly from the back.

She felt deliciously foreign and familiar all at once. The way she welded against him was like it was made just for that.

It was hot and the smell of sex was strong in the room. Skin slapping skin and restrained grunts acted like background noise for their little sinful deceit. The man came first, straining and cursing against the euphoric bust. Dorian was whispering and spewing curses in a voice even he didn't recognize. His possession had taken full control, and for the time being, Reagan was all his. The sight was enough to take Dorian over the edge. His knees gave out and he collapsed on the sofa, completely spent.

Reagan sat down on the cold leather of the couch, her dress still bunched up at the waist. "Thank you, baby," she said, leaning on Dorian's shoulder. "You don't know how much I needed that."

Dorian sighed, willing his breathing to slow down. "Who the hell was that anyway?"

"Hell if I know."

"What happened to Kenny?"

The question had Reagan laughing. "I sent him home," she said. "Told you he wasn't my type."

Dorian debated if he wanted to ask the question that was burning in his mind and decided to anyway. He had to know. "Why did you stop seeing Myles?" He braced himself for the answer, already dreading the words she had yet to say.

"Because that's your friend," Reagan answered, looking up at him. "I just couldn't keep doing that to you. I love you too much."

Relief had Dorian's smile spreading. Marriage aside, he was just happy Myles wouldn't be getting any more of what was his. And as twisted as it was, as much as he tried to avoid it, that's what Reagan was now. His.

Chapter Eighteen

"Ma, you sure you okay?" Dorian asked for what seemed like the hundredth time. Even through the phone, her cough sounded worse, and painful. He didn't like the sound of that.

"Son, what did I say?" Teresa cleared her throat. "Your mama is tough. Don't you forget it."

Her voice didn't carry as much authority as he was used to, but he would let it go for now. Better to not stress her about it. He would make a point to talk to Rochelle, see if anything had changed since their last conversation.

Dorian sat back in his chair. His mind was consumed with thoughts of Reagan. Here he'd been thinking he was content with the stability of marriage. The first taste of something new and fresh, it was as if he had been a starving man all along.

"Son, you listening to me?" His mom brought his attention back to the conversation. Dorian silently cursed himself. Damn, he was really distracted.

"I'm sorry, Ma. What did you say?"

Teresa sighed. "I was saying did you get that situation worked out? You know, the one that had you over here pissed at the world, but you didn't want to tell your mama because you were afraid I would worry? But you got me worrying anyway? That situation?"

Again, another vision of Reagan brought a smile to his face. "Yeah," he answered. "I got it all under control, Mama. Promise. You don't have to worry about me. I'm supposed to be worried about you."

"You know that's not necessary. You just take care of yourself, okay?" She sounded genuinely concerned. "I'm serious, Dorian. I don't want you getting into any trouble."

Dorian had to laugh. He was a grown-ass man. Maybe he liked a little trouble. But he would cut off his left foot before he said something like that to Teresa Graham. "Yes, ma'am," he said instead. "I love you, Mama."

"I love you too, son. I love you so much."

They hung up before Teresa could lapse into another coughing spell.

Dorian took care of a few action items on his to-do list in preparation for his consultation. According to the chart, Ms. Nicole Peach was getting a complete round of cosmetic procedures from head to toe, ranging in the ballpark of upward of $200,000. Hopefully, she wasn't like Ms. Davis.

One thing that disgusted him about his profession was folks trying to talk themselves into getting procedures they didn't want just to make someone else happy. Dorian had thought about the idea of getting an in-house counselor to speak to his patients. Of course, it would be a free service, but he thought it would be worth the investment. That way he could feel at peace when he wheeled these people into the surgery room. Not that he'd had a disappointed patient yet. He prided himself on his knowledge, skills, and abilities.

"Dr. Graham." His assistant Pam buzzed him on the intercom

phone. "Your two o'clock has checked in and is back in the exam room."

"Thank you, Pam."

Dorian gathered his things and carried the woman's file with him. He was still studying her preliminary forms as he gave a few knocks on the door before opening it.

"Okay, Ms. Peach, I'm . . ." Dorian glanced up and damn near stumbled when he saw, not a Nicole Peach but Reagan sitting on the exam table. She had disrobed, her clothes in a neat folded pile on the chair by the window. Her hands rested in her lap, her legs crossed at the ankle. Her breasts, which had already had enough work and looked absolutely perfect, sat at attention in the chilled room.

Dorian quickly closed the door behind him and leaned on it. "Reagan, what are you doing here?"

Reagan's smile bloomed. "Hi, Dr. Graham," she said, clearly engrossed in her role-playing. "The form said I could put a false name if I didn't feel comfortable putting my real name."

Dorian was amused. "True. And what can I do for you, then?"

"I'm here for my consultation," she said. "I have an appointment, Dr. Graham. Or should I call you Dr. Feelgood?"

"Well," he said, leaning against the door, "show me what you want me to do."

Reagan hopped down from the table and took a step in his direction. "Well, for starters," she said, grabbing her breasts, "these are much, much too big. They're heavy. Don't you think? Feel them."

Dorian chuckled and obediently cupped her breasts. He kneaded them gently, his face scrunched like he was deep in thought. "I think I see what you mean," he said. "Though I must say, I rather like the size. A perfect mouthful."

"Really?" Reagan's head cocked to the side as if in surprise. "Okay, what about this?" She did a pirouette on her bare feet, turning to give Dorian a full-on view of her backside. "Too big? Too little?" She did a little wiggle.

Dorian was getting harder by the second. This was some sexy-ass foreplay.

"I think that's perfect too, Ms. . . . What did you say your name was?"

"Peach."

"That is certainly fitting. Well, Ms. Peach, I think your peach is also perfect. I'm tempted to take a bite."

Reagan was clearly enjoying her little tease as she stepped back out of his reach.

"Okay, well, last one," she said. She hiked up her leg and rested her foot on Dorian's lap. Using her toes, she gently massaged him awake until he stood firm against the pressure. She slowly rubbed her leg, from her ankle up to her thigh. "You don't think these legs are too . . . I don't know. Open?"

Dorian had had enough. He rose then and clicked the lock on the door. "We should do something about that," he said, beginning to unbuckle his belt.

Reagan laughed as she backed up and let him lift her back on the table. "Oh yes," she purred. "We should definitely do something about that."

Chapter Nineteen

He had fucked up. Bad. Reagan was addictive, and Dorian couldn't get enough of her.

Weeks later and he was making up excuses to leave work, just so he could go home and sex her senseless before his wife got home. Much to Claudia's disdain and Kenny's confusion, Reagan had even started coming up to his job throughout the day. Sometimes multiple times a day.

"Bringing you lunch."

"Wanted you to hear this song."

"Saw this mug and thought of you."

It could seem suspicious, but under the guise of his "lil' sis," no one could really say her intentions were anything other than pure. Which gave them free rein to indulge in each other. And the two had definitely been taking advantage.

On and under his desk, in the restroom, conference room, janitor's closet—Reagan's nimble body was always on the ready.

With Dorian sexing Reagan more and more, his intimacy with his wife was becoming less and less frequent. Which was how it had to be. Reagan was the jealous type, and she had already made it clear she didn't want her man screwing his wife. At first, Dorian thought it impossible to withhold from Shantae without raising obvious red flags. A few times he even had to bust a quickie in the middle of the night to appease her.

Unfortunately, compared to Reagan's voluptuous curves and freaky porn-star tricks, sex with Shantae was becoming more and more of a chore. Nowadays, he couldn't even finish and had to pull out due to exhaustion. It was laborious, and eventually, Shantae stopped asking for it at all. Which was just fine with Dorian.

Now, Valentine's Day was rolling around and Shantae had suggested they go away for the weekend, but Dorian couldn't do that to Reagan. He tried not to think about how messed up that sounded. So he feigned like he was too busy at work to get away.

When he got home that night, fully expecting to see Reagan naked and waiting for him, it was Shantae who greeted him at the door in nothing but a see-through teddy and apron.

"Hey, baby," she said, giving him a long, passionate kiss. Surprised, Dorian pulled back, masking his disappointment with surprise.

"Wow. What are you doing here?"

Shantae smiled and twirled, the short lace skirt billowing up enough to give a peek of her ass cheeks. "Since you couldn't get away for our Valentine's weekend, I wanted to bring it to you."

"Thanks, babe." His eyes darted around the kitchen, though he had a feeling Reagan was long gone. "Should you be dressed like that with your sister here?"

"Oh, I sent her away." Shantae turned around and walked back to the stove, her black heels clicking against the hardwood with each step.

Dorian snuck a quick look at his phone. Reagan hadn't called. "So, I get you to myself all weekend?" he fished, pulling off his coat.

"Aaaall weekend, babe," Shantae exaggerated and tossed a flirtatious wink over her shoulder. "You're all mine." She dipped her finger in whatever was simmering in the pot and turned around, her finger stretched out in Dorian's direction. "Come taste this, babe. I tried a new sauce for the lamb, but I don't know if I like it."

"Um, one second, sweetie." Dorian made his way toward the stairs. "I just got off, so let me shower really quick before we get the evening started."

Shantae licked her lips. "Oh yeah. Get it all nice and clean for Mama to taste." She giggled and turned back around to finish prepping her meal.

Dorian darted up the stairs and closed their bedroom door. He then went into the bathroom and closed that door as well. Quickly turning the knob to the faucet, he made sure the water was on full blast before pulling out his phone and dialing Reagan's number.

She answered on the first ring. "What the hell is she doing?" She sounded as if she had been crying. "Dammit, Dorian, your wife is ruining everything. I had something planned for you for Valentine's Day."

"I know, baby, I'm so sorry. I didn't know." Dorian stepped farther from the door. The water was loud, but he lowered his voice anyway. "This was a shock to me too. You know I wanted to spend today with you."

"Then leave. I'm at a hotel. Come see me."

Dorian sighed, rubbing his hands over his face. "You know I can't, baby."

"Why not?" Her whine definitely belied her age.

"Baby, let me try and get away, okay?" Dorian offered. He didn't know how, but that was the best he could do.

"You promise?"

"Yeah."

"I love you."

Dorian hesitated, as he always did when she uttered those words. "You too." That was his usual response and one that seemed to satisfy her. As always. Reagan blew kisses through the phone and hung up.

Dorian undressed and stepped into the shower, but stress had him just standing there for a moment, letting the water beat against his tense muscles. He knew there would be a time when both his life and his secret life would collide. He should've known it was entirely too good to be true and the shit wouldn't last. But he had insisted on riding until the wheels fell off. Now what the hell was he supposed to do? There was no way he could be in two places at once.

Dorian emerged from the shower and picked up his phone again. This time, he dialed another number, all the while trying to work out the details in his head.

"What's up, man?" Roman greeted.

"Hey, I need a favor. You busy?"

"A little. You know Bridget done hooked up something for Valentine's Day. What you need?"

Dorian pulled back his phone to check the time before placing it back on his ear. "Can you call me in like thirty minutes?"

"For what?"

"It's a long story. I just need to get away for a minute." Dorian blurted out the first truthful-sounding lie that came to his head. "I forgot to get Shantae a gift, and I need to get away without the shit looking obvious. So, call me and say some emergency came up at work and you need me to do something."

Roman laughed. "Man, you crazy, but yeah, I got you."

"Thirty minutes, Roman."

"Yeah, man. Just get Shantae what I got Bridget. This big-ass *dick*."

Dorian rolled his eyes at his friend's weak attempt at humor. "Thirty minutes," he repeated again and hung up. He sent a quick text to Reagan to let her know he would be there in an hour, made sure the ringer on his phone was turned completely up, and threw on some sweatpants and a T-shirt. He tucked his phone in his pocket and trekked back downstairs to wait for the night to play out.

Shantae had already plated the meal in the dining room and was pouring them each a glass of wine when Dorian entered.

The lamb looked and smelled heavenly, braised on a bed of rice with steamed cabbage on the side. A bottle of Roscato was chilling in a bucket of ice next to the table and she had set out a small gift-wrapped box and a card beside his plate.

"Smells delicious, baby," Dorian said, taking his seat at the table. As discreetly as possible, he placed his phone on the table as well.

Shantae grinned as she joined him. "I wanted to do something special for you," she said. "I know we haven't been on the best of terms lately but, Dorian, I want you to know how much I love you. We got us." She lifted her glass and Dorian did the same, clinking them together.

"We got us," he repeated.

"What do you think?" Shantae asked, as soon as he took a bite into the lamb. Truthfully, Dorian was sure it was great. But anxiety had numbed his tongue because he couldn't taste any of the flavors, just counting down the minutes until he was sure his phone would ring. He nodded and smiled, forking another huge helping in his mouth. His stomach was bubbling, and it was a wonder he could swallow anything at all.

When Dorian was sure Roman should be about to call, he stood with his plate in hand. "Let me get a little more. You want seconds?"

"Not just yet. Saving room for dessert."

Dorian carried his plate back to the kitchen taking slow, calculated steps. He stood at the stove, deliberately taking his time in piling more food on his plate. Sure enough, he heard the familiar jingle of his phone resonating from the dining room. He held his breath and waited.

"Dorian, your phone." Shantae's voice rose over the shrill ringtone.

"Who is it, babe?" he called back.

"Roman."

"Can you answer it for me please? It's probably nothing important." He stood in place, listening as Shantae greeted his friend on the phone. Then her footsteps as she joined him in the kitchen.

"He says it's important." She held the phone out to him. "Something about paperwork at the hospital."

Dorian feigned a confused frown before accepting the phone.

"Hey, Ro. What's up, man?"

Roman laughed. "Is that good enough?" he asked. "Or do I need to come over there with tears on bended knee?"

Dorian's eyes slid to Shantae. She was waiting and watching patiently at his side. He cleared his throat. "Well, did you get them to sign off on the procedure?"

"Man, you really playing it up." Roman was completely tickled by the circumstances.

"Damn, man, now?" Dorian continued his role-play, ignoring his friend's laughter. "All right, all right, here I come." He clicked the phone off and turned to Shantae, his eyes already filled with regret.

"What's wrong?"

"I'm sorry, baby. I have a procedure for next week and didn't sign off on the authorizations." Dorian shook his head in mock annoyance. "I need to run back to the office really quick to get the papers."

"Why now, babe? It's Friday night. It can't wait until Monday?"

Dorian shook his head. "I'm afraid it can't. She is being admitted in the morning."

"Does she even need the surgery?" Shantae teased with a pout.

"Tell her like you tell me, she is beautiful and doesn't need her tummy tucked or her breasts bigger."

Dorian chuckled. "I'll use that one in my next consultation, babe." He kissed Shantae's forehead, ignoring the dejected expression. "I won't be long, sweetie. I promise. And hey, we got all weekend, remember?"

"I know, but . . ." She sighed and nodded in understanding. "Okay. Just hurry back, please."

Dorian lifted the back of her hand to his lips to kiss it. "I will," he promised and nearly broke out in a run to grab his keys, shoes, and coat. He just hoped Reagan was up and waiting for him.

⟶•⟵

"It's a shame," Reagan said, her fingers toying with the hair on Dorian's chest. They had just finished round three and were now cuddling in the hotel's king-size bed. Somehow, "hurry back" had turned into four hours, but he just couldn't bring himself to leave, and Reagan damn sure wasn't letting him go. He knew Shantae had been calling, but he had put his phone on vibrate and left it in his pants pocket in the other room of the suite. He would just have to deal with the consequences later.

He pulled Reagan closer, loving the feel of her body against his. Her skin was still slick with sweat and her favorite position was her leg thrown over his so her pussy could rub on his thigh.

"What's a shame?" he asked.

"You and my sister," Reagan said. "A shame y'all are still together after all these years when you're so clearly in love with me."

Dorian sighed, already hating where this conversation was heading. "Reagan, let's just enjoy this moment. Don't ruin it."

"How am I ruining it?" She lifted her head from his chest, her tresses tickling his shoulder with the movement. "You do love me, don't you?"

"Reagan, please."

She let out a frustrated sigh and turned over, breaking their contact. "Fine, I won't mention it anymore. Damn."

Dorian leaned over to kiss her bare shoulder. "Can't you just appreciate that I'm here now? I could be at home with her, but look where I am. Right where I want to be."

Reagan warmed at the tender words and she raised her arms over her head, the gesture lifting her breasts closer to Dorian's face. "You right, baby. Show me again how much you want to be here. You know how much I crave you."

Dorian leaned in to lick her nipple but stopped short when something caught his eye. Reagan had her eyes closed so he took the opportunity to peer closer, sure he wasn't seeing what he thought he was seeing.

"Reagan, what the fuck is that?" he snapped. Angry, he sat up, snatching Reagan's arm with him.

"What are you . . ." She trailed off when her eyes followed his down to the tender flesh inside her elbow. The scars were healing, but the razor-thin impressions had left white welts in her chocolate skin. Embarrassed, she snatched her arm out of his grasp and tossed her legs over the side of the bed.

"Reagan, since when do you cut yourself?" Dorian jumped up too so he could catch her before she darted into the bathroom. "You promised me you wouldn't do anything stupid. You promised." He was clutching her by the shoulders now, squeezing and shaking at the realization.

"It's not stupid," Reagan shouted in tears. "I do it to cope with the pain."

"What pain?"

"You and Shantae. Dammit, Dorian, how am I supposed to feel?"

"I don't believe this shit." Dorian threw up his hands in frustration. "Who am I with all the damn time? Who am I having sex with? Who am I sneaking off to be with? What the hell else do you want me to do, Reagan?"

"But you're still with her! You're still married to her."

"But you knew this when this shit started, Reagan. Don't act brand new now."

"I'm not acting brand new." Reagan turned and stormed into the bathroom. "But shit changes, Dorian."

"Ain't shit changed. *You* changed. Don't want to deal with the situation, then leave me the hell alone."

It came flying toward Dorian's head before he had time to duck. Thankfully, the object wasn't too big, but the news was big enough to suffocate him. The little pregnancy test landed window side up, and the pink plus sign glared back up at him, validating the proof that yes indeed, shit had changed. For the worse.

Chapter Twenty

Shantae's name flashed across his cell phone for the fifth time, but Dorian rejected it once again. He sighed, sitting back in his office chair, and pressed his fingers to his eyes. He knew he should feel bad for ignoring her, especially after how he had been acting lately, but he was too preoccupied with Reagan. And at the moment, he was waiting on her very important phone call.

Dorian swiped the screen to reject his wife's call once more. Then, thinking better of it, he flipped open to his text messages and shot her a quick **I'M IN A MEETING. CALL YOU BACK IN A BIT.**

He was partially surprised Shantae was even calling at all. Ever since he had stood her up on Valentine's Day, she hadn't really had too much to say to him.

He had finally made it back to the house after coddling Reagan for a bit. Of course, Shantae had been furious, and he couldn't really do anything but toss out some half-assed excuse about car trouble that he doubted she even believed. But with Reagan's pregnancy announcement still weighing heavy on his mind, he didn't even have the energy to try for a better excuse. He vaguely remembered Shantae still cussing his ass out, but that had been nearly two weeks ago, and between him and the two sisters, the tension in the house was like a thick fog. Somewhere, his life had fallen apart, and he had no idea how to get it back on track.

Sighing, Dorian glanced at his phone again, anxious for Reagan's number to come up on the screen. Still nothing. The notification signaled Shantae had left a voice mail message this time. Curiosity outweighed his apathy, so Dorian dialed into his voice mail box to listen to what she had to say.

"Hey. It's me." Her voice was low and Dorian's heart broke when he could easily detect hurt over the anger. *"Listen. We really need to talk. Can you come straight home after work? Maybe we can go somewhere for privacy, but I have some things to say, and it may or may not change us and our marriage. I'll talk to you later. Bye."*

Dorian sat the phone back on his desk and leaned forward, resting his head in his hands. Dammit. he knew it was only a matter of time before Shantae would get restless. He prayed to God she wouldn't ask for a divorce.

He loved his wife, even though it didn't really seem like it, since he had been thinking entirely with his other head the past few months. But if it came down to choosing, there was no choice to be made. Shantae was his wife. She still had his heart.

Of course, Reagan wouldn't like it, but she would get over it. He had some love for her to a degree, but it wasn't like the special bond he shared with his wife. He and Shantae had been through hell and back.

Anyway, after today, Reagan probably wouldn't want to have anything else to do with him.

"Man, you don't hear me talking to you?"

Kenny's sharp voice snatched Dorian out of his thoughts, and he glanced up to see his friend framing the doorway. "Oh, my bad," he said. "I was thinking about something."

"I could tell." Kenny came on in and sat down. "You all right? You seem distracted."

"Just women problems."

"Who, Shantae? What happened?"

Dorian shook his head. "Nah. It's other stuff. No big deal."

"If you ask me, both them sisters probably a little cuckoo." Kenny emphasized his statement by twirling his index finger around his temple.

Dorian had to chuckle. "Why you say that?"

"Shit, if Shantae's anything like Reagan, I don't know how the hell you survived this long."

The statement piqued his interest, and Dorian realized he never really asked him about their little date. Reagan hadn't said much either, except she sent him home early. He didn't know why he even cared, but since Kenny had put it out there . . .

"You never even told me how the date went anyway. What happened?"

Kenny rolled his eyes. "Man, that bitch is on some crazy shit. One minute, she's a mute. Not talking, not really listening to me. Just staring off into space. I'm asking her questions and she really ain't got much to say. So, I'm thinking, okay. She's shy. Then the next minute, she's in tears. Claiming she can't ever do anything right. Can't find a man. Then, she gets angry at me. Talking about I only wanted to go out with her to get some, and that's all niggas cared about. All this shit, Dorian, in a matter of minutes. I mean she went through seventy-six personalities before the waitress even brought our appetizers."

It should've been funny, but Dorian could only frown at the story. He was listening but his mind kept flashing back to when Reagan had been committed to the hospital and Roman had mentioned possible mental health issues. Here again, someone else had noticed something about that girl.

"Aw, man, I'm sorry," Kenny said, noticing Dorian had lapsed into deep thought. "I know that's your baby sister. My fault. I didn't even think about that. I wasn't trying to disrespect you or anything."

Dorian dismissed the apology with a wave of his hand. "Oh no, that's not it," he assured him. "I was just thinking about what you said and was trying to see if I ever noticed her acting like that."

Kenny shrugged. "I don't know, but it was damn sure awkward. Then we had a few drinks at dinner, and I think she had loosened up toward the end there because she seemed calmer. I almost got caught up, though."

"What you mean?"

"Shit, going home to my girl smelling like Japanese Cherry Blossom and sex." Kenny chuckled again as if reliving that brief moment of paranoia. "I had to jump in the shower quick." If he had been looking, he would have seen the flicker of anger in Dorian's eyes.

Dorian felt his blood beginning to boil and he had to count to ten before speaking. He knew he didn't hear what Kenny had just said. "Sex?" he repeated, choosing his words carefully. "Oh, you and Reagan sexing and shit?"

Kenny cursed under his breath. "Shit, my fault again, man. I keep forgetting that's family for you. I'm not even thinking. Just talking like how we do."

"So, that's a yeah?"

Kenny's breath was reluctant. "Yeah, man. We did."

Dorian didn't even know he had moved. He just remembered suddenly being on the other side of the desk, Kenny's neck between his fingers, and using his other fist to decorate his friend's face. They fell to the ground, toppling over chairs, and Dorian could only see red as Kenny struggled to dodge his punches.

"Hey, man, what the—" he spurted before Dorian knocked the rest of the words down his throat with a fist to his mouth. All he could think about was Kenny sexing Reagan, feeling her walls, touching on her body. Then Kenny's face morphed into Myles's, and Dorian punched even harder. The images were flying in rapid succession and were enough to have jealousy fueling his adrenaline, and he was damn near dragging the man across his office.

"Dorian, what are you doing?" Claudia's high-pitched voice broke through and seemed to snap him out of his daze.

Baffled, Dorian looked down to assess the damages. His own hands were sore, and his knuckles were bruised, but other than that and being a bit winded, he was fine. He couldn't say too much about Kenny, on the other hand. His friend's face was swollen. Blood trickled from his nose as well as his busted lip to splatter on the white dress shirt he wore under his gray blazer. He groaned as he sat up, his hand reflexively grabbing his side to massage his tender ribs.

"Shit." Dorian climbed to his feet and could only stare at Kenny's perplexed and bruised face. "Damn, man. I'm sorry."

"What the fuck is wrong with you, man?" Kenny coughed and spit out a glob of blood, the crimson red spot immediately staining the ivory carpet. He readjusted his tattered suit. "All this over that crazy bitch?"

Dorian opened his mouth and closed it again. He wanted to explain, wanted to rattle out an excuse of feeling disrespected because Reagan was his little sister. But looking again at Kenny's face and the mess in in his office, even that excuse wasn't strong enough to substantiate such a horrible fight. Especially with his good friend.

"Oh, my God." Claudia's hands were to her lips as she watched Kenny wobble to his feet. "Kenny, are you okay? Do you need me to call someone?"

"I'm good, Ms. Claudia." Kenny gave one final glare at Dorian before turning and hobbling from the office.

Claudia looked to Dorian as if waiting for an explanation, but he had none. He was at a loss. Not to mention his body was aching from Kenny's defensive blows and rolling around in a brawl like they were two kids on the playground at recess. Panic was beginning to claw at him. He was losing control of the situation. Plain and utter jealousy at its finest. He had been okay with them going out, but knowing that Reagan was having other men was enough to shred his sanity.

Dorian lifted one of the chairs and plopped down in it, massaging his hands. "Ms. Claudia, can I have something cold to drink, please?"

Claudia snorted. "Hmph. What you need is a good stiff kick in your behind. In this professional place, fighting like some common thug. You already know how white people think of us, and you and Kenny just go and give them something else to talk about. You ought to be ashamed of yourself. Get your own damn cold drink." And with that, she turned and stalked off down the hall.

He deserved that. He knew he did. And he did feel ashamed. Not to mention embarrassed. How was he going to explain his behavior to Shantae? To Kenny? To his coworkers?

Deciding he needed air, Dorian grabbed his keys and phone and headed down the hall.

Claudia wasn't at her desk, so he quickly scribbled a note about leaving for the day on one of her Post-its and stuck it to her monitor. He then took the elevator down to the parking garage.

Dorian sat in his car for a moment, staring at his phone. He needed to call Shantae. They did need to talk. And more importantly, he needed to completely get rid of Reagan. She was destroying his life. Speaking of which, he saw she had called twice and sent a text. Damn, he had forgot he was waiting on her call. He read the simple **CALL ME** message first before dialing her number.

She picked up on the first ring as if she was expecting him. "Hey, baby."

"Hey. Is it done?"

Reagan sucked her teeth. "Damn, no 'how are you? Are you feeling okay?' Just straight to it, huh?"

Dorian squeezed his eyes shut. "Reagan, please. I've had a hard day."

"And I haven't?"

"That's what I'm trying to see about. Did you do it?"

"Yeah," she said, in a huff. "I did. You happy now?"

Dorian bit back a response. Actually, he was. When he had first suggested abortion, Reagan was completely against it. She had cried on his shoulder about wanting to have their love child. Needing to have a piece of him always. He had tried several tactics, asking how could she want to have another child, already having one who pretty much was now being raised by her parents. He had even resorted to threatening he would never see her again if she continued to refuse the abortion. Eventually, she gave in and he had quickly handed over the money for her to have the procedure. Now, hearing her affirmation had Dorian sighing in relief. One less complication he had to deal with for the time being.

"Are you okay?" he asked, finally. "How are you feeling? In pain or anything?"

"Oh, *now* you care?"

"Reagan, I don't need the fucking attitude. For real."

"So? You just made me get an abortion. I have a right to have a fucking attitude."

"Oh yeah? Well, I just got into a fight with my friend over your grimy ass, so *I'm* not in the fucking mood," Dorian snapped back.

"What are you talking about? Fight with who? And who the hell you calling grimy?"

Dorian stretched his fingers, feeling them beginning to cramp up. "Kenny. Remember my friend, Kenny, who you went out with? You just give it up to anybody, huh?" Disgust filled his gut when Reagan just remained quiet. "Yeah, that's what I thought. So, he wasn't lying, huh? You were."

"Baby, it's not like that." Reagan's tone had softened. "It just happened, and it didn't mean anything. I didn't even want to. I was just so angry and hurt you let me go out with him. Like you didn't even want me. Like you didn't even love me."

"I don't love you, Reagan," Dorian yelled, banging his fist on the steering wheel. "Stop saying that. Stop being so damn extra. I can't handle that shit."

"Baby, what am I doing?" Tears thickened her voice as she wailed into the receiver. "Please don't be mad at me. Can't you just come home so we can talk? I'm at the house. Shantae's not here. Let's just talk. I don't want to fight with you."

"Reagan. Hear me good. I need you to get your shit and get the hell out of my house." Dorian's words seeped through clenched teeth. "This shit is done."

"But I just had the abortion for you, Dorian."

"I don't give a fuck. How do I know the shit was even mine? It could've been Kenny's. Or Myles's. Or hell, ol' boy you brought to my house that night."

"Dorian, baby—"

"Get the fuck out, Reagan. I'm serious. We are over." Dorian clicked the phone off, not surprised when it immediately rang in his hand, with Reagan's number flashing across his screen. He rejected the call and it rang again, and again. She called twenty-four times before Dorian was able to get to his block list to block her number. He then punched in his wife's number and waited for her to pick up.

"Hello?" Shantae answered.

"Shantae. Babe, it's me. Where are you?"

"I'm at work, Dorian. Why? Did you get my message?"

"Yeah, that's why I'm calling. Can you take the rest of the day off and let's go somewhere so we can talk?"

Shantae sighed. "Yeah. Where do you want to meet?"

———◆———

Dorian went all out and chose a spa near the house. He knew it was extreme, but after the fight with Kenny and the blowup with Reagan, he needed to realign his focus. And his focus was his marriage.

He almost told Shantae to meet him there but then he reconsidered and told her he would pick her up. When she stepped out of the bank in one of those signature suits that flirted with both sexy and professional, her hair swirling with the cool breeze, it reminded him of when they had first started dating. It was definitely something about Shantae's aura that kept him coming back. Somewhere along the way, he had forgotten that.

She approached the car, and he quickly got out and rounded the hood to open her door. He watched the surprise register on her face. "Dorian, what is all this?" she asked, her voice weary.

"Just get in," he said. "Please." She sighed but obliged without another word.

Dorian drove with leisure. The windows were down to let the comfortable breeze drift through, the radio soft enough for conversation but loud enough to have Shantae nodding along to the music. When he placed his hand on hers on the armrest, he felt a silent victory when she didn't budge at the casual gesture.

After a short drive, Dorian eased the car up a brick driveway and under the arch of a stone building. A *Spa Amor* sign hung suspended between two columns, and large windows allowed a glimpse of the elegantly decorated reception area. A valet was already opening her door and extending his hand to help her out. "Welcome to Spa Amor," he greeted before rounding the hood to the driver's side. Another victory. He saw the ghost of a smile playing on Shantae's lips and he felt himself simmering with excitement. This just might work in his favor.

Inside, candles, plush cream couches and ottomans, lap throws, and glass shelves adorned the lobby. Someone had lit the fireplace, and a mellow flame cracked as it licked a stack of firewood, filling the room with the smell of hickory.

Dorian headed to the reception desk while Shantae wandered to a set of French double doors toward the back of the room. She peered through, admiring the pool, hot tub, and rock formation waterfall, all surrounded by an assortment of palm trees, hammocks, and patio furniture. They were shown down a spiral staircase where the young attendant led them to their respective areas.

The men's changing room carried the same luxury and high-end finishing as the rest of the mini resort, from the deep, chocolate lockers lining each wall to the floors patterned with tiles in rich shades of rust and sage. When Dorian removed his socks and shoes, he could only smile as the underfloor heating radiated gentle warmth. As instructed, he changed into the monogrammed spa robe, savoring the distinct smell of honeysuckle that infused the locker room and drifted suggestively into the attached bathroom. Damn. The depth of this serenity had his body nearly throbbing in appreciation.

He had booked them a couples massage and had to praise himself at his great idea. He didn't realize his body was as badly bruised as it was until now. At first, Shantae had seemed vaguely impressed by his suggestion they have a couples spa day, but one thing she had loved about him, at least in the beginning, was his spontaneity and his charming ways. Dorian could only pray her mind wasn't already made up and she wasn't just biding her time, looking for the right moment to destroy their marriage and his heart.

The attendant led them into a European-style room, dimly lit with a range of earth tones and two massage tables. "If you two will get comfortable on the tables," she said, adjusting the lighting on the wall, "your masseuses will be in shortly."

As soon as the door closed, Dorian watched Shantae turn her back to him. "What's the matter," he teased. "You afraid for me to see you naked?"

"Nah," she said, simply. Dorian should have expected the cold response. The sudden spike in tension nearly had the room vibrating. She loosened the belt on her robe and let it slip from her shoulders to pool at her feet. Then without another word, she lay on the table and turned her face to the wall as if creating her own shell of privacy.

"Babe—" he started.

"Dorian. Please. Not now."

He nodded. Fair enough. Without another word, he climbed on the table and waited in silence. Pretty soon, a young man and woman walked through the door, dressed in identical crisp, white T-shirts and white cargo shorts. His masseuse was Kelly, a young blonde with petite hands and a sunny smile. Kelly wasted no time going to work on his sore muscles. He closed his eyes, enjoying the feel of warm oil dribbling on his back. He couldn't be sure if Kelly was actually trying to hold a conversation with him, and honestly, he couldn't care less. Instead, he focused on his body beginning to hum with her delicate presses, her fingers gliding over his skin like satin.

The room set a relaxing ambience with the smell of eucalyptus wafting around them. The harp music and wave-crashing instrumentals drifted low through an in-ceiling speaker and helped to calm the thoughts racing through his mind.

After fifty minutes, Dorian and Shantae dressed in their swimsuits, cream-colored monogrammed spa robes, and matching slippers before being led to the Jacuzzi. In the middle of the afternoon on a Tuesday, they pretty much had the place to themselves.

"That felt so good," Shantae said as soon as they had eased into the Jacuzzi. The steam surrounded them, and the bubbling hot water was pleasantly soothing on Dorian's body. He sat across from her on the bench and watched her lay her head back on the lip of the Jacuzzi, sighing luxuriously. Right there, that relaxed look on her face with the first few beads of sweat peppering on her forehead, that was his Shantae. His love. So easily distracted with Reagan, he hadn't realized how much he had missed her until that very point.

"I love you," Dorian said.

Shantae lifted her head and stared at him. "Do you? It sure hasn't seemed that way for months now."

"I know, babe. And I'm sorry. I don't have an excuse." He averted his eyes, uncomfortable with the way she was scrutinizing his face.

"What changed, Dorian? What happened?"

Dorian shook the image of Reagan riding him out of his head and merely shrugged. "I think we just started drifting apart. I'm not really concerned with the why. I'm more concerned with what we need to do to get back to where we used to be."

Shantae's face was flushed and wet, but Dorian couldn't tell if it was from sweat, steam, or tears. "I'm not sure if we can, Dorian."

Dorian felt his heart quickening and he shifted across the water to sit beside her. He kissed her cheek, tasted the salt, and knew she was indeed crying. Knowing he was the cause, he could only wrap his arms around her shoulders and curse himself for his stupidity.

"I don't want to divorce you, Dorian," Shantae said, looking up into his eyes. "I really don't. I wanted the happily ever after with you. The kids, the dog—"

"And we can do all of that, babe," Dorian said, almost desperate. "If that's what it takes. Let's have kids. Let's get a dog. Whatever you want to do."

"Kids? Now? Look at us. We are broken."

"We can be fixed, Shantae. You mentioned children before, and I'm sorry for not being as receptive. But I'm open to it now. Whatever you want. We got us, remember?" He kissed her response away and she moaned, parting her lips to receive him. Dorian poured all of his love and passion into the kiss and reached between her legs to slide her bikini bottoms to the side.

"Dorian, wait—"

"Shh." He covered her mouth with his once more. If a baby would save his marriage, he was willing to do that. This time, not with Reagan. With his wife. With his happily ever after.

Chapter Twenty-one

Only two times Dorian had ever cried. One was after he heard his father had been killed in the line of duty. He remembered his dad hadn't made his basketball game at the rec center that Wednesday night. Not that he was starting or anything, but still, at the tender age of six, he just wanted his dad to be out there in the stands cheering him on like all the other dads. And when he finally got to play in the fourth quarter and his dad was nowhere to be found, he remembered being so damn pissed that he ended up missing both free throws.

His dad had come home later that evening and tiptoed into his room. At first, stubborn anger had prompted Dorian to pretend to be asleep, though he was wide awake and had been for hours. But then when his dad started to leave, Dorian had jolted up in the bed, unable to hold in his discontent any longer.

"I thought you were coming," he said, his young voice elevated with emotion. It wasn't too often his dad disappointed him, and maybe looking back on it he had overreacted. But that didn't register then. All he knew was that his hopes had been shattered.

Officer Graham had, of course, apologized and assured him he would be at Dorian's next game, which was that upcoming Saturday. He was killed Friday night. It wasn't until years later, until he was much older, that Dorian was told the truth. His dad was a ladies' man, and while he should have been getting prostitutes off the street, he was keeping them in business. But the tears had already been shed and it was in the past. That was the first time he had ever cried.

The second time was now.

Dorian held Rochelle as the choir launched into a soulful rendition of "His Eye Is on the Sparrow." It was enough to sting. She was sobbing and nearly crumpling to the floor. Knowing it was inevitable didn't make the pain any less. Dorian, on the other hand, let silent tears trail down his cheeks. He wanted to be angry but didn't know who to be angry with. God? For calling his angel home, as the reverend had already assured him? His mother? For not wanting to continue chemo and letting herself slowly deteriorate? Himself? For not listening, for not being there, for not being more persistent about her treatments?

This was different than when his father passed. That was sudden, abrupt. Officer Graham had been literally snatched from this world, and it was completely unexpected. One could only wonder if he was doing right, would he have met the same fate.

His mother had died that same day. It had just taken all these years for her mind to catch up to her heart. From the time she was diagnosed with cancer, he had time to prepare. And yet he never could have prepared for living without Teresa Graham.

Rochelle was able to compose herself enough to give the eulogy. After all, she had been his mother's aide and caregiver for over four years. He should have known she was going to take his mother's death harder than most. But she gave them a few heartfelt words, even some humorous stories of his mother that had the audience chuckling. Teresa didn't have many friends or family, but the ones who knew her certainly remembered her jokes and laughter.

It was a small funeral, only about fifteen people. Mostly old coworkers, a few church members, and some retired officers from the force that came to show their respects because she was Officer Graham's widow.

Shantae sat beside Dorian on the hardened pew. She didn't make a sound, nor did she cry, but she was gripping Dorian's hand so tight her knuckles turned white. He didn't expect her to have much emotion for his mother. The two had never gotten along. But she was supportive just the same, and for that he was genuinely appreciative.

So when she pulled him to the side after the funeral to explain she needed to leave, he was surprised.

"For what?" he asked.

"I'm sorry, babe. Work stuff," she answered. "There is a lot of fraud stuff going on since our network was hacked."

Dorian glanced around as people waited idly before everyone convened over at the grave site. "This is my mother's funeral, Shantae," he said in shock. Was she really leaving for a work-related issue? "It can't wait?"

Shantae seemed equally surprised by his reaction. "I understand that, babe. I've been here for you the entire time. But this is my job. I could get fired."

Dorian shook his head, appalled. "Bet," he said and left her there in the middle of the church.

Even the forecast seemed appropriate for a funeral. The sky was overcast with the impending showers the meteorologist assured would come early afternoon. A low rumble of thunder could be heard in the distance.

As Dorian stepped out into the brisk air, a few people who he didn't know approached him to pay their respects. "She was a lovely woman." "She's gone on to glory." "Haven't seen you since you were a kid." He shook hands and nodded to be cordial, all the while finding it interesting that he had seen none of these faces since his mom had been diagnosed with lung cancer. Interesting how they were in attendance today, boo-hooing and hollering over her open casket like they had caught the Holy Spirit in Sunday service.

A few people were already gathering in their cars to follow the hearse when Rochelle walked up, blotting her face with a tear-stained tissue.

"Dorian," she said, her hand gentle on his back. "I want you to know I'm here if you need anything, you hear? Your mom was like a sister to me."

He wrapped his arms around the woman's limp shoulders, resting his head on top of her salt-and-pepper bun. "I know. We're definitely going to miss her."

"I've taken care of a lot of folks, but it was something special about that Teresa Graham. This one . . . it just hurts." Rochelle's voice cracked under the gravity of her words.

Dorian took the opportunity to reach into his pocket and pulled out a check, neatly folded in half. He pushed the paper into the palm of her hand, already prepared for her firm refusal even before she started shaking her head fiercely.

"Rochelle, please," he said. "I would not feel right if you didn't take this." It was a year's salary for her, but she didn't have to find that out until later when she looked at the zeros. "And I know she left you something in the will too, so you don't have to worry, you hear me? You're family."

Rochelle clutched her fist tight over the check, her eyes now watering in earnest gratitude. "Bless you," she whispered and gave him one final hug before she started down the stairs to the chauffeur.

Dorian felt Shantae touch the back of his neck, and he rested his hand on hers. "I'm glad you stayed," he murmured, closing his eyes as she began kneading the tension. "I need you."

"That's why I'm here."

Dorian's eyes snapped open and his head whipped around. Not Shantae but Reagan peering through a black birdcage veil affixed to a clip hidden in her curls. She smiled at his shock. "Don't act so surprised."

Dorian's hand was still on hers and he held it now, pulling it off him. He led her over to the side of the church steps, out of the way of oncoming traffic.

"What are you doing here, Reagan?" he hissed.

"I just wanted to see you." She lifted her hand to stroke his face before he quickly snatched out of her touch.

"Now is not the time."

"Why not? Shantae is gone." Her smirk spread. "Want to take me in the bathroom really quick?"

"Reagan—"

"What? I can be quiet." She lifted her arms this time and Dorian clutched her wrists, his grip almost desperate.

"You need to go."

"But I want you."

"This is my mom's funeral," he snapped. "This shit has got to stop."

Now it was Reagan's eyes that seemed to flare at his sharp tone. "You said you love me."

"I don't. I love Shantae."

"Bullshit." She lifted her voice an octave and immediately giggled when Dorian shushed her.

"Now is not the time," he repeated, his voice almost pleading. "Go home. We'll talk about this later."

She seemed satisfied for now. "Promise?"

"Yeah."

"Give me a kiss, then."

Dorian opened his mouth to let loose a few choice words he probably shouldn't have been saying at the house of the Lord. Since this bitch was putting on a show, he was going to set her straight. He stopped short when he saw Myles, Neil, Roman, and Bridget approach.

Reagan heard them too and she grinned, tossing Dorian a wink and puckering her lips in a silent air-kiss. Then she turned and held out her hand to Myles.

"Hey, baby," she cooed as his arm wound around her waist.

Myles gave her a quick peck on the cheek, completely oblivious to the events that had just taken place. "Hey, D, I'm sorry about your moms," he said, his voice sincere.

"Yeah, Ma Dukes was an angel, man," Roman expressed, his eyes downcast. "Mean as hell. But an angel."

Bridget punched Roman's arm, but the little remark had Dorian relaxing into a chuckle. "You right about that. But I appreciate it, y'all. For real."

"Where is Shantae?" Bridget asked, glancing around.

"My sister had to work," Reagan spoke up. "Didn't she, Dorian?"

Dorian frowned, confused at the intrusive comment. "Yeah," he said. "Emergency."

Bridget didn't bother hiding her obvious disdain for Reagan as she rolled her eyes.

Something strange was definitely going on with Reagan. But the shit was stressing him out more than necessary. And all of that extra, he really didn't need. Not from Shantae and sure as hell not from her sister. Dorian massaged the beginnings of a headache throbbing at his temples. Right now, he was supposed to put his mama in the ground. He would have to sort through Reagan's bullshit antics later when he had the time, energy, and patience to put this girl back in her place.

The feel of death was so thick it nearly suffocated him. Dorian shuddered, struggling to warm his body at the eerie chill prickling goose bumps on his skin. Funny. As many times as he had gone into Teresa's room, now all eight hundred square feet of the elaborate master suite felt like a casket.

Dorian emptied the drawers, placing silk blouses and cashmere sweaters in neat stacks on the bed. He didn't know what to do with all of his mother's things, but he figured packing the house was the least he could do.

Afterward, he roamed around, taking in the home he had grown up in. It didn't feel the same. His footsteps seemed to echo even louder in the large house. He shut his eyes and took a breath to calm himself. It felt like just yesterday they were moving in, both on the heels of grief but wanting to build toward their future, just the two of them. Dorian remembered he didn't care for the house too much. It was too big, too lavish, too much of everything he wasn't. His mom had always wanted a big, fancy house but could never afford one. Not until Cop passed, of course. Dorian didn't think the house ever really became a home. Even now, it felt like more of a tomb.

Needing to talk to someone, he pulled out his phone and punched in Shantae's number. It went straight to voice mail. Damn, he knew he shouldn't bother her. Not when she had made it clear she was busy. He flipped open his messages and quickly sent her an **I LOVE YOU** as a makeshift apology for how he reacted at the funeral. He knew his emotions had been raw. She had been there for him. She had always been there for him. He was wrong to make her feel otherwise.

Dorian debated if he should text Reagan. He had even typed out **CAN YOU CALL ME** and his finger was hovering over the Send button. It was tough, but he couldn't bring himself to do it. So he quickly put his phone away.

Chapter Twenty-two

Dorian struggled to swallow his disappointment as he shifted the phone to his other ear. "You sure you can't get off a little earlier, babe?" he asked.

"I'm sorry, sweetie," Shantae apologized once more. "I am really swamped at work, and there is no way I can leave now. I promise I got you tomorrow."

Dorian plopped on the sofa, eyeing the clock, which read 6:23 p.m. He had been really looking forward to their date night. After their talk a few weeks ago, he had been putting all his energy into making his marriage work, starting with their weekly date night tradition. He had wanted to surprise her this time with reservations to Sip-N-Paint since she had been hinting about wanting to do it. But he understood it was a busy time of year for her at the bank, especially with the recent hacking that they were finally able to get under control.

"What time do you think you will be home?"

"I don't know, sweetie," Shantae said. "Late. You don't have to wait up. I'll try and finish up as quickly as I can."

"Okay. Love you. If I fall asleep, wake me when you get home so daddy can take care of you."

Shantae giggled. "Oh, well then, you know I will wake you up. Love you too, babe. We got us?"

"We got us, boo," Dorian said, before disconnecting the call. He relaxed in the cushions. Might as well make himself a sandwich or something. Maybe find something to watch on HBO. Since he had been spending as much time as possible with Shantae, it felt weird actually being by himself. Funny how much he was missing his wife at the moment. He couldn't wait for her to get home so he could climb up between her legs.

Over the past few weeks, Dorian had become more and more excited about the prospect of a baby with his wife. He didn't even realize he had a desire to have kids, especially after Reagan got pregnant. But he felt it and he was sure Shantae had felt it too. That talk was just the fuel to reignite their fire. They had been all over each other ever since, and Dorian couldn't be happier, or more in love. Plus, he knew without a shadow of a doubt they weren't doing that hall pass anymore. The shit was enjoyable but destructive.

The doorbell startled him awake. Dorian sat up, wiping the sleep from his eyes. He didn't even realize he had dozed off until his eye caught the clock again, squinting to see it read 9:17. Rising from the sofa and stretching his bunched muscles, Dorian made his way across the living room to the door.

"Damn," he whispered, after peering through the peephole. He hadn't seen Reagan since his mother's funeral. She had moved out the day of the abortion. He had been surprised she had actually listened without putting up a fight, but sure enough, he and Shantae had come home from the spa to find her loading a rental with her things. Shantae had begged for answers while Dorian had just looked on in silence. Reagan hadn't said anything to either one of them, just crying and packing her trunk. When she was done, she had peeled out of the driveway so fast, it was a wonder she didn't turn the little Ford Focus on its side.

Dorian had checked his blocked calls and messages, but she hadn't so much as bothered him with a text, even after the little stunt she pulled at his mom's funeral. Maybe it was an asshole move, but Dorian had actually been satisfied how the whole situation had resolved between them. He knew it was ultimately for the better. But now here she stood on his front porch, the angle from the peephole providing an up close and personal view of her distraught face.

"I know you're in there, Dorian," Reagan said, folding her arms across her chest. "I called my sister and she said I could come by and get some more things because you were home."

Dorian hesitated for a few moments longer before he flipped the locks and pulled the door open.

She looked like crystal. He was surprised at his own description, but it seemed fitting, both in fragility and in pallor. She also looked thinner than he remembered, and she wore exhaustion hard as shown by the bags under her eyes and deep-set stress lines creasing her forehead. She hadn't bothered with makeup or, hell, even a comb to her hair, by the looks of the raggedy ponytail. The baggy gray sweat suit she wore looked foreign on her, given her usual revealing attire.

Dorian leaned against the doorjamb, at a loss for words. At first, he didn't want to see her again. But now, after seeing the physical proof of the emotional pain he had caused her, he wanted to just comfort her. But tell her what? It was going to be all right? It wasn't. That they could go back to their little affair? They couldn't. So confusion had him frozen in place.

"You can let me in, you know," Reagan said, when he hovered in the doorway. "It's cold out here." The wind whipped coils of her hair around her face as she waited patiently for him to move.

He did and Reagan stepped into the foyer, closing the door behind her.

"I just need to get a few things I left," she announced. She started to walk past, and Dorian put his hand on her stomach to stop her. Remembering the pregnancy and abortion, that was when the regret swallowed him and he had to take a steadying breath.

"Reagan, I'm sorry." His voice was a whisper. "I never meant to hurt you. I promise I didn't."

"D." The simple syllable spoke volumes. She let it hang between them like a thick cologne, welcoming the comfort. He took a step toward her. She shuddered with the weight of his presence, though he didn't touch her. Reagan stepped away, putting an arm's distance between them. She sniffed, blinking back tears of her own. "How could you do that to me, Dorian? One minute we had a good thing going and the next, you just throw me away like some bitch in the street. Like what we shared ain't mean shit to you."

Dorian nodded. It was true. He felt like shit because every word was true. "I should have handled it better," he agreed with a nod. "I was a jerk to you, and you didn't deserve that." Reagan didn't say anything, just looked at him with red-rimmed eyes, and Dorian opened his arms. At the end of the day, she was still his sister-in-law. He had seen this girl grow up right before his eyes, and playing with her heart was selfish. He had been riding high on avoidance the past few weeks, not seeing Reagan, not communicating with her. But now all of the memories and emotions came rushing back to wring him out until he felt like a shell of a man.

Reagan stepped into his arms for the hug and for a brief moment, they held the embrace. Completely non-sexual. Nothing more than a tender exchange of reconciliation. But then, Reagan sighed, and her body shuddered under his and Dorian felt that familiar shift. However miniscule, it was enough to have his body rising to life, and he stepped back.

"Don't be mad," Reagan murmured, brushing a few loose strands of her hair behind her ear.

"Mad? At what?"

Reagan didn't say anything, just pulled the right sleeve of her sweatshirt to her elbow to reveal the fresh razor cuts to the inside of her arm. Pieces of the slits were still bleeding, so he knew she must have done this recently. But even more than that, it was the number of them zigzagging down her forearm. There must have been forty or fifty cuts in various stages of healing. A big difference from the six or seven when he had first discovered she was a cutter.

Dorian snatched his eyes away from the image, his heart breaking even more. He might as well have taken the razor to her arm himself. "I'm not mad," he said, choking on the words. "I'm just so damn sorry. For hurting you. For making you do this. It's all my fault."

He felt Reagan's arms circle his waist and she laid her cheek on his back. "I still love you, Dorian," she murmured, her voice muffled against his T-shirt. "That's why I haven't bothered you. I just want you to be happy. If it's with my sister, I want that for you."

He started to respond but stopped when he felt her featherlight kisses on the back of his neck. His manhood was completely awake now, throbbing between his legs and damn near begging to be unleashed on the young vixen. "We can't do this," he moaned, though he was too weak to move.

"Shh. One last time, Dorian. Then I promise I'll be gone for good. You owe me that much, don't you?"

She was right. He felt compelled to give in because of the shitty way he had treated her. It would ease the guilt. Or maybe that was just his excuse to entertain the forbidden fruit one last time. Either way, he found himself lifting her into his arms and carrying her up the stairs while their tongues wrestled with each other.

The first door at the top of the landing was his and Shantae's bedroom, and he had to stop at the threshold. Damn, it was bad enough to fuck Reagan again, but in the bed he shared with his wife? The shit was foul.

"In there," Reagan urged, climbing down from his arms. She backed into the bedroom, keeping her eyes trained on his while removing her clothes. Completely naked underneath, she lay back on the satin sheets and spread her legs wide. Taunting him. Beckoning him. When Reagan threw her head back and shut her eyes, for a brief moment, she looked just like Shantae. Their features were oftentimes so similar that the right angle, the right lighting could damn near make someone confuse the two. But right now, in this moment, this was Reagan, and he wanted to ravish her just one more time. Needed to for his own peace of mind and even more for his guilty conscience.

He was across the room in two strides, her delicate folds twirling on his tongue. She moaned and grasped the back of his head, encouraging him to feast more, deeper, faster. Pretty soon, Reagan was emptying herself of that delicious nectar while her screams echoed through the walls.

"I need it rough, babe," she said breathlessly as Dorian fumbled with his belt buckle. "Don't make love to me. Save that for Shantae. Fuck me. Punish me. I deserve it."

Dorian did as he was told, snatching her to the edge of the bed by her legs. He entered her hard and grimaced when she yelped in pain. "Am I hurting you?" he asked, stopping in mid-stroke.

"Don't stop," she whimpered, using her feet to guide his hips.

He was rough, animalistic, gripping her wrists to pull her against his rapid thrusts. Reagan gasped and braced for the assault, arching her back as he began pumping once more. His other hand reached between her legs, which brought her crying out as she rode the next orgasm. She was screaming his name like a sweet melody on her tongue as she chanted I love yous in various octaves.

The headboard banged against the wall in tune to their freak show and Dorian quickened his pace, feeling the edges of his own orgasm surfacing.

He mumbled a slew of curse words of his own as he gave one final thrust before emptying himself, the release leaving him weak. He collapsed on her back, exhausted.

"Damn, babe," Reagan said through a shaky breath. "Damn, I'm going to miss you."

Dorian chuckled. He was damn sure going to miss her too.

After they cleaned up, Reagan helped Dorian change the sheets and light some candles to mask the stench of sex. Then they stood at the door and hugged one more time. "You take care of yourself," Dorian said.

"You too, big bro." Reagan winked at the comment and, giving him one final kiss, stepped out into the night.

Chapter Twenty-three

Dorian glanced up at the knock on his office door. His new receptionist, Emily, stood in the doorway with Shantae by her side. The young college student was no Claudia, but she was a temporary replacement since the older woman had retired. Dorian had to say that he wasn't surprised when she had presented her resignation only days after the knock-down, drag-out fight. He didn't even blame her. Things had gotten way out of hand, and his professional reputation was stained. Plus, his friendship with Kenny was permanently damaged.

"Dr. Graham, your wife insisted on surprising you," Emily said with a wistful smile.

Dorian nodded and rose to greet Shantae. "That's no problem, Emily. Thank you."

Emily nodded and left, closing the door to give the couple some privacy.

"Hey, babe," Shantae said after they exchanged an intimate kiss. "I think your little receptionist has a crush on you." She giggled as Dorian waved his hand.

"Please. Ain't nobody thinking about that girl. I'm interested in you. What's up? This certainly is a pleasant surprise."

Shantae lifted a to-go bag with two Styrofoam boxes inside. "I was hungry and figured you were too. Lunch?"

Dorian grinned and began moving items on his desk to make room for the food. He was neck-deep in a new project, but it was after 1:00 and his stomach was growling.

"How are you feeling?" he asked as they ate. Shantae had complained of stomach pains and nausea earlier that week. He tried to keep the hope out of the question, but he knew it was more than obvious why he was asking.

Shantae stabbed at her salad with a fork and forced a thin smile. "I'm not pregnant, if that's what you're getting at," she said.

Dorian stared into his food to hide his disappointment. "You sure?" he asked. "I mean, you took a test or something?"

Shantae nodded, keeping her eyes downcast.

"Aw, baby, I'm sorry. You know we can keep trying."

"What if I don't want to keep trying?" Shantae murmured.

Dorian's face deflated. "You don't want kids?"

"That's not what I'm saying. Maybe we should just wait awhile. It's becoming a bit nerve-racking."

Dorian opened his mouth to respond when another knock came at the door. He swore under his breath. "This damn new assistant," he muttered, shaking his head. "Come in."

He turned just in time to see Emily enter with two police officers on her heels. "Sir," she said, tossing a fearful expression to the cops. "They insisted on seeing you."

Dorian's heart quickened and he already knew his legs felt like rubber, so he didn't even bother standing.

"Dorian Graham," the taller officer said, reaching to his waistband.

Dorian recognized the gesture. He had watched one too many

episodes of *Cops* and *Law & Order* to not know what they were there for. The question was why. He remembered the fight with Kenny. The one he had neglected to tell Shantae about. Damn, had his ex-friend really filed assault charges or some shit on him? Fear had him speechless as he looked from his wife to the police.

It was Shantae who stood up, her hands on her hips. "Officers, what do you want with my husband?"

"Are you Mrs. Graham?" the officer asked.

"Yes."

That was enough to have Dorian standing to intercede. They were there for him, and the last thing he wanted was for Shantae getting in trouble. Especially over some shit he caused. Maybe he could talk to Kenny. Try to reason with him that this shit was beyond extreme. "Officers, I'm Dorian Graham. What is the problem?"

Dorian caught a glimpse of the handcuffs at the officer's waist as he took a step forward.

"Dorian Graham, we need you to come with us. We just want to ask some questions."

"Listen," Dorian held up his hands as they continued to move in his direction, "Kenny and I just had a little misunderstanding. I'll be happy to give you my side of the story."

The officers exchanged looks before one spoke up. "No, Dr. Graham. I'm afraid this has nothing to do with Kenny. You are a person of interest in the assault of Reagan Reynolds."

Chapter Twenty-four

Dorian felt the beginnings of a migraine at his temples. He took another breath to calm his nerves and frustration before repeating himself for the sixth time. "Listen. I don't know what you're trying to do here, but you're not going to make me confess to something I didn't do. I didn't hurt that girl."

The officer that had been persistent in his interrogation was Officer Williamson, an aging black man who seemed to direct his caseloads' worth of anger toward Dorian. He sat across the table, drumming his fingers on a manila folder. He had long since stripped out of his blazer and now had the sleeves of his button-up rolled to the elbow due to the excruciating heat in the tiny room. Or maybe the heat was due to Dorian's panic. The longer he sat in that room, the more he felt he wasn't leaving outside of a pair of cuffs.

"Listen, dude. I get it." Officer Williamson sat up, lacing his fingers together. "You're one of those guys with everything together. You got the wife. The big house. The fantastic job. Right?"

Dorian kept his lips shut. He was a cop's son. He could tell he was being led into a trap, so he didn't even bother responding.

"And wifey's fine-ass sister comes over and you just figured, what's the harm, right? She's young and stupid. A ho. Who is going to believe her?"

Dorian wanted to reach across the table and shake the man. "No. Man, that's not what happened at all. Aren't you listening to me?"

"So, you saying you didn't sleep with her?"

"No, I'm not saying I didn't sleep with her. I'm saying I didn't hurt her." Dorian's voice rose in irritation.

Officer Williamson nodded and rubbed the hair on his goatee. For a moment, it looked as if he was actually believing Dorian's story. "So, tell me this, Dorian," he said. "How did she get the bruises?"

"What bruises?"

"So, you didn't give her any bruises?"

Dorian's mind flashed back to the sex. Sure, he had been rough, but he didn't remember leaving any marks. "Reagan asked me to give it to her rough," he said, still confused.

Officer Williamson flipped open the folder and slid it across the table so Dorian could take a good look. He snatched back in horror. There were photos. All of Reagan's body in various angles. All emphasizing the blue and purple discoloration on her chocolate skin. Close-ups of her thighs, her arms, her wrists. There was even a side angle capturing her jaw that had swollen up twice its size.

Dorian shook his head, sliding the folder back across the table with enough force that the pictures went scattering to litter the floor. "Man, I don't know who the hell did this," he fumed, gesturing to the photos. "But it damn sure wasn't me."

When the officer remained silent, Dorian rushed on. "Did y'all check into her baby dad, Terrell?"

"Who?"

"Her son's father. She sometimes was afraid of him. He may have done this shit, man. I don't know, but it wasn't me."

The officer shook his head. "I think she would know if her son's father did this to her. She specifically said you."

"Nah, I didn't."

Officer Williamson cocked his head to the side on a frown. "Now, I thought you said she asked you to give it to her rough."

"Not this shit. I don't know who did this. She didn't look like this when she left."

"Right. It does take a moment sometimes for bruises to show up."

Dorian stood up, his chair toppling to the floor. He felt like he was suffocating, and fear had him pacing the tiny room like a caged animal. What the hell had he gotten himself into? He could lose everything. His practice. His wife.

The sudden memory of Shantae's face in his office when he was taken away almost left him nauseous. Pure and utter shock had marred her face, followed by disgusting hatred that could only be expressed in her eyes. She hadn't bothered to utter a word. What the hell was he going to tell her? Was she even going to believe him?

"Look." Dorian turned from where he had been hovering in the corner. His voice had changed to one of pleading desperation. "Man-to-man. This girl is crazy. She attempted suicide and had to be hospitalized. She's a cutter. Did you check her arms?" Dorian pointed to the inside of his elbow. "Look at her arms and you'll see the cuts. She did that shit to herself. I know I fucked up by having an affair with her. But I've never hurt her. I swear on my life."

Officer Williamson nodded, but kept his face neutral. "Why would she be doing this to you, Dorian? What does she have to gain?"

"She just wants to ruin me. A fucking nutcase scorned. She got upset when I told her I wanted to work it out with my wife, and now she's trying this revenge shit."

"I see. So, she's crazy?"

"Yeah. That's what I'm trying to tell you."

"And still you slept with her again?"

Dorian blew out an annoyed breath. He knew what it sounded like. Shit was bad. "Are we done with the questions? Can I go now?" he asked.

Officer Williamson nodded as he rose and began gathering the pictures in a neat stack. "Thank you for your time, Dorian. We'll be in touch. Oh, and I'm sure this goes without saying," he added. "If I were you, I would refrain from trying to contact Ms. Reynolds."

Dorian wanted to roll his eyes. Like hell he was going to refrain. They would be lucky if they didn't find Reagan's body somewhere after this setup she pulled.

They offered to drive him back to his office to get his car, but Dorian didn't want to be around the police a second longer than he had to.

By the time he finally emerged from the station, it was well after 7:00. The sky was dark with a gentle wind chilling the air. Dorian had his phone on him, and he used it to call an Uber. Then he sat on the steps of the station to wait. His fingers itched to dial Shantae, but he already knew she wouldn't pick up. It was probably for the better anyway. This was a conversation they needed to have face-to-face. He just prayed she was willing to hear him out and that their marriage could survive in the end.

The Uber dropped him off back at the office, and not even bothering to go up, he immediately went down into the parking deck and hopped in his truck.

More than anything, he was scared. Dorian recognized the feeling of fear clutching his chest, strong enough to give him pains. What if Shantae didn't believe him? Worse, what if the police didn't? He could rot in jail over Reagan's crazy ass. He really had never thought himself a violent man, especially when it came to women. But dammit, if the police weren't on his ass and Reagan wasn't already battered, he was tempted to give her a reason to bring up some charges. Because he wanted to beat her ass to the point she was unrecognizable.

Shantae's car was in the driveway when he pulled up to the house. It was dark, with the exception of the porch light and the light shining through the curtains in the master bedroom. Time to get it over with. Dorian took a breath for strength and to calm his racing heart before opening the garage door.

His steps were slow and deliberate as he made his way through the kitchen and up the stairs. He braced himself, half expecting to have to duck from some object Shantae was going to hurl his way. To his surprise, she was sitting up in bed, scrolling through her phone. She looked up when he entered the room and, without a word, sat her phone on the nightstand, crossed her arms over her chest, and glared at him.

Dorian's mind went blank, but he knew he better start talking while he had her attention. "Know this, Shantae. I did not attack your sister. I swear."

Shantae nodded, her voice calm. "But did you sleep with her?"

He wanted so badly to lie. Already had one lingering on the tip of his tongue. But the more he watched Shantae, the more he knew she wasn't about to believe shit other than the truth. Anything else would be an obvious lie, which would probably lead her to believe Reagan.

"Let me explain—"

"Yes or no, Dorian? Did you sleep with my sister?"

Dorian's shoulders fell in defeat and he nodded. "Yeah."

Shantae pursed her lips and snatched her eyes away. Dorian wasn't sure, but he thought he saw the first glimmer of tears before she turned her head.

"It started out with that damn hall pass, Shantae—"

"Oh, so I guess it makes it better?" she snapped. "Because I seriously doubt it was a one-time thing."

Dorian didn't answer, which was answer enough.

"Oh, my God. Dorian, how could you do this to me *again?*" she went on. "Didn't you cheat enough when we were dating? You promised me you would never hurt me again. Especially after we got married."

Dorian hated that he couldn't read her. She was teetering somewhere between anger and hurt, but how far the pendulum swung in either direction, he just couldn't tell. She was doing a damn good job of keeping her composure, which was hurting his heart even more. She was on another level. She was just too damn . . . calm. Dangerously calm.

"Baby, I just need you to believe me," Dorian said.

"About what? That you didn't beat her or that you've been having an affair with her?"

Dorian grimaced as she slapped him with the facts. It sounded even worse. "Both," he said finally. "If there was ever a time I needed you, it's now. We got us, remember?"

"No. Fuck you and fuck us, Dorian. Get out."

He couldn't bring himself to move. He knew what she said, but the thought of leaving seemed so permanent, and his marriage couldn't be ending like this. "What?" he stalled.

"You heard me, get the fuck out!" Shantae yelled, and this time, she picked up the table lamp and threw it in Dorian's direction. He ducked as the ceramic shattered against the wall within inches of his head. The shade bumped his shoulder on its descent to the floor, with the other broken shards cluttering at his feet.

Shantae had turned her back to him but he could see she was holding her arms to calm the subtle trembling. She sniffed but still didn't turn around or say anything else.

Dorian started to head toward the guest bedroom but thought better of it. Shantae needed space. And if he could be honest with himself, he didn't trust her right now to be in such close proximity to where he slept. Not bothering with any clothes other than the ones on his back, Dorian trudged back to the garage. A hotel would suffice for the night. That would give him time to think and privacy to call Reagan to see what the hell she had to say.

———◆———

"You have reached me. You know what to do."

Dorian felt his blood boiling at the sound of her voice. He had made two attempts to call Reagan from the hotel phone, but to no avail. Reagan was slick and manipulative, and he didn't know why he expected her to answer, knowing what she was doing.

The beep had him opening his mouth to leave a message, a slew of cuss words and threats already on the tip of his tongue. But then, remembering how Officer Williamson had warned him about trying to contact her, he thought better of it and slammed the phone down.

His work clothes were uncomfortable, and having brought nothing else, Dorian stripped down to his boxer briefs and lay in the stiff hotel sheets. Sleep was out of the question. The uncertainty of the entire situation left his mind and heart restless. His body was hungry, but Dorian felt like food wouldn't settle in his stomach. So he just lay there, listening to the muffled thumping and bumping of the hotel guests above him.

The cell phone's vibration was loud against the wood tabletop and Dorian picked it up to read the caller ID. It simply said UN-KNOWN. He swiped the screen to answer the call, prepared to dismiss whoever it was.

"Wow. You picked up."

Dorian sat up at the voice. "Bitch, you've got some fucking nerve—"

"Whoa there. You want to calm it down a bit, Dorian? I'm the victim here." Her laugh echoed in his ear and only heightened his anger.

"Reagan, what the hell are you doing? This shit isn't funny. You could cost me everything."

Reagan sucked her teeth. "Well then, maybe you should've thought about that before you did it."

Dorian bit back another curse. He would have to appeal to her emotional side. He had been dealing with Reagan long enough to know. So, she wanted to play games? He could play right along with her. "Baby." His voice was softer and thick with charm. "How can you do this to me? To us? I thought you loved me?"

"I do, Dorian. But you brought this on yourself."

"I'm no good in jail, Reagan. If you love me, you'll drop these charges. You know I would never do anything to hurt you."

"But you did."

"But I didn't mean to."

Reagan sighed and suddenly she sounded further away. "I'll drop the charges," she said with a sigh. "But on one condition."

"What? Anything, baby."

"I'll tell you in person. Meet me tomorrow. I'll text you the address."

Dorian had to ignore his anxiety. He wanted this done and over now, but if he had to kiss Reagan's ass, so be it. "Okay. Don't forget, Reagan. I want to meet up and settle this."

"Oh, we will."

Click.

Dorian pulled the phone away from his ear. No telling what Reagan wanted, but he was prepared to give her damn near anything to make this thing go away. He just hoped he could do whatever she asked, and it wasn't anything stupid like marry her or give her another child. Otherwise, she was about to have a whole other problem on her hands.

Chapter Twenty-five

The sports bar was in an uproar. Apparently, some basketball game had brought out every man in Atlanta. They nursed shots and Coronas around the crowded bar or sat munching on hot wings at the high-top pub tables. Every seat was in view of an angled flat screen, all showing the same game currently in progress. An occasional three-pointer or foul call had unanimous cheers and slaps of high fives, even a few exchanges of money as the gamblers made good use of the anticipation. A mixture of weed, cologne, and liquor hung in the air like a stale blanket, and someone had turned down the music enough to hear the game announcers.

Dorian's boys had already arrived and were seated at a high-top table close to the bar. They had apparently been there for a good bit. Bottles of beer, shot glasses, and half-eaten trays of appetizers and chicken bones cluttered the table.

Dorian had debated calling them after he hung up with Reagan. Hell, he had been holding a lot of secrets from them, and at this juncture, it seemed like it was too late to solicit any type of help or advice. But then again, he just needed to vent. They wouldn't judge. They would keep it real with him. At the end of the day, they had too much history behind them and he hoped they would support him through all this bullshit. The only one he was really concerned about was Myles. Technically, he and Reagan were in some kind of relationship. But Dorian would hate to know he had managed to let her come between their friendship.

"Man, what took you so long?" Roman greeted him first.

Dorian took a seat. "Traffic."

"What you mean *traffic*? In your driveway? You live right around the corner," Myles teased with a laugh.

"I'm not at home," Dorian said.

His friends stopped laughing, realizing Dorian's somber mood. It was Neil who finally addressed the elephant in the room.

"You good, my friend?" he asked. "What's up? Did something happen?"

Dorian flagged a nearby waitress. "Let me get a Corona," he said. She nodded and flounced off to get his drink. No one said anything else just yet, but he felt all eyes on him, watching and waiting.

He didn't speak again until he got his beer and nearly finished the bottle in one gulp. Reagan's words were still fresh on his mind, and he didn't realize his jaw was clenched until it started to ache.

"I messed up," he started, keeping his eyes downcast. "And shit has gotten bad."

He kept his story very basic, giving just the relevant details at first. He met a girl, he used the hall pass with her, he tried to break it off, she wasn't having it, and now she had the cops on him. For now, he conveniently left out Reagan's identity. He would stall as long as he could, though it wasn't like it made the story sound any better.

"She did what?" Roman was frowning as he too was trying to

process everything. "That's some obsessed *Fatal Attraction* shit, D. How the hell you get tangled up with this chick?"

Dorian took another swig, polishing off his drink. Shit sounded even crazier when he thought of everything in its entirety. He couldn't believe he had been so damn stupid. And over what? Sex? Lust? There had to be a special pit of hell for guys like him. And to top it off, messing up a good thing—no, a great thing, with his wife.

"Man, the police showed me those pictures of her and had my ass shook because I *know* she's lying. That's the messed-up part." The images of Reagan's bruises flashed in his mind and he slammed his fist down on the table, startling all of them. "The hell I'm gon' do? This bitch is trying to put my ass under the jail."

"Damn," Neil muttered, at a loss for words. "You got a lawyer or something?"

"Of course I got a lawyer. That ain't the point. The fact that I'm even being accused is the bullshit. Do you know what could happen if this gets out? Even just being accused will ruin everything I've worked for. I just started my practice not too long ago."

"And what about Shantae?" Neil mentioned, his voice quiet. "What did she say?"

Dorian shook his head. "She put my ass out. She ain't trying to hear none of it. I didn't even get a chance to . . ." He trailed off on a sigh. It didn't matter. He already knew she was as good as gone. Hearing that kind of news had hurt her in the worst way. Not to mention shattered whatever little trust she had in him. Hall pass or no hall pass, there was no excuse or justification in the world she would accept, he knew.

"The bitch sounds crazy," Roman said, shaking his head.

"Who is she?" Myles said. "I can get some homegirls to pay her snake ass a visit."

Dorian sighed. He needed to get it all out. No use still trying to lie about it. "Reagan," he muttered.

"Huh? What about Reagan?"

Dorian's eyes already held the apology even before words left his lips. "Bruh, I didn't even know she was your girl at first. I didn't . . . I told you I fucked up. She was off-limits."

Myles's face remained neutral. Dorian wouldn't have known he had even reacted if it wasn't for the vein throbbing at his temple. His face registered a combination of disbelief and anger. And right there under the surface, pain. Dorian saw it, and it made his own heart ache. His boy really cared for that girl. Even though she wasn't shit, he loved her anyway.

"Damn," was all Neil murmured. "Just . . . damn."

Dorian started to say something but caught the movement out of the corner of his eye. He should've known it was coming. But still he was too slow and didn't have time to block the punch before it landed like a piece of steel against his jaw. The rounded knuckles of Myles's fist were fueled with such force that it sent him flying out of his chair and tumbling to the hardwood floor. Dorian gasped, struggling to take a breath from the brief spasm. He felt dizzy and his face was throbbing as he climbed to his feet, the puffiness of swelling already tightening the skin from his eye to his chin.

And there Myles stood, towering over him, fists clenched, as if daring him to retaliate. If it had been anyone else, he and his boy probably would've been throwing blows just like him and Kenny. But Dorian knew he deserved it. So, after picking himself up, he just stood there and waited among the steadily growing crowd surrounding them with anxious eyes and cell phones, ready to capture what they figured was about to go down.

It was quiet. Even the TVs sounded like they had been put on mute because the action in the bar was better. All that could be heard was heavy breathing roaring in his ears, and Dorian realized it was his own. At the continued silence, he chanced speaking again. "I ain't got no excuse, man," he said, his palms out in surrender. "I ain't got nothing left. I'm sorry."

Myles shook his head, and an expression of pure hatred furrowed his eyebrows. "Reagan is your karma," he said after a minute or two. "I hope she gives you everything you deserve."

And with that, he left.

Dorian stooped to pick up his chair, Myles's last words resonating with him until they left him sick. What if she already had?

Chapter Twenty-six

Dorian hadn't even bothered trying to sleep. Just lay in bed taking deep puffs of Black & Mild after Black & Mild and getting lost in a daze. His mind felt as stifling and foggy as the smoke, and by the time morning light had broken through the hotel's blinds, he was in no better shape than when he had checked in the night before.

The glass from his tequila rested on the nightstand beside him. At the time, it was comforting to indulge in the complimentary en-suite bar. But now the mix of alcohol and nicotine had him feeling nauseous, not to mention light-headed.

Dorian put the butt of Black & Mild out in the cluttered ashtray and picked up the phone. He didn't know what time it was, but the twenty-four-hour room service was a welcome blessing. He didn't have a piece of appetite, but he needed food in his stomach and a distraction from waiting. Reagan had insisted she would text him a meeting place, but as of yet, his phone was empty of notifications. He wanted so badly to call his wife, but he knew there was no point. Hell, he didn't even know if he still had a wife. But one thing at a time. Dorian needed to reason with Reagan and get her to drop these ridiculous charges. Then he could beg for Shantae's forgiveness.

The room service arrived, and Dorian positioned himself on the bed with his omelet. He forked pieces of egg and bacon into his mouth, but he might as well had been eating cardboard. About half was all he could stomach, and he sat back, frowning when there was still no text from Reagan. Maybe she had been bullshitting him during the call. But what the hell kind of games was she playing? Each excruciating second that ticked by with only the deafening silence to lull him had his anger increasing. But outweighing the anger was pure fear. He was scared of this bitch and the power she currently held that could destroy him. The knowledge had his stomach bubbling, no thanks to that dry-ass omelet he had just forced down.

His phone vibrated and Dorian snatched it up. Sure enough, there was a text message from an unknown number. He assumed it was Reagan when he read the simple address, followed by *5:00*. Dorian glanced at the clock and rolled his eyes. He had all day to marinate on this bullshit meeting later. He was tempted to text back that they needed to meet earlier, but he didn't want to risk Reagan throwing up her hands at the whole thing. He hated how he had to play this game by her rules, but he had no choice. For now, he had eight fucking hours to kill.

Dorian ended up going by the house. He had been in his work suit ever since the police took him down to the station for questioning, and he needed a good shower and a fresh change of clothes. More than that, he wanted to see Shantae during the visit. Disappointment had his heart falling when he saw the garage was empty.

She hadn't touched anything, which was maybe a good sign.

No boxes or luggage packed. The bed was neatly made, and there was even the faint smell of coffee still fresh in the air from where she had apparently made some that morning. Dorian hadn't known what to expect, but his hope was revived when he saw she hadn't immediately changed the locks, packed up her things, or set fire to his.

Dorian showered and put on some jeans and a long-sleeve shirt. Then, just in case, he tossed a few essentials in a duffel bag, along with another set of clothes. Hopefully after today, he would have a better idea whether he should come back home or make the hotel his temporary living quarters until he found another place to say. Damn Reagan for putting him in this position. But then again, he knew he was just as much to blame. That fact was leaving a bitter-ass taste in his mouth.

Dorian settled down on the couch. It was funny. Shit felt like déjà vu. The night of the hall pass, he was sitting in this same place staring at the Christmas tree, trying to psych himself up to go have sex with Reagan. Now here he was, staring at the same spot. The tree had long since been put away, but just like that damn corner, his life was now empty, thanks to the wrong, crazy-ass woman.

A knock on the door had Dorian snapping out of his daze. He rose, his face creased in curiosity. Who was knocking on their door on a Wednesday afternoon? Instead of the peephole, Dorian bent back the bay window blinds, which gave a perfect angle to the porch. The person was turned away from the window, but Dorian would have recognized the body frame anywhere. Question was, what the hell was Kenny doing at his house?

It was around noon, and one look at his usual business attire let Dorian know he must have come over on his lunch break. When he turned, his face was in full view, so if there had been any lingering doubts as to the visitor's identity, they were completely erased. Kenny's face had healed from the fight and his expression carried impatience as he rang the doorbell this time. He then glanced down at his watch and back to the street.

Dorian stood back from the window. A mixture of anger, hurt, and confusion tugged at his heart. So much so that he was tempted to open the door and resolve the uncertainties once and for all. They hadn't spoken since the fight. Not even a text message. If Dorian was honest with himself, he knew it was his pride, and Kenny, he was sure, was being stubborn, so neither had bothered to initiate contact.

The doorbell rang a few more times before Dorian finally heard footsteps as Kenny stepped off the porch and walked back to his car. Moments later, he drove away. He had come for someone, that's for sure. Which begged the question, just who was Kenny there to see? Him? Reagan?

Or Shantae?

⇒•◇•⇐

Dorian pulled up to the address Reagan had texted him. A furniture store? What the hell did she want him to meet her at a furniture store for? It was already five minutes till, so he parked his truck and climbed out.

Reagan was already there, waiting on a bench outside the entrance. She was dressed casually in some jeans and sneakers, and her hands were shoved in the pockets of her short winter coat. Dorian saw from his distance her jaw was still swollen, but even that didn't stop the smirk that spread when she noticed him walking toward her. For that, he wanted to punch her in her damn face.

"Hey, boo," she greeted as soon as he was in arm's length.

Dorian scoffed. "'Hey, boo'?" he mocked. "Bitch, you filed charges on me and you acting like shit is gravy."

"Damn, you're hostile. You should sit down. And stop being so aggressive before it makes you look even more guilty."

"What? Makes me look guilty? To who?"

Reagan pursed her lips but didn't respond. Instead she said, "So what's up? You called me, wanting to meet. What do you want to talk about?"

"Are you serious? Why the hell did you say I beat you, Reagan? You know damn well that shit isn't true. Now I could lose my job, my wife—"

"Fuck your job and your wife. What about me?"

"Bitch, what about you? All this bullshit you causing because I didn't want you?"

To his surprise, Reagan burst into laughter. It sounded somewhat slurred because of her swollen mouth, but that was definitely a laugh seeping between her lips. "Little boy, are you serious right now? You think I went through all of this because of revenge?"

Dorian's anger dissipated and he stood there confused. If not revenge, then why?

"You are really on your own sack right now," Reagan went on, seemingly tickled by the whole conversation. "Fuck you, Dorian. You ain't no damn good anyway. A dog-ass cheater ever since I've known you. What the hell am I going to do with you? I can get sex from any damn body."

"So this?" Dorian gestured to her mouth. "All of this was for what?"

"You can't be that stupid," Reagan said. She paused as if waiting for a response and cocked her head to the side. "Well, damn, maybe you are. Money, Dorian. It's always been about money. And you have plenty of it."

The pieces were trying to fit, but for some reason, Dorian couldn't accept the picture it was making. No way that could have been Reagan's one and only motive.

"Took a little longer than I anticipated," she went on. "But, hey. I'm a very patient person. I knew it was only a matter of time."

"Wait." Dorian shook his head trying to clear his jumbled thoughts. "So, you got me mixed up with the police so you could get money?"

"Dorian, I took you up on your hall pass so I could get money," Reagan clarified. "These past few months were all part of the plan. Your stubborn ass just took too damn long."

"But the suicide attempt, the whole affair, everything?"

Reagan nodded and rose. "Hard to believe, I know," she said, her voice laced with pity. "But no, sweetie. I've never had feelings for you. I just needed some money. I told you before, I have to move around a lot. Well . . . to make a long story short, I fucked some high-profile guy out of a lot of money and I need to pay it back. Plus, live a little comfortably, because I'm honestly tired of the hopping around. So, I need to be broke off. That's where you come in." Reagan nodded her head across the street and Dorian turned to see the Bank of America. Of course. She had been strategic with her planning this little meet-up. "I'm going to keep it simple. A little money and I'll disappear. All charges dropped."

"How much?" When she quoted the figure, Dorian was sure if she had drop-kicked him in his throat, it would have been less shocking. He stood for a moment before he heard laughter. It took him another moment to realize it was his own.

"You owe some guy all that money?"

"I didn't say that," Reagan said. "I've always been a greedy bitch. I put in a lot of work with you these past few months. I need restitution. Pain and suffering and shit."

"You crazy as hell," he murmured. "I should've known that shit after your ass attempted suicide."

Reagan rolled her eyes. "Oh please. Didn't nobody attempt no damn suicide. I cut myself way too far from the artery. Plus, if I wanted to die, why did I call my father? Why didn't I just do it?"

Dorian remembered Barbara insisting Reagan had just done it for attention. *How right she was.* "What about the pregnancy?" he asked, his eyes darting down to her belly. It was well hidden under the coat she wore.

"I needed money to hold the guy over," Reagan admitted. "You were taking too long and he was getting impatient."

This was entirely too much. He needed some hard liquor to maybe make this shit easier to digest.

"Now," Reagan pulled her phone out of her pocket to glance at the screen, "since you've got all your questions answered, I need you to go get my damn money. The bank closes at six, so you now have one hour."

"Reagan, don't do this," Dorian didn't give a damn if he was begging. She was about to deplete every one of his saving accounts. "How do you think I even have that kind of money?"

"Boy, don't play me for stupid." Reagan turned up her lips in a doubtful scowl. "I know exactly how much you have in your bank accounts, combined from your dad and your mom's life insurance. Where do you think I came up with that figure?"

Dorian could only stare in shock.

"Fifty-nine minutes," she snapped. "I suggest you go. I don't have all fucking day."

"And if I don't?"

Reagan shook her head. "You don't want to go there. Aren't you staying at the Residence Inn near downtown? Isn't it a coincidence I am too? I would hate to go back to the police station tonight to make a follow-up report. Apparently, my perpetrator found out where I was staying and attacked me again for running my big-ass mouth."

Dorian's stomach flipped at the threat. "No way in hell anybody would believe that shit," he said, trying to convince himself.

"Maybe not now," Reagan said. "But that's nothing a few more self-inflicted bruises couldn't fix."

Now he knew this girl was all the way on another level of crazy. But standing there watching Reagan with her face healing from where she had broken her own damn jaw, or had someone do it for her, all just to frame him and milk him out of money, he knew she would do it again.

His hands were tied. He was dragging his feet across the concrete as he made his way to the bank. The whole time, he was racking his brain for a way of out this mess. Some way he could escape with her dropping the charges that wouldn't require him going broke. The only thing he kept coming back to was killing her.

It was almost closing time, so the bank was nearly empty. A few people stood at the teller counter and one stood hunched over the table completing a form. Dorian grabbed a withdrawal form from the tray and the pen attached to the table by a thin silver chain. It took him three times to actually fill out the form correctly, because his mind kept running over possible scenarios.

In the end, Dorian was no closer to a solution than before and he relented, carrying the slip to the line. He had never considered himself a rich man. Not by any means. He had scrimped, saved, and earned every penny of the stacks of money scattered in three different savings accounts. He had plans to travel with the money, just he and Shantae, flying and cruising from coast to coast, country to country. Now it was going to be used to pay off this bum bitch's hustling mistakes and probably new shoes, purses, and extensions. Was that the cost of his freedom? It pissed him off he was in this situation, but it pissed him off even more that he'd put himself there. And now there was absolutely nothing he could do about it.

Of course, he had to see the branch manager, due to the large sum he wanted to pull out. Sitting in the office, verifying and reverifying his identity, being asked a million questions about why he no longer wanted to do business with them. Dorian answered them all in brief, simple responses. He just needed this to be over. Each torturous minute that ticked by as the manager stepped away only to return with more forms and questions left him in sheer agony. Finally, they brought him his money in duffel bags, handing them over with as much regret as he had taking them.

Night had fallen when he exited the bank, his accounts completely wiped clean. Reagan had moved her car outside the door, and as soon as she saw him, she popped her trunk. Her eyes seemed to dance in delight as she got out to watch him load the money in the back.

"I thank you, Dorian," she said once he was done.

He didn't say anything, only slammed the trunk door hard enough to rock the entire car.

Reagan didn't bat an eye at his temper. "Well, it's been real, sweetie. I'm on my way to the station now to drop those charges, so Officer Williamson will be off your ass, I promise."

The anger had completely fizzled, and Dorian just felt empty. Even emptier than his bank accounts. He felt completely used and exhausted from the manipulation. Stress had tightened his chest to the point it was almost unbearable to breathe. But it was over. At least he prayed it was over. With Reagan, he could never be sure.

She seemed sincere as she stood there and promised to drop the charges. But then, she had seemed sincere for months. If she stood true to her word, the charges would be dropped, and he could try and rebuild his marriage with Shantae. He would have to explain every single thing. At this point, it wasn't even about the money anymore. Yeah, that shit hurt to his core. But more importantly, he just wanted his life, his freedom, and his Shantae. Time would help him get over the rest of the bullshit.

"So, that's it, huh?" Dorian said as Reagan prepared to hop back in the driver's seat.

She turned and shrugged. "Yeah, pretty much. This is where

we part ways. Like I promised, you won't ever hear from me again."

"Are you happy?" Dorian wanted to know. He stood there, shivering in his coat and sweats, and he felt completely robbed and broken, in more ways than one.

Reagan looked at him. He caught it, one brief flicker of sorrow in her eyes before she quickly masked it with an eye roll. She slid in the seat and slammed the door shut. Then, as if she were considering something, she rolled down her window.

"I wasn't the only one, Dorian," she muttered, her eyes direct on his. "Just so you know. Don't think this is over, sweetie."

Dorian's eyebrows drew together, and he felt like he was going to collapse right there on the sidewalk. "There is more? Reagan, you promised me this was all it was going to take to make this go away."

"Go home, Dorian," she said. "Get some rest. You look like hell." Rolling up her window, she drove off, the little white car breaking a corner and disappearing into the night.

Dorian's phone rang and he pulled it out of his pocket, absently glancing at the number rolling across the screen. "Hello?" he answered.

"Hey, man," Kenny said. "How is everything?"

Dorian sighed. He was damn near stunned silent at the events that had taken place, leading up to him handing over damn near every penny of his money to Reagan. No words could describe the shit feeling that was rolling around in his gut. There was no way it could get worse. "Long story," he murmured. "Just a lot of shit going on. I feel like I'm in the *Twilight Zone.*"

"Yeah? Is this about the fight? Reagan?"

"I don't want to talk about it," Dorian muttered, trying to keep his temper down. "Hey, man, I'm sorry about the fight. I was wrong to do you like that."

Kenny chuckled. "Hey, it's cool. I don't know what the hell is going on with you and that bitch, but mark my words, she ain't nothing but trouble. Stay away from her."

Dorian remained silent. If only he had known that months ago. "Listen, you came by my house earlier," Dorian said, not bothering with subtlety. "I was there but I got to the door kind of late. Who were you looking for?"

Kenny hesitated and blew out a heavy breath. "I'm sorry to have to tell you this, man," he said. "There has been some talk around the building. I don't know how true it is, but I hear they're trying to take your medical license."

Dorian just stood there in disbelief, his brain unable to form the proper words for a response. That had to be a lie.

"I came by to tell you," Kenny went on. "I just wanted to give you a heads-up anyway, so you would know."

"They're not doing that," Dorian said. It was a mistake. Had to be. "Under what grounds?"

"Sexual misconduct," Kenny said. "Man, was Reagan really one of your patients?"

Immediately, Dorian's mind flashed back:

"What can I do for you, Ms. . . . What did you say your name was again?"

"Peach. I'm here for my consultation," she said. "I have an appointment, Dr. Graham. Or should I call you Dr. Feelgood?"

He had sexed her right there on his exam table, not thinking anything of the visit other than she was getting her usual fix. He had been so blinded that never did he think she just needed to get on his papers for yet another piece of her plan to completely destroy him.

Rage had Dorian throwing his cell phone on the pavement with enough force to send it shattering into pieces of plastic, glass, and metal.

Dorian glanced down the empty street. Reagan was long gone, but like a hurricane, she had come barreling through, leaving destruction in her path, leaving him holding the shattered pieces. His only hope now was that when he got home, he and his wife could work through this. "We got us" was more than just their mutual understanding. Now it was his lifeline.

It was right then his mom's words came back to haunt him and remind him he was more like his father than he realized. *"You got your father's blood. But greed was his downfall. Had to have his cake and eat it too."* And just like his father, he had been destroyed.

Chapter Twenty-seven

Reagan stretched out on her lounger, the sun tinting her skin to a beautiful bronze. Her face was hidden behind huge-framed sunglasses, but behind the tinted lenses, her eyes zeroed in on her son building a sandcastle only a few inches from the water. Every so often, the waves would crawl close enough to splash his little legs, and he would squeal in delight as he ran up the beach only to return to his spot to have the little game repeated. She chuckled. He had never been to the beach. Neither of them had.

For the past six years, Reagan felt like she had done nothing but move from couch to couch, man to man, hustling to make ends meet and ducking and dodging men she had made broken promises to. Her poor child had never had a real home, and so often, she was tempted to send him to her parents in the hopes they would have some stability. But she knew it was only a matter of time before she had coordinated the ultimate payoff. And damn, did it pay off.

After paying off her debts, Reagan was still sitting lovely. Now she and TJ were laying out in the Dominican Republic, and she couldn't be happier. She had always wanted to travel. Not that "on the run" shit she had been doing so some crazy dude didn't put a bullet in her head, but real travel. For pleasure. Her son deserved it. She deserved it.

Reagan undid the strings on the top of her crocheted bikini and turned on her side. She had just about dozed off when a voice had her peeking out from her glasses.

"Girl, why didn't you wait for me?" Shantae huffed as she laid out her towel on the lounger next to her sister. Her beach hat flopped in the light breeze and a matching set of sunglasses hid her face as she feigned a pout. "I told you I was coming. Damn, you're so impatient."

Reagan giggled and flipped on her back. "I told you to hurry up. TJ was anxious to get to the water. You wanted to lay up in the hotel all morning."

"I'm enjoying my freedom," Shantae said and even the glasses couldn't hide the exaggerated wink.

Reagan could only shake her head. She had to admit, at first, she was surprised when Shantae approached her about the idea while she was in jail. Thanks to their pre-nup, Shantae couldn't divorce him without walking away with nothing. There wasn't even a cheating clause included in the damn document. So, between the two sisters, they had come up with the perfect scam.

Everything had been well thought out. The affair, the attempted suicide, the cops, how Reagan was always in the right place at the right time to play on Dorian; hell, even how she knew how much money he had to begin with—Shantae had planned it all. She had been the puppet master, and Reagan had played her role. It had worked like a charm and they had split the money.

Shantae had sent Dorian his divorce papers the week before she boarded the plane to Punta Cana. Sure, she loved him. Always would. But after the continuous cheating when they were dating, then the pre-nup the night before their wedding, somewhere along the line, their relationship had changed. She had been the one to mention the hall pass, curious if he would even be interested. And she'd had some reservations about using her sister at first. But when he had indulged in the full-blown affair, it only served as a reminder that she needed to get the money she was technically entitled to and leave. After all these years, Dorian still wasn't shit.

"I'm thinking I want to go to Alaska next," Shantae said as she lay back, content. "I hear it's beautiful."

Reagan nodded. "Cool with me. We got us, right?"

Shantae had to giggle at the slogan she had with her sister. It had been theirs long before Dorian was in the picture. He had just adopted it as theirs, but it never meant the same when the feelings weren't mutual.

"Yeah, we got us," Shantae agreed and let her eyes close.

When Reagan was sure Shantae had dozed off, she threw her feet over the side of the lounge chair and used her toes to fish in the sand for her flip-flops. She headed up the walk toward the hotel, nearly out of breath by the time she reached the lobby. She murmured a greeting to a few of the hotel attendants as she made her way to the bathroom. The baby was sitting on her bladder, so speed was of the essence. She squatted over the toilet to relieve the pressure and had to sigh as she felt her muscles relaxing.

Reagan knew it was only a matter of time before Shantae asked questions, which was why she knew they were going to have to go their separate ways soon. She was only showing a little, but her sister would go off if she found out she was pregnant by Dorian. *That* was completely unplanned, but Reagan had seen it as yet another opportunity. She had indeed asked for abortion money to pay down some of her debt, but she knew she wasn't going to get rid of his baby. It had started out as a plan, but Reagan had messed around and caught feelings somewhere along the way. She knew she could never be with Dorian, especially now after their little scam. But she could relish the fact she would always have a piece of him—not to mention steady child-support income for the next eighteen years.

THE MARRIAGE PASS

Briana Cole

ABOUT THIS GUIDE

The information and questions are included
to enhance your group's reading of
Briana Cole's *The Marriage Pass*

Statistics

It is estimated that **4% to 5% of people living in the U.S. are currently participating in what is known as consensual or ethical non-monogamy**, a practice in which partners maintain more than one sexual or romantic relationship with each other's knowledge and consent. For comparison, that means non-monogamy is about as prevalent as the number of Americans who identify as LGBTQ, which is estimated to be about 4.5% of the American population.

Using two separate samples based on the U.S. Census, Haupert and colleagues found that fully **one-fifth of the population in the United States (21.9 percent in the first sample and 21.2 percent in the second sample) has engaged in consensual non-monogamy at some point in their lives.**

Types of Consensual Non-Monogamous (CNM) Relationships

* **Polygamy** – a form of marriage consisting of more than two persons. The most common form of multiple partner marriage is
  o *Polygyny* – a marriage of one husband and multiple wives, who are each sexually exclusive with the husband—most common form of multiple partner marriage
  o *Polyandry* – a marriage of one wife to multiple husbands

* **Open** – Open relationships are varied enough to be an umbrella term for consensually non-monogamous relationships based on a primary couple who are "open" to

sexual contact with others. The most common form of open relationship is that of a married or long-term committed couple that takes on a third (or sometimes fourth or fifth) partner whose involvement and role in the relationship is always secondary. Swinging, monogamish, polyamorous/polyfidelitous, and anarchistic relationships can all be considered "open."

- **Swinging** - involves committed couples consensually exchanging partners specifically for sexual purposes.

- **Monogamish** - Popularized within the last few years by author Dan Savage, _monogamish_ relationships are those in which a couple is primarily monogamous, but allows varying degrees of sexual contact with others.

- **Polyamory and Polyfidelity**
  - _Polyamory_ - a relationship style that allows people to openly conduct multiple sexual and/or romantic relationships simultaneously, ideally with the knowledge and consent of all involved in or affected by the relationships.
  - _Polyfidelity_ - similar, except that it is a closed relationship style that requires sexual and emotional fidelity to an intimate group that is larger than two.
  - _Polyaffective_ - emotionally intimate, non-sexual connections among people connected by a polyamorous relationship, such as two heterosexual men who are both in sexual relationships with the same woman and have co-spousal or brother-like relationships with each other.

- **Relationship Anarchy** – the belief that relationships should be bound by rules aside from what the people involved mutually agree upon

Key Values for CNM Relationships

- Trust
- Communication
- Consent
- Mutual Respect

Transitioning to a CNM Relationship

1) Be clear on what you want
2) Learn more about the possibilities
3) Ask lots of questions
4) Take it slow
5) Be prepared to learn as you go
6) Be prepared for jealousy
7) Schedule check-ins
8) Always choose your own adventure

Discussion Questions

1. Have you ever thought about someone other than your partner during sex?

2. How do you feel about "hall passes" (Permission to sleep with someone else)?

3. What is your personal definition of an "open relationship?"

4. Do you believe you can romantically be in love with more than one person?

5. How would you feel if you could have different relationships and share experiences and knowledge with several people?

6. What is your biggest regret in your relationship history?

7. What does "commitment" look like to you?

8. What pitfalls do people commonly experience when opening a relationship or starting to explore non-monogamy?

9. What does success in a relationship look like to you?

10. Do you enjoy variety in your sex life?

11. Is it difficult to remain faithful to one partner today? Why or why not?

12. How do you typically respond to jealousy and what are your jealousy "triggers?"

13. Do you trust your partner?

14. Is cheating a deal breaker in a relationship?

References

psychologytoday.com/us/blog/the-polyamorists-next-door/
201905/updated-estimate-number-non-monogamous-people-
in-us

psychologytoday.com/us/blog/the-polyamorists-next-door/
201407/7-different-kinds-non-monogamy

ossacollective.com/open-up-your-relationship-questions/

thecouplescenter.org/better-understanding-open-relationships-
and-non-monogamy/

bustle.com/articles/155289-how-to-explore-non-monogamy-in-
your-relationship

exploringyourmind.com/know-seven-types-of-non-monogamy/

time.com/5330833/polyamory-monogamous-relationships/

healthline.com/health/polyamorous#terms-to-know